D0715889

Cardiff Libraries
www.cardiff.gov... ...ries
Llyfrgelloedd...
www...

YOU CAN'T HIDE

ACC. No: 07038817

YOU CAN'T HIDE

SARAH MUSSI

Hodder
Children's
Books

HODDER CHILDREN'S BOOKS

First published in Great Britain in 2019
by Hodder and Stoughton

1 3 5 7 9 10 8 6 4 2

Text copyright © Sarah Mussi, 2019

Excerpt on p.312 from *The Magician's Nephew* by
C.S. Lewis, published 1955, © C.S. Lewis

The moral rights of the author have been asserted.

All characters and events in this publication, other than those
clearly in the public domain, are fictitious and any resemblance
to real persons, living or dead, is purely coincidental.

In order to create a sense of setting, some names of real places have
been included in the book. However, the events depicted in this
book are imaginary and the real places used fictitiously.

All rights reserved.
No part of this publication may be reproduced, stored in a retrieval system,
or transmitted, in any form or by any means, without the prior permission in
writing of the publisher, nor be otherwise circulated in any form of binding or
cover other than that in which it is published and without a similar condition
including this condition being imposed on the subsequent purchaser.

A CIP catalogue record for this book
is available from the British Library.

ISBN 978 1 4449 1788 8

Typeset by Hewer Text UK Ltd, Edinburgh
Printed and bound in Great Britain by Clays Ltd, Elcograf S.p.A.

The paper and board used in this book are made
from wood from responsible sources.

Hodder Children's Books
An imprint of
Hachette Children's Group
Part of Hodder and Stoughton
Carmelite House
50 Victoria Embankment
London EC4Y 0DZ

An Hachette UK Company

www.hachette.co.uk
www.hachettechildrens.co.uk

You might think that if victims just leave their abusive relationships that will resolve the problem. Unfortunately, statistics seem to consistently show that victims are at more risk of being killed by their abusers in the weeks and months after they have left, often despite all efforts to relocate and disguise identities.

Source: Refuge.org.uk

For Finn, because he deserves the truth.

BEFORE THE EXODUS

Downstairs the lounge door slams. I freeze. I listen. Then I lean out over the landing rail to capture every sound. The scrape of a chair drags across the floor. A silence follows, hollow, unnerving.

'Please,' shrieks Mom.

A muffled sound like meat thumped down.

Shouting.

Loud. Frightening.

His.

More shouting.

'Please.' Softer. Sobbing.

Something crashes. Low words. Then more shouting. The snap of something breaking.

Glass shatters.

I tell myself to run up the next flight of stairs, bolt myself in the attic, hide under the spare bed, cover my ears, squeeze my eyes shut.

Run.

My legs don't listen. Blood pounds against the tissue of my temple.

Run.

But instead my feet turn and shakily go down the stairs.

You must stop him.

He may kill her this time.

Don't go there. He may kill you too.

My hands don't listen either. They brush across my face, smear wetness. Then they reach out towards the door handle to the lounge.

A shriek cut short. Another kind of thud, like a hammer hitting soft wood.

A long high-pitched scream.

Mom.

I feel sick and cold. I want it to stop.

Run.

Hide.

He will kill you.

I see the livid scar tissue across the back of my hand. Look at what he's capable of. He'll do worse than scar you this time.

Phone the police? They'll get here too late. I'm too scared. There's no time. Film him?

Don't be stupid.

Mom always said: If it gets bad, just run, baby girl. Run. And don't look back.

I turn the door handle.

Don't think. Just act.

Trembling, I stop, pull out my phone.

Quickly I yank down the door handle and kick it open.

My mom's face. Pale. Bloody.

A shout. Curses. An object hurtles through the air.

My legs, having got this far, threaten to give way.

'STOP IT,' I scream. 'I'm filming. I'm streaming it to my friend. She's calling the police!'

SHOUTING. SWEARING.

I hold firm.

He pushes me. I don't back off. He reaches for my phone. Shoves his hand at my head. Tries to snap my neck back. But I'm too quick. My legs are suddenly alive; like wild creatures they flare into speed. I'm flying towards the kitchen.

From behind the kitchen table, with the back door open, I scream, 'THE POLICE ARE COMING! THEY'RE GOING TO GET YOU!'

He stops as if an idea has suddenly struck him, like he's remembered an appointment, pretending he's not scared of the police. He turns on his heel, kicks over the hall stool.

At the front door he yells, 'YOU'RE FRIGGING DEAD.'

Slams out.

Gone.

Mom on the sofa.

Shaking legs.

Blood. Bone white. Her arm weirdly misshapen.

I bolt the front door. Heartbeat. Heartbeat. Bolt the back door.

I dial 999.

Shaking fingers.

'Ambulance,' I whisper. Breathe. Breathe. I need air. 'I need an ambulance — come quickly.'

AFTER THE EXODUS

One year later . . .

Dear Finn,

It's been six weeks since the accident.

Today is the start of week seven. I feel strong enough to write to you. There's so much I need to say. I'm going to imagine you are inside my poor damaged brain and tell you everything as I think it. I'll make a start.

You are already in my heart.

WEEK SEVEN

since the accident

I pray you, in your letters,
When you shall these unlucky deeds relate,
Speak of me as I am; nothing extenuate,
Nor set down aught in malice. Then must you speak
Of one that loved not wisely, but too well

William Shakespeare – Othello

MARS BLACK

1

Venice Ward, Room 4, The Shore Center for Medical Care
I hide my hands.

They're ugly.

I don't mean just unattractive.

I mean ugly.

Scarred.

Burnt.

Discoloured.

My auntie (who is not actually my aunt) reminds me it's because of what Mom's boyfriend did. I know she's right. But I don't want to believe her. I prefer to believe they're burnt and scarred because I'm a hero. Your hero. A hero who pulled you, Finn, from under a burning bough at Mac's bonfire party, when you were nine and I was too.

What is truth anyway?

It's just a construct.

The truth is what we believe.

I'm going to tell you the truth, Finn, the whole truth, what I believe and what I've been told. That's the least I can do.

You see, my burns remind me of how much I love you, and how much you love me. And what a small sacrifice beautiful hands are, in the face of life and love.

I know you love me. It's not just gratitude for perhaps saving your life. You love me so much, you would die for me. I'm your muse. You told me so.

That is the truth.

I don't know why nowadays, in this medical center, I hide my hands.

2

I'm very tired of Auntie Gillian.

She insists that I face the facts. As if they have a truth of their own. She's been visiting me every day since the car accident. She reminds me what the facts are about my hands. That when I was younger, before Mom and I escaped from the UK and got here to Massachusetts, my 'stepdad' asked me to do the washing-up. Being a kid, I told him exactly what he could do with all those dirty plates. Apparently he marched me to the kitchen, flung all the soiled crocks in the sink and boiled the kettle. Then he held my hands over the mess of plates, smeared with half-eaten lasagne.

And poured boiling water over everything.

And kept boiling.

And kept pouring.

I was in hospital for ten days and off school for two and a half months. The scarring fused the tissue to the bone in places. I find it hard to flex my fingers. Auntie Gillian insists that if I am to recover I must not mix up realities. I must hold tightly to the truth and figure out the reasons behind all the lies. She's right, of course. I do remember everything that happened in the UK perfectly well, even if I'd rather not. Aunt Gillian encourages me to document every horrible incident, every abuse we suffered before we came to live with her. Otherwise I will be of no use as a witness. I didn't tell you about everything that happened in the UK, Finn. I wish I had.

So here is some of it.

It seems Mom was too scared to leave my stepdad after he burned my hands, until she'd formed a foolproof exit strategy. So we carried on living under his roof for another six years.

Those six years were awful.

I've had to work very hard at forgetting them.

Sometimes that wasn't so easy.

Like when he broke her arm.

OK. Breathe.

Calm down.

I'll get to the details when I feel a bit stronger.

3

I was really proud of my poor scarred hands until the car accident. Even though I told you lies about them. They were still a symbol of you and me. Now I hide them and that worries me.

The accident. I can't remember that so well. Just snatches like so many half-remembered things. I was down by the interstate railroad. I was alone. And I didn't have a phone. There was a car. I think. I wish I could remember everything.

The rail plates were shaking and the air was charged with a kind of electricity.

'Just keep on trying and trust the brain,' says the doc.

'For God's sake the train's coming,' someone yelled.

'The brain will work it out – just don't get so mad at it . . .'

I couldn't move.

'Your hip has healed well since the op; your brain will too. Memories will come – when they will.'

The car. So heavy.

I try to remember.

PUSH!

I must remember.

Mom, what has he done to Mom? The tracks rattle. The moon's all hazy. The train's coming.

The voice of Aunt Gillian drills in. 'You must remember! You *absolutely* must. Everything at the trial will depend on what you say and your state of mind.'

I feel it through the sea air, through the centre of the earth.

What will it be like, to be free at last? Feel the whoosh as my life extinguishes.

I thump my head back on the pillow. What else happened? So many flashes of memory, but I still can't seem to link them up.

Why didn't I have a phone? Why haven't I got one now?

And why is remembering so important to Auntie Gillian?

Where is Mom? Why don't I know?

But I have remembered something. The hazy moon. There was a moon that night and the whole stretch of trackway was lit up.

OK, so there was a moon.

So what use is that?

4

So Finn, as I said, I've been in this medical center now for six weeks. I can't tell you anything about the first two of them. I was in a coma. The next two weeks after that are hazy. Very muddled. The last couple of weeks I've been gradually more awake, though very disorientated and weak.

I still get very tired, but I'm improving.

When I get out of here, I'll live with Auntie Gillian again. Auntie Gillian says she's kept my room exactly as it was, because she's sure I will recover.

Gillian is a silly name. It even sounds silly. Sillian. It is probably one of those ironies of life that Gillian is actually the least frivolous person imaginable. Plus she is not my relative except in the eyes of God apparently. Plus also her full name is Gillian Obedience Lament Makepeace, which is not frivolous at all.

I'm just remembering something else. Strange how these thoughts come in bubbles.

Sea breeze. Chain-link fence. Tall shoots of grass. Hazy moon. And the shadow of someone else.

Mom and the police.

That hazy moon.

Then darkness flows in.

GET THE CAR OFF THE TRACKS!

The train's coming.

Tremors. Low like a rumble of thunder.

Then shaking.

A pain somewhere. Thrown aside, rolling, breaking. The train exploding past. Hot air blasts my eyes. My ears implode.

Lightning strikes.

The noise fades to white.

There you are. You see, memories come when they will. I should trust my doctor. *I will remember everything. Even if I don't understand the urgency.*

I told you my name was Alexia. I like being called Lexi. Aunt Gillian insists on calling me Alexandra. My full name apparently is Alexia Clarke. Aunt Gillian is an elder for the Living Faith Tabernacle for the Reformed Puritan Church. My mother does not live with us any more. Actually, I don't live with us any more. I live in this medical center. For now.

I'm sticking to the facts.

And as well as all that, since we're discussing facts, you should know something else. Alexia Clarke is not my real name.

I can't tell you my real name. That is a secret, which is not just mine. So I can't share it until I have permission. I'm so sorry about that. I'm not sure who I have to get permission from. It's just better if I don't tell you. Though actually I prefer Lexi anyway. And I'll always be Lexi to you, Finn, won't I? I can't tell you who it will put me in danger from either, not his real name anyway. It would take more than a million car accidents to wipe his memory out, though.

Breathe. Stop hands from involuntarily trembling.

OK. The truth. The facts. I'm in danger from my stepfather.

Breathe. Though strictly speaking he is not my stepfather. *Stop. Calm yourself.* Let's call him . . . Charlie? That's it, deep breaths. Charlie is a name that can minimise anyone. He'd hate to be called Charlie. *Calm down. He can't get into this place.* It is a bit melodramatic to keep referring to him as Him. Plus he doesn't deserve that kind of status. *I hope one day he knows I called him 'Charlie'. I hope he gets so angry he bursts.*

Exhale. That's better.

Now you'll want to know where I grew up, won't you? Every doctor I see asks me the same questions.

'Hi there, what's your name?'

'Where do you come from?'

I'm not sure if they really don't know or have forgotten.

I always say, 'UK. Littlehampton.'

Or maybe they are just testing, to see if the car accident left me with permanent brain damage.

Littlehampton is just the kind of place I want you to imagine I come from anyway. Generic. Fish and chips. Seaside. Entirely forgettable. If you haven't been there, and have a poor imagination, even better.

5

My long-term memory is still intact. At least I am sure of that. I can remember mostly everything, up until those last five weeks just before the accident. I sit here remembering and not remembering, tucked into these stiff, scratchy hospital sheets.

Whilst I remember: the quintessential smell of floral disinfectant wafts around me, chemical freesia and synthetic white musk.

I go over and over everything in my head, just to be very sure I've got all the details straight. I don't want to forget anything mysteriously overnight. That's one of the reasons I'm retelling everything for you too, Finn. It will preserve everything, for both of us, you see. And it'll be some kind of an explanation. Apparently they'll need to know everything at the trial as well.

Plus you deserve the absolute truth.

I'm not sure what the trial is all about. I'm not sure if I've done something wrong. Aunt Gillian does try to tell me, but I can't seem to remember what she says. Anything to do with the accident just evaporates within seconds. I only know that it's very, very, very important. And I must remember what happened.

Anyway, I know these things:

When we ran away, we left England entirely. Mom thought it'd be safest to put the Atlantic between Charlie and us. The planet Pluto was too near, if you want my opinion. We got on a plane and moved to the east coast of the USA (you know where, obviously).

Charlie. The thought of him makes me really shiver.

We left everything behind. Especially the things we loved most. That is the only way to leave without a trace, apparently.

If you start secreting away your heart's treasures, then you will attract suspicion. You have to leave everything very conspicuously lying around. Not too conspicuously, of course. You can't be crass about it. Your best, most expensive pair of shoes can be carelessly tossed aside on the first-floor landing. Your laptop can be abandoned wide open and running in your room. I even suggest tipping the left foot of one expensive shoe on to its side, so that it cannot give any hint that its owner has just walked out.

For ever.

This gives you more getaway time.

I left my books and my games, my make-up, my mirror, my PJs, my school books, my teddy and my cell phone. Especially my phone. I didn't pack that in between my science homework and GCSE exam past papers, on the day we left. I 'forgot' it beside my bed on purpose. He knew I'd never go away and leave my phone. It was Mom's idea. A tactic to assuage any suspicion.

We left on a Tuesday and I don't have PE on a Tuesday. So even my sports bra had to be deserted.

I know what you're thinking.

But he would.

Those cold slimy fingers.

You just really need to understand about Charlie, Finn.

I was so scared of him. And there was no way we could oppose him. He was a very careful man. His blows never left a bruise. Usually. Unless he was really mad. Then nobody left the house till the injuries had faded. We wouldn't dare to. He was a good liar too. The police sometimes looked into things, but he had the gift of the gab and could talk them round. He knew Mom and I would back him up. We'd be too terrified not to. God, he was such scum. He'd drilled us both on what to say. That's why I'm sometimes not sure I believe what Gillian tells me about the hot-water incident. I think Charlie would have been way too careful to burn me like that.

But maybe I'm wrong. Aunt Gillian says he did it. It was one of the things that puzzled me when I started to come out of the coma. Why were my hands so scarred? Auntie Gillian says I was probably hanging on to the bonfire fantasy, because the truth was too awful. I was very confused those first few days. I couldn't even recognise Auntie Gillian. Faces are still a problem.

I think I was hanging on to it because of you, Finn. I don't want ever to have lied to you.

I must face facts. I lied to you about my hands.

I'm so sorry.

Anyway, Charlie was clever and cruel and controlling. He'd smell you. He'd try to catch you out in a lie – to see if you'd used perfume – had a boyfriend – gone shopping with a mate – been swimming (that telltale whiff of chlorine) – even been to McDonald's. He had a good sense of smell. He boasted he could tell whether you'd eaten a Big Mac or just had the fries. He'd close in on you and sniff all down your neck.

Hang on. Got to stop. It's pretty hard to remember all that stuff. OK. Deep breaths.

The truth is he'd smell me, and search me, every day before I left the house, and again when I came back in.

Yes, right down to my bra.

Hang on. OK. Breathe.

It's OK.

We left. Flew the nest. Ran for our lives.

IVORY BLACK

6

Massachusetts Last Spring

I need a break from remembering Charlie. I'll tell you about my arrival in our coastal town. That's way more positive.

My Fresh Start in Massachusetts!

Welcome to me starting my new life after Charlie. Thank God.

With a new name.

With a new school

In a new country.

Totally unsearched.

Totally lovable.

Totally safe.

Having left the past totally behind.

Here we are, Mom and me after the Great Escape. We are in a smallish, yet famous, coastal town in Massachusetts. You know it well – its beachfront and well-heeled residents, its religious myopic focus – so there's no need to describe it. You don't know how I experienced it, though. I'll help you with that.

Mom and I were graciously welcomed back in by her church elders despite the fact that sixteen years ago Mom had to escape from them. It seems escaping is her forte. She was pregnant on that occasion.

You're probably all too familiar with this town's puritanical past, how religious and judgemental and provincial and conservative it is. So no need to judge Mom too harshly, about running away whilst being unmarried and pregnant, I mean.

Anyway, try to imagine you are me, so that you can see everything through my eyes.

This coastal town is not too different from Littlehampton, but 'it's warmer here than you're used to.' Those were my mom's words. She warned me. 'You'll need light things. Cotton tops. Shorts. It's late spring. Your legs are to die for, kid, but don't wear your shorts too short. Got it?'

I got it. Shorts for the beach only. Never show too much skin, even on a hot day. Long dress and hat for church. Keep shoulders covered.

Yes, this coastal town. I remember how we arrived.

We drove in along a tree-lined boulevard. The trees bowed and waved graciously at us. Then past a mall. Some stores. A high street. A beachfront. A railway station. A saloon that had been repurposed as a community hall. A grid of residential houses that merged into the distance. I saw a shadowy hill far away. I heard the crash of waves. I smelt the quiet air of respectability.

Everyone smiled. I felt vaguely that I had arrived in a film set. The elders of the church came out to meet us at our reception point. Auntie Gillian was one of them. She generously volunteered to host us at her home. 'You are to call me auntie,' she proposed. 'Your mother and I are sisters in the eyes of God.' Then everyone gave us warm handshakes, fresh lemonade, home-baked cookies and the acknowledgement of our broken existence from the safety of their perfect lives.

And we thanked them.

And sipped the lemonade.

And nibbled the cookies

And prayed with them.

For they had rescued us.

And we were eternally grateful.

7

Well, here we are now at my new school.

Crowded canteen. No space in the library. Students stacked four storeys high in a vast, noisy building. Dress code very conservative. No tank tops. No midriffs. No pants (girls). DEFINITELY NO SHORTS. No make-up. No designer labels. We can peer into the classrooms, overhear conversations; here's one small group of senior girls.

'Who's the new girl?'

'Which new girl?' Studied indifference. Kisses teeth.

'The cute one.'

'Call that cute?'

'Well, hot.'

'So you need glasses.' Tosses hair. Rolls eyes.

'Yeah, cool, guess you're right.' Shrugs. Hangs head.

'You. Guess. I. Am. Right?' Eyeballs in face.

'Sorry, Jules, I know you're totally right.'

'Thank you!'

'Sorry. My bad.' Attempts at groveling. 'I just think she's pretty, that's all.'

'Pretty boyfriend grabbing. Did you see the way she looked at Finn?'

'Yep, I saw it.'

'Did. You. See. All. That. Eye language!'

'Kind of.'

'Not. O. K.'

'But Finn's got you. He'd be crazy to look at anyone else.'

'That's not the point.'

'I know.'

'She has got to be put in her place Very Firmly.'

'Yep, buddy, I agree.'

'She's ho-nasty and we'll let her know it. Every. Single. Day.'

'You're right.'

'Obviously.'

And here I am a few hours earlier, standing in the schoolyard being the new girl, before school starts, loitering without intent, trying to look cool. I'm resplendent with all my possessions: one set of dress-code-compliant school clothes, one borrowed school bag and lunch pack, courtesy of the Living Faith Tabernacle Charity Aunts, and one pair of ugly hands.

This is the first day of my new independent life. And what is a new beginning if you don't make a clean break?

I am trying to be optimistic. I am going straight into twelfth grade. Nobody will ever know my secret past, because it is a secret.

A secret I will never tell. In case Charlie finds out and comes after us.

Please don't ever let him find out.

Luckily, I cannot be traced anywhere ever, anyway. This is because I leave no clue. This is because I have no fingerprints. And that is very ironic, isn't it? In scarring my hands so badly, he lost for ever the power to trace me out.

Here are some of the details I should have told you, Finn.

Example:

We are in the kitchen. I'm peeling the potatoes. Mom has got the roast on. It's a Sunday. We are pretending to be a normal family, cooking lunch. We're pretending we're happy. Mom has got the radio on and is singing along. I'm smiling and wearing an apron. I have plans to make a floury cinnamon apple bake for pudding. We have even vacuumed the house just like a normal family.

We are certain there is nothing wrong.

Everything is in its place.

Everything is as it should be.

But his anger comes out of nowhere.

It smashes into the floor tiles, crashes the furniture about, rebounds off the ceiling.

'What the hell do you call this?' he yells. He picks a pack of pre-chopped and prepared vegetables from the kitchen counter. 'I don't eat pre-packaged crap.' He throws it in the bin. 'What kind of a moron feeds anyone this shit?' He crosses to the cooker.

I freeze.

'I thought you liked mixed veg.' Mom tries to back away.

'Me?' He breathes fire at her. 'LIKE boiled soggy vegetables? Is that your idea of Sunday lunch?' He picks the pan from the top of the cooker, lifts the lid and throws its contents into the sink. The boiling water splashes, hisses. I'm trembling. He kicks out at the furniture, upturns a chair. Potatoes roll onto the floor.

Mom has gone ashen pale. Her hands shake.

'I'm sorry,' she starts.

'YOU'RE SORRY?' He places his hand on her chest and shoves her backwards. She stumbles on the upturned chair and falls, cracking her back on the wall as she goes down.

'Stop it,' I yell.

He whirls round. Fireballs ignite. He steps towards me.

'Please,' yells Mom. 'Please. I'm sorry. It's not her fault. We were just trying to cook lunch.' Mom is struggling to get up off the floor. Blood. I think she's bitten her lip. The potatoes smash beneath his boots.

'You're sorry?' he yells again. 'You're always sorry. What is it you've got to be so sorry about?' He steps menacingly towards her. 'You think I don't know?' he continues.

'I don't know what you mean,' stammers Mom.

'You don't know what I mean,' he mimics. 'It's always the same with you, isn't it?'

'Stop it!' I yell again.

'Tight as little thieves, aren't you?' he says, whirling round on me. 'You'd happily murder me and then back each other up.'

We both stare at him.

'I'm not hanging around here with you witches.'

He slams out through the back door.

'You wait till I'm back!' A parting threat.

Left to terrify us.

And Mom and I are truly terrified.

We stand there frozen. Minutes pass before we can pick up the potatoes. Wipe up the smash. Hours before we can sit down in the front room. Neither of us feel like eating. We wait, while he drinks.

We know he's drinking.

We wait for him to come back again and finish what he's started.

8

I am disappointed.

School Day One and I stand in the schoolyard of Coastal Town High School Academy. I am totally despondent. I had hoped to find friends. But it's obvious that the school is full of cliques. It will be hard to break into any of them. You do have a small advantage when you're new though, if you can pretend well enough.

You get to choose who you are and who you want to belong to. You can choose to be sporty, or clever, or you can hang out with friendly airheads who giggle hilariously at everything in a completely vacuous manner. Or you may be able to join those shunned, overweight, lonely losers lurking about in the least noticeable corners of the library.

Or you can suck up to the female dogs. The clean, lean, hair-straightened, dyed-blonde, long-legged, sharp-tongued, mean vampires.

You can create for yourself an entirely new history.

Your new name will never be questioned.

In addition to the group you want to join, you also have to choose your boyfriend. To be the perfect American teenager you need an American boy by your side. Maybe you want the dark-haired goth. Or the sporty jock. You must choose carefully – who you are with is just as important as who you are. So there was also that to be decided. But *that* was an easy decision.

Because there was Finn.

You will have to get used to me referring to you in the third person, by the way. At least for a while.

You see, I must tell you the truth and it's easier if I do it without apologising for it every minute. Back then I thought of you as 'Finn'. So that is the way I must tell my truth.

Except that I *am* truly sorry for what happened, whatever it was, and part of the penance is not to spare myself. Aunt Gillian drills this point into me.

And I did decide about you, right on that first morning.

You were the only person who welcomed me. Do you remember? You were shooting baskets all alone before school, at the rusty old pole with the rim and no net. Remember by the fence, in the furthest corner of the schoolyard, where the alder tree grows?

I sat down on a nearby bench. I was tired of standing alone in the open savannah of the schoolyard.

You were practising. You shot a few bricks. You frowned. It looked like you were going to give up.

'Last try,' you muttered.

Miraculously the ball rolled round the rim, and just when we were holding our breaths, fearing it'd be another brick, it swished through the basket.

You whooped.

You turned to me and smiled.

I smiled back.

'Welcome to Coastal High!' you hollered.

I didn't even know your name.

You didn't know any of mine.

I remember that morning so clearly. The sudden rush of sweetness.

I thought about that smile all through morning prayers.

And each time I thought about it, I looked at you.

And each time I looked at you, you looked back at me.

You smiled.

I smiled.

And I found out in Coastal Town High School Academy, you were considered the hottest, coolest, sexiest, tallest, cleverest, fittest boy in the twelfth grade. And you were awesome at art.

And kind.

And I decided about you there and then.

I decided that you would be mine.

On an existential level. Obviously.

And the fates seemed to favour my decision.

Because when I left assembly, we found ourselves crushed together in the corridor. You leaned into me. I leaned into you. Electricity sent jolts of energy between us.

If I close my eyes, I am right back there.

'You look just like Janey Morris,' you whisper. 'For real.'

'Janey who?'

'Janey Morris, the model for the Pre-Raphaelites?'

'Oh,' I say.

'Proserpine, Goddess of Spring and Empress of Hades,' you say.

I'm lost.

'Born to be painted.'

'Oh,' I say again, in confusion.

'So I have to ask you.'

I laugh. I get it. He likes me. He's going to ask me out.

'One day will you let me?'

'Excuse me?'

'Paint you?'

Then the river of students parts us, and I feel strangely marooned and strangely rescued, all at the same time.

I must find out all about you.

And I do.

Your name is Finn and you are admired and talked about by every girl in the academy. You already have a girlfriend. Your girlfriend is Jules Bridges and she is the queen of the female dogs. I have already named them the Dogettes. She is the alpha Dogette, gorgeously pretty, long blonde hair, tiny waist, big blue eyes. She is all rattlesnake and quagmire. Venom and razorblade. But I know, as I walk through those corridors, that she is alarmed. I am her bête noire.

She has felt the energy between us. She has seen the way you looked at me.

And she fears I will take from her everything she possesses.

And I will try to, because she, like Charlie, is a bully. And you should not belong to a bully. Nobody should.

I will take you, because you have called me to be your muse. Because I held my breath with you by the deserted basketball pole so your luck could change.

The Fates threw us together. And I decided about you.

Way before I knew of her.

She is malice and poison. I can see it in the way she glares at me. She sizes me up for butchery. I can see she's thinking: anyone approaching anything like her level of pretty needs to be spatchcocked.

But I will not be glared at. I will not start my new life being bullied. I have waged war on all bullies.

So I harden myself. I prepare for her assault. She is a mosquito to me, annoying, but not threatening. I am a monster from the fire. I have survived the torments of enforced isolation. I have seen my beloved mother torture herself at his command. I have seen her mangled on the floor. I have endured the daily insults of a much more powerful abuser than her, and I have stood firm.

Example:

Instinctively I duck.

The bottle comes flying across the living room floor. It leaves a trail of beer sprayed high over the wall, over the sofa, over the rug. It crashes into the laminate flooring. It gouges out a huge dent then rolls under the table. Mom screams. She is splattered in flying beer.

And I stand firm, then fetch her some kitchen roll.

Oh yes.

I have survived the heat of boiling water and the cold of being locked out on a winter's night. I can lift my scarred finger and incinerate Jules Bridges with a blast of brimstone.

And I can choose to belong to anyone I want, even her precious Finn.

Finn the Awesome.

Finn the Artist.

Finn the Kind.

That is one thing I learned from Charlie. Once you choose someone, it really doesn't matter if they choose you back.

And that's what Jules doesn't understand.

She is doomed.

With people like her, if possible, I will strike first, and strike hardest.

As I stow my stuff in my school locker, I steel myself. If I know bullies, they don't go down without a fight.

Yes, I want to make friends, but not with her. If you make any effort to be liked by a bully, you are cursed to lick boots for ever, to put up with them borrowing all your money, your best clothes, your ideas, your phone, your lipstick, your reputation, your secrets, while they rubbish you to others.

And I can't allow that.

My secrets must go to the grave with me.

My secrets are the grave.

Here's what some of my secrets are like:

Mom and I sit huddled in the garden shed. She puts her arm around me and whispers, 'Don't worry, baby girl.'

How can I not worry?

'Maybe he'll just go straight in and fall asleep on the sofa,' she whispers, 'then we can go back in.'

We sit together in the darkness and hold hands. The garden shed smells of damp earth and worms and graveyards. Somewhere in the darkness overhead spiders weave spells and earwigs crawl out of cracks. It's cold. My heart is beating so hard I'm sure it will give us away. Mom squeezes my hand tighter. 'He'll just think we're asleep. I know he will,' she says.

We both know he won't.

The sound of a car turns into the drive. Brakes squeal. A car door squeaks open, bangs shut. Heavy feet crunch on gravel. Low curses as he fumbles for his keys.

We don't speak. We wait in the darkness. The front door slams. We can hear shouting. The noise of something crashing, breaking. The kitchen light goes on. A square of yellow appears on the frosty lawn. Charlie swears. He shouts for Mom.

Mom squeezes my hand.

'No,' I say, 'you can't go in. He'll think you're asleep; he always does.'

I can feel the tension in her. To disobey when he calls . . .

'You can't leave me.'

She doesn't leave me.

We sit together in the freezing, spiderweb dark until all noises stop and even then we dare not go back into the house.

LAMP BLACK

9

Venice Ward, Room 4

Every day I try to inch my memory forward a little. Most days it works and I reclaim something, some little extra particular.

I know that's the key, remembering what happened in detail and why.

That's what Auntie Gillian wants. At every visit she pushes me a little harder. 'We are running out of time,' she says. 'If you don't remember all will be lost.'

I don't know what will be lost, but I know it's serious. Aunt Gillian is never dramatic.

Not everything is useful though. Bits of memory lie scattered in my mind like lost jigsaw pieces. Some of them don't fit anywhere. I haven't got the whole picture at all.

Today I will work some more on **Day One of New Life in Coastal Town High School Academy.**

CHARCOAL GREY

10

Massachusetts, Last Spring

OK, so, first day and I have not decided about anything except Finn (and Jules). I have not decided about which clique to join, which teachers to like, what after-school clubs to join. I shall wait and learn and listen for a while.

I will not be unsociable. I will try to make friends. I'm going to be positive. Friends are great. What I long for most in life is to have a best friend. Someone I can share all my secrets with. All the secrets that I cannot share.

That is a contradictory dilemma, which I am perfectly well aware of. But I shall try, nevertheless, to find such a friend.

My first period is math, and then it's science. Math is totally important for my standardised test. I'll have to take that at the end of the semester. I'm a whole year late in sitting it. I'm off schedule. Out of balance. Another of the consequences of running away from Charlie. Thankfully I'm going to be allowed to sit the SAT with the juniors.

The SATs, that's what counts here, if I want to get into college, that is.

It's a standardised test in math and English and writing, used for college admissions. I determine to practise hard for it.

If I do really, really well at the test, the school says there's still a chance colleges might look at me, though most of the seniors have already applied or got places.

I cross my fingers. *Please let me get into college.*

Of course, there are still all the everyday quizzes and tests and essays in all the other subjects. I have to do well at them too. They'll contribute to my overall grade from the school, my GPA. Colleges totally look at that as well. So I have to be good.

Very good.

I *do* want to go to college.

Anyway, I survive math without incident, and head to science. There doesn't seem to be a seating plan in the science lab, so I put my bags down on the end of a row, where I figure nobody really has a vested interest in sitting. I'm early. I wait nervously. I tilt my bag at an apologetic angle, just in case it's somebody's special place. Sort of: *Is it OK for me to sit here?* Like I said, however contradictory, I want to make friends.

One of the first groups of students to arrive are the Dogettes, led by Jules. She marches straight up to where I've put my bag and says, 'That's my space.'

'But Jules?' One of her friends tries to drag her to a different bench.

Jules shakes off her hand and pushes my bag to the floor.

Pencils and books spill out.

I step back and start to pick up my stuff.

A tall girl with a thin, yellowish kind of face and funeral-straight black hair watches me from the other side of the science lab.

Jules sits down where I'd put myself. Her friends hesitate.

'We are sitting here today,' Jules announces.

I finish packing my bag. Nobody helps me. I stand there unsure.

After a minute or so the girl with the funeral-straight black hair walks over.

'You're a newcomer, aren't you?' she says.

I am not going to apologise for being myself. I am not going to apologise for being new. I'm not going to apologise for selecting a seat that wasn't anyone else's special seat either.

'You can sit by me if you want,' she says.

I don't know if she is the class pariah, a lonely loser, or just friendly at this stage, but I am not in any position to refuse a kindly offer right now. Plus, I do need a place to sit down.

'Thanks,' I say. I shoulder my bag and follow her to the end of the next row. She nods at a space next to her. On her other side sits a round, plump-cheeked, freckle-faced student. She has that straw hair which is neither orange nor red, nor auburn, nor dyed. It just looks odd. I figure I am in with the weird bunch.

'Claire,' she says. The straw-hair girl shoves her shoulders past the thin girl's chest, elbows her out of the way, and sticks her face forward. 'Hi, I'm Claire,' she repeats. 'I see you've met Maggie.'

'I see you've already quarrelled with Jules,' said Maggie.

Ah! So that's it! That's why Maggie came to my aid.

I raise an eyebrow.

My enemy's enemy is my friend.

'Jules, you know, the Queen of Them.' Maggie rolls her eyes.

'I'm not sure what I did wrong,' I say. Although I *do* know and it wasn't where I'd chosen to park myself either. 'She doesn't seem to like me.'

I hide the real reason from these new friends. Of course she doesn't like me. She's seen Finn and I have looked into each other's eyes and found each other. She is afraid.

She *should* be afraid.

'Wow, you're, like, British!' says Claire.

I instantly like Claire. She doesn't care about Jules. She's just focusing on me. I give her a big happy smile.

'She doesn't like anyone who won't lick her butt,' says Maggie, sticking to the 'we hate Jules' theme.

'OK,' I say. So I'm no butt-licker.

'She'll HATE it that you're British,' says Maggie.

'My mom's American,' I say. Should I be trying to fit in?

'I just love your accent!' gushes Claire.

'I'm sorry that a run-in with Jules had to be your welcome to science at Coastal High.' says Maggie. 'We're not all like that.'

'Don't worry, she doesn't deal with us,' soothes Claire.

I raise an eyebrow again.

'Because Mags has about a zillion brothers and cousins and uncles and most of them have got, you-know,' adds Claire, 'his-tor-ee.'

'History?' I say.

'With the law,' laughs Mags. 'But I'm OK, honest; I won't steal your pencil.'

I smile and hold my pencil case close to my chest, my hands around it. In jest obviously.

Claire laughs, and suddenly it's really easy to sit down by them. This is how it should be.

The science teacher starts to hand out notes. Claire whispers across at me. 'Because of Finn, you know, that's why Jules is hating on you. Cos you're real pretty.'

I smile. Claire is so sweet. But of course I know Finn was why Jules was on the attack.

Claire doesn't wait for me to ask more. 'She thinks that Finn belongs to her,' she concludes.

'Well, he does,' says Maggie.

Claire continues, 'He doesn't belong to anyone except himself.' She snorts as if that is obvious. 'But Jules has put a picket a mile high all around him. Anyone who even peeks over it at him is likely to get her eyes scratched out.'

'Look, no eyes,' I say, and cover my face with my hands.

'That won't help,' says Maggie. 'Like Claire says, you're way too cute.'

'And British,' adds Claire. 'But wow, what happened to your hands?'

'I know, they're not cute.' I hold my hands out.

'OMG,' says Maggie. 'How did you do that?'

As quick as a flash I say, 'A fire.' It is the first thing that comes into my head.

But somehow it feels like the truth.

I don't want this focus on my hands, so I nod at the bunch of boys who have come in and are now sitting on the back row. They're all playing superstar cool, like nobody in the room is looking at them. 'So, which one of them is Finn?' I ask, all pseudo innocence.

'I'll give you one guess,' says Maggie.

'The handsome, tall, fit one?' I say.

'Uh-huh,' says Mags.

'You see, you do have eyes!' says Claire.

The class buzzes. The teacher at the front stands with his hands behind his back, waiting.

'Are you going to Bobsy, Crystal and Ethan's party next weekend?' whispers Claire.

I shake my head, puzzled.

'All the seniors are invited.'

'You should come,' hisses Maggie.

'You going?' I ask.

'Hell yes!' says Claire.

'OK,' I say. 'If I'm invited.'

Maggie opens her mouth to say something.

I whisper to Claire, 'Is Finn going?'

'Ladies, please,' prompts the science teacher.

Claire shoots me an OMG look.

I shrug and smile.

Maggie, Claire and I settle down ready to listen.

A party. *I'm already invited to a party!* And it's still Day One! I sneak another look at the back row.

Finn sneaks a look back.

I smile.

He smiles.

I want to carry on smiling.

'Janey Morris,' he mouths.

Maggie digs me in the ribs, and shakes her head. Then nods at Jules.

Jules is watching.

I refocus.

Science.

Not parties.

Focus on science. Not Awesome Finn the Artist. Not Crystal and Bobsy and Ethan's party. I breathe in, I steady my smiling heart.

Science.

I am totally hoping that science in Massachusetts is the same as science in the place I've come from. I want to do well. If I do well, I can go away to college. Nobody will know me at college, and I will be away from Mom too. She'll be able to stop worrying so much about me. She needs to focus on herself. And I'll be one more step closer to my heart's desire. Freedom. From everything. Everyone. Anonymity. Independence.

Safety.

No Charlie.

No Charlie.

I let myself in.

It's three days since we slept in the shed.

Just an ordinary weekday. I've been delayed at school by our head of year. She called a meeting to discuss our sixth-form options. She's been going over expectations and application protocols. I'd forgotten about staying late after school. I sent a text to Mom and Charlie on the group messenger. I knew that was risky.

I'm never allowed to stay late at school without Charlie's express permission.

The moment I open the door I can tell something dreadful has happened. There's a stillness. An uncanny, eerie quiet. It slips down the stairs and flows under the doors. Its chill swirls around my feet.

'Mom?' I whisper.

The house should be full of life. The TV should be blaring, doors should be being opened and closed, crockery rattling, dishwasher washing, washing machine tumbling. Even the fridge seems weirdly silent.

'Mom?' I say again. I stand frozen in the front hall, unable to move forwards or backwards.

I don't know whether to step outside and call the police or check the house.

'Mom?' I say a bit louder.

At last, a distant whimper, somewhere from upstairs. I take the stairs two at a time, race up to the front landing.

The bathroom, it's coming from the bathroom. The door is ajar. I push it further. There's Mom sitting on the closed toilet seat, her head in her hands.

'Don't look,' she says. 'Darling? It's OK. It's OK. I'll be OK.' Her voice catches. 'Please just hand me a cold flannel.'

I wet a flannel in the sink and pass it to her. She puts it over her face and then lifts her head.

There is blood on her blouse. She presses the cold flannel to the side of her face.

'Let me call the hospital?' I say. 'Let me get a taxi. I'll take you there.'

'No,' she whispers.

I know better than to try to persuade her. I know a lot better than that. Any attempt to get help from outside will only make everything much, much worse. It is better to press the cold flannel against her black eye, to wash the cut on her split lip, sponge the blood out of her blouse. To make her a hot cup of tea with plenty of sugar and some paracetamol. To let her lie down for as long as it takes, until she can leave the house and nobody will suspect a thing.

This is how we live.

In hiding.

In fear.

And wounded.

I shake my head, trying to dislodge the memories. Focus on science.

The teacher starts.

Stay focused.

We refer to diagrams. We complete exercises. We read through theorems. I breathe a sigh of relief. This is the same stuff. It's going to be OK. I pretty much think I can put science in the bag. I settle down to grapple with the rest of the topic. I even finish early and start doodling. I like drawing mazes. Before long the break bell rings and we're done.

We leave the science lab. Maggie tugs my arm. 'Hey, come on, I'll even let you share my crackers.'

'And I'll tell you all about Crystal's party, you little British newbie,' says Claire.

I smile; it's nice to have friends.

Enjoy it, I tell myself. After this you're on your own.

Maggie and Claire are gone. I pick up my Living Faith bag.

For a second I stop. I listen through the laughter and the whooping. I hear through the walls of the canteen. My mind shoots across the wide Atlantic Ocean.

Into the heart of England.

Straight to Charlie.

He is going through our stuff.

He is piling and labelling and searching.

He has found Mom's old photo album and the pictures of her as a child.

He is thinking.

His thoughts steam into the corners of the room, like toxic thunderclouds they hover.

Lightning strikes.

He reaches for the phone.

'Ben, you work for a travel company. Can you get me timetables for flights leaving for New York on a Tuesday?'

Pause.

'Really. Thanks, mate.'

Pause.

'From every airport in London. Also Bristol and Birmingham?'

Pause.

'Can you send me a link to that?'

Poison starts to drizzle down.

'Thanks. I owe you one, pal.'

Charlie nods. Replaces the phone.

'I'll find you,' *he whispers.* 'Run all you like, but you can't hide.'

11

It's third period. Art.

Again, I have nowhere to sit. That is not totally true.

There are a few spare chairs. But I have no one to sit by. Mags and Claire don't do art.

I hesitate at the front of the class while everybody else gets out their folders, sits at their spots. I scan the room. No Jules. And no Finn. I still continue to wait. The teacher is occupied, cleaning up after the break. He casts a glance over his shoulder, sees me still hovering by the front table. 'I'll get around to you soon,' he calls. 'Be creative, sit down.' He waves a busy arm.

I relax and step to the nearest empty table. I sit. It is only when I feel the electric stare of everybody in the room that I realise I've made a massive faux pas.

The door swings open.

Latecomer.

Finn sweeps into the room. A lightning bolt, fiery, beautiful.

He lays his folder down on my table.

I gasp, expecting Jules to enter too.

But the teacher crosses and closes the door.

And Finn smiles at me. Sunshine, warm, friendly.

The rest of the class giggle.

And no Jules enters.

Fate has interceded a second time. I'm not at the wrong table at all.

'We meet again, Janey Morris,' Finn says.

He pulls out his chair and sits down. Opening up his folder, he rifles through it, pulls out papers. Spreads his drawings before me. Flowing lines. Lifelike faces. Incredible. Beautiful.

My eyes widen. 'Wow!' I whisper.

'Now will you let me draw you?' he whispers.

The teacher brings me a copy of the course requirements. 'Welcome to art,' he says.

I stare mesmerised at Finn's drawings.

'We're doing our practical projects, studying old masters. It's a part of the fine art component and an important contribution to your overall grade. You will have to team up with someone to do the pair work. I suggest, as you're at this table, you pair up with Finn, who currently has no partner.

'OK, Finn?'

Finn is looking at me through a lock of hair that has flopped across his face. Stormy smiles in blue skies.

The teacher doesn't wait for an answer. He put the course requirements down on the table.

Finn brings his chin up. He sends me a conspiratorial look, then eyeballs the art teacher. The teacher eyeballs him back, presses his lips together until they form one tight line and says: 'You have to do paired work. She's sitting here. Up to now you've refused to work with anyone. And now there's no one left to pair up with.'

He pauses. The whole class have stopped work. They're watching.

'Take it or leave it. But if you want the grade you better get with it.'

Finn laughs. 'No sweat,' he says. 'I was saving myself for her.'

The class giggles again.

The teacher laughs, realising he's just been had.

'Did you bring your portfolio from your former high school?' the teacher asks me.

I shake my head.

41

'Can I contact them to get it?'

I start to panic.

'Oh yeah, I forgot. I have it,' I lie.

'Bring it in when you can.'

I mentally write off the weekend. I'll have to redo every piece.

Finn turns to me. 'So, Janey Morris?' he asks.

'My name's Lexi,' I say.

'Well, Janey Lexi,' he says, 'welcome to art. We have to work together; do you think you can work with me?'

I glance at his drawings. I take a deep breath. 'I'll try not to bring your grade down.'

He smiles. 'Art is not all about grades.'

A wide ocean of possibilities opens up, and I'm at sea.

'I'm quite good at art,' I say, sticking to the safe shorelines of grade boundaries. 'And grades mean a lot to me. I need them. I need to get to college. I mean I'm relatively OK,' I say. I don't want him to think I'm bragging. I feel flustered. I look down at my hands.

He casts an eye down too.

I've purposely worn long sleeves and I've hooked a thumb through the sleeve cuff to make sure my burns are covered. Ninety per cent of them. But a telltale ridge of knuckle betrays me.

I snatch my hands away. 'They're not as bad as they look,' I say. 'I can use a pencil.' I shove my fingers into my lap. 'And a paintbrush,' I add.

He turns his head away. A strange tightening flits across his brow. A dark memory. He hesitates for a moment, as if he is trying to recall something that won't be summoned.

42

'Sorry,' he says at last, 'sorry. I didn't mean anything by looking. I've got a good feeling about this. We'll make it work. And of course grades are important to me too. I'm planning on art school. Brief yourself on everything. You can ask me anything.'

I nod my head.

And my heart starts dancing.

I start reading the course requirements. None of it makes sense. I read the same sentence five times. I doodle a whole complicated series of passageways on some scratch paper, without realising what I'm doing. Finn has the most amazing grey-, green-, blue-, brown-flecked eyes. Finn has the most amazing smile. Finn can draw like Michelangelo. Finn has the straightest teeth. And the squarest chin.

I'm mesmerised.

I am at sea on a wide, wide ocean.

I can see now why he is the fittest, hottest, coolest guy in the school. I cannot believe I'm going to have to do an art project with him. WE ARE GOING TO WORK TOGETHER. I read the same sentence again. It still makes no sense.

Finn has a girlfriend.

A strange inner witchy thought suddenly warns me off.

Don't go there, Lexi. Keep your head down. Do you hear me? Forget all about Finn. Keep your mouth shut. His girlfriend is trouble.

'So have you cracked it yet? Lexi-Jane?' he says. Somewhere behind his question an ocean floods in.

And I'm drowning.

I dismiss the witchy warning. 'Not quite,' I say; my voice is hoarse.

'First impression?'

Handsome. Solitary. Bold. Talented. Kind. Dangerous. Sexy.

'What have we got to do?'

I force myself to read the paragraph yet again. My pulse races and I feel sweaty.

'I think we have to study some famous masterpieces and do a rendition or media transformation of them, taking into account something about historical context—' I break off. I'm waffling. *I don't know what we have to do.* I think it's something like that.

'Yeah,' he says, 'but I'm telling you now, I do not do Picasso. And I do not do abstract. I want stuff with long flowing lines. Like the Pre-Raphaelites. I want life. I want passion.'

'OK,' I say, 'maybe we could do some Michelangelo?'

He draws like Michelangelo.

But Finn is drawing again and I do not think he hears me. He does not raise his head. Instead his hair flops back in front of his face. And he draws. He is so awesome at art. He is doing a line drawing of a storm at sea.

He is suddenly indifferent to everything. Absorbed. Complete. I might as well not be there.

I carry on looking at the course requirements, trying to read through the protocols. I know nothing about art. The words cartwheel in front of my eyes. There is no way I'm going to pass this grade, not unless I can make Finn love me more than anyone else he's ever met.

Where did that thought come from?

Don't go there, Lexi.

Don't be afraid. *He will be yours.* I learned that from Charlie. If you choose someone there is no way they can escape you.

Even if they seem totally indifferent.

Finn doesn't look up from his drawing.

'If you don't like abstract art – what about impressionism?'
I say.

I'm so out of my depth.

And he is so absorbed he doesn't answer.

'Or life drawing?' I say, desperately trying to get it right.

'Yeah. I like life drawing,' Finn drawls.

Oh good. He's listening.

'But only if you will be my model.' Finn flashes me a look
that instantly undresses me.

OMG.

A wave of fire.

Why did I say that about life drawing?

My cheeks!

Life drawing!

Posing in the nude.

WEEK EIGHT

since the accident

But I will wear my heart upon my sleeve
For daws to peck at: I am not what I am.

William Shakespeare – Othello

RAW UMBER

12

Venice Ward, Room 4, The Shore Center for Medical Care
Visiting hours in this hospital start from 11:30 a.m. onwards.
If you ever get this document, Finn, and can forgive me,
please come. I miss you so much.

Since I regained consciousness, I never know who will
visit me.

I get a sense that someone coordinates the visits. Crystal
and Aunt Gillian never *ever* come at the same time. Either they
both have a psychic ability to avoid each other, or somebody,
somewhere organises their timings. I am never kept
informed. I do not know how to prepare myself.

I hope today it's Crystal.

I want it to be Crystal, though I can't remember her well.
Did we become friends at school after her party? I want her
to help me remember more about the things that led to
the accident. You see, I have a deep fear that somehow the
accident was my fault. Auntie Gillian has gone completely
silent on the subject and can't be drawn or coaxed into
telling me anything any more. Every time I try, she puckers

up her lips like she's sucking lemons and says: 'I've told you all I know, more than once before, and I don't intend to keep on repeating myself. Nothing I've said speeds anything up. In fact I think it slows you down.'

Of course, to my knowledge, she hasn't told me anything at all. So I don't accept that as an answer. And I keep badgering her. But if I go too far, I get a full religious cautionary response like: 'You have made your bed; now you must lie in it. Proverbs 1:31.' Or: 'It seems your penance is to discover the truth and not spare yourself from it.' Or: 'You must ask for forgiveness from God. Only then can you be absolved of your sins.'

Great. And not very reassuring. Apart from: 'I will pray for you. And pray that your memory returns in time to spare us all.'

No concrete details.

But Crystal is different. Crystal is very beautiful. She has wild thick auburn hair, all frizz and electric, and green eyes. Though sometimes they are violet. She tells me she has a rainbow of coloured contact lenses to choose from. And her hair is chestnut blonde sometimes. Really pretty. It reflects the setting summer sun. When I think of her hair, I don't know what colour it is. It just seems to shine when she enters the room.

Anyway Crystal always tries to help me remember.

And Crystal is slim. Way slimmer than any Rubenesque painting. Am I right, in remembering you liked Rubens? And she seems to float, to skim rather than walk, to glide even. When she first visited, I was struck by that.

'Lexi,' she says as she enters. Her voice is deep. Her tone: chocolate and cream with a hint of the Irish.

'Lexi,' she says, and lays a hand on my shoulder. And I must look into her eyes and sink into their indigo midnight over Arctic oceans.

'Crystal,' I stutter.

I am so glad it's Crystal.

Beside Crystal, Aunt Gillian is cheap towelling and rag rug with no fabric conditioner.

'You look *so* much better,' Crystal says.

Do I? I am lifted up on a rush of happiness. I look better. I will be better. I will remember everything. In time for the trial too. Suddenly the cream-painted, plastic-floor-tiled hospital seems so much more iconic.

She smiles.

'Soon you'll be walking again and—'

I cut across her. 'I walked yesterday,' I say. 'The nurses got me out of bed and made me do ten steps. They followed with this.' I point at the tubes and drips.

I don't know why I draw attention to them. It is inglorious and revolting to be catheterised and tied up to a drip.

I shrug as if to say – this is what being human entails. Though Crystal is scarcely human; she is all angel wings and spirit.

She smiles. 'Wow,' she says, 'that is so awesome. Soon you'll be out of here and doing cheerleading!'

I'd like that, but my legs ache so badly after today's walk. It'll be decades before I do any cheerleading.

'What's happening at school?' I ask.

'It's summer vacation, dummy!'

'No news of Finn?' I don't know why I bother asking. I know there'll be no news of him.

'He's gone.' Crystal rolls her eyes, as if that's what's expected of all boys who've recently graduated high school.

I know he hasn't gone. What I don't know is why nobody will bring me news of him.

'I've brought you make-up,' says Crystal, 'so you can always look your best, just in case.'

She dumps her handbag on the bed and rustles around inside it, until she retrieves a plastic bag with 'Coastal Drugstore' printed on the plastic.

'What of Mags and Claire? Have you seen them?'

She tips make-up out on to the bed: eyeliner, mascara, lipstick, blusher and nail polish. Then she says, 'Look, I'm here, isn't that enough?'

'Sorry.' That was so tactless of me.

She smiles. 'OK, rest up your head on the pillow, and I'll make you look beautiful.'

She gives me a gentle shove on the chest and I flop backwards. She tucks my scarred hands out of sight under the hospital sheet.

'I have questions,' I say. 'I want to go over things.'

'Close your eyes,' she orders.

I want to remember as much as I can.

'How did we become friends?' I say. I untuck one hand and wave it around as if to say – her, here, me, her caring enough to come and visit and make me look beautiful.

'Shush,' she warns, 'or I'll smudge the line.'

Branches scrape gently against the windowpane.

'OK, I'll stay still, but tell me. Was it at your party?'

50

When I first came round from the coma, I had no recollection of anyone except Mom and Finn and Charlie. Even visits from Auntie Gillian were a surprise.

'You were pretty wild at my party you know,' she says.

Crystal's party.

Suddenly I remember. That's when everything started.

Finn and me at Crystal's party. Of course.

'We were friends, despite all the fuss after the party,' she says. 'It hurt me at first when you couldn't make me out when I visited you here. I stuck up for you, you know, when all that happened. I don't mind now. I'll do what I can to help you anyway.'

'Thanks,' I say. 'My bad. It's faces, I can't seem to remember them. I'm sorry.'

'There, you look awesome,' says Crystal.

'Can I open my eyes?' I ask.

'OK, but you must keep still, because your eyebrows are a mess.'

I peek out. Crystal is twisting some threads with a determined look.

The chrome of the metal bed winks at me. The squeak of trolley wheels echoes somewhere in the door-slapped spaces of a remote corridor.

'I really do want to go over things,' I say. 'I need to remember. And the thing with faces is really worrying.'

'Shall we start with the accident?' says Crystal.

'OK.'

I sigh. Crystal always wants to start with the accident, but she can't tell me anything about it, as she wasn't there.

'Do you remember anything new?'

'No.'

Actually that's not true. 'Yes,' I correct myself.

Crystal leans forward with the threads ready. 'Tell!' she demands.

'There was a hazy moon.'

'Anything else?'

I shake my head.

'Who was there? Did you see anyone by the light of that hazy old moon?'

'I don't know,' I say. 'Just the hazy moon and the train tracks and the car, I think, and then nothing.'

Crystal leans over me and says, 'Really, stay very still now.'

She starts threading my left eyebrow. It hurts as the hairs are twisted out.

'You're never going to remember it,' she says. 'Maybe you're trying so hard you're imagining things. I'm sure that night there was no moon at all.'

Funny what we remember. I have no recollection of Crystal, yet I remember a hazy moon that wasn't there. And I can relive every moment of School Day One with Mags and Claire as easily as if it were this morning.

Yet Mags and Claire never come to visit.

I frown.

Why don't Mags and Claire visit?

And where is Mom?

Was it because of what happened at the party?

I must remember.

I really must.

BURNT SIENNA

13

Massachusetts, Last Spring
School Day One, After Home Time

I wait in the school yard for Mags and Claire.

They promised to meet me, show me around town. I don't want to go back to Gillian's. I know Mom would probably like to have me home, so she can quiz me about my day, vent a little, catch me captive in the cold north wind of her pain, clutch me close and breathe her fears down my neck.

So glad you are home safe, honey. So glad. So relieved. Whenever you are out, I think Charlie has got to you. I can't stand it. Now you're here. We're both here. You are more precious to me than life itself. I'd kill to protect you. Did you lock the hall door? I'm so, so sorry about everything. So, so sorry. Are you sure you haven't been online?

And on. And on.

She worries and worries over me.

Until soon she is whispering how Charlie will find us and creep into the apartment in the dead of night with a massive hunting knife, and how he will tie me up and make her watch him stab me repeatedly, before he strangles her.

Over and over.

Until the sound of a passing train drowns her out.

I love Mom, but sometimes it's all too difficult.

And I want to escape into being a teenager and invincible.

And we are over three thousand miles away from Charlie.

And I have made a clean start. I have met a glorious artist who wants to paint me, even though he has a toxic girlfriend, and I have two new friends and I want to see what a coastal town in Massachusetts has to offer.

So Mom can wait.

Just this once.

We walk down to the shore. The sea is grey, all wet slate. The sky sends dark shadows over the waves. Sunlight breaks through in patches. A salty breeze stings my cheek. I know from the way its tugs at my hair that I'm going to have to wash away brine and spray as soon as I get in.

Mags buys us all ice cream. It runs down the cone and drips through my fingers. I twist the cone around. The biscuit stuff is soggy and cheap, the colour of woodchip. The ice cream is runny and tastes of synthetic vanilla, like a chemical car air freshener. But I am walking down the seafront, with my arms linked between two new friends, and we are laughing and dizzy with excitement. It is the best ice cream I've ever had.

And I think I'm a little bit in love.

With my glorious, kind artist, my strong-headed, friendly god. His smile has melted ice caps in my soul. His welcome has made me see how things could be, in a world free of Charlies.

He has redeemed men-kind and that delights me. Someone like Finn would never stalk me, never spy on me. He would be absorbed in his art. His passion for beauty would bathe his every action. He would never smell my clothes and accuse me of vile acts. He would see only my loveliness and perfection. My freedom would be safe.

Just imagining it thrills me.

And suddenly I am happy. Free of shadows. And stained by cheap ice cream.

'Let's walk all the way down, past the pier and up the road to Gallows Hill,' says Mags.

'Gallows Hill?' I say.

'Up there.' Claire points to the headland on the far side of the bay. 'Across the train tracks and along the cliff path.'

I squint into the distance. I see the dark promontory of land, the hill behind.

'It's really not as far as you think,' says Mags. 'Come on. It's gonna be a great view.'

'And it's not gonna rain,' says Claire.

I'm not so sure; clouds seem to be gathering.

'Let's dance around the site of the old gallows and call out to Bridget Bishop,' says Claire.

'And we can have more ice cream on the way back,' says Mags, 'or doughnuts.'

'Or fries.'

'With sweet chilli,' says Mags.

'And ketchup,' adds Claire, 'plus mayo.'

'You have a deal,' I say. 'As long as you don't mind me dancing totally left-footed.' I kick out my left foot and hop a few steps. 'Who exactly is Bridget Bishop anyway?'

'Bridget Bishop was a witch and they hanged her here, maybe. The remains of the gibbets,' says Mags, 'have long gone. There's only a bench up there. But, be not disappointed! The ghost of Bridget Bishop and all the others are really gonna be watching your big left foot.' Mags pulls a mwahahaha scary face. 'And with May Day coming next week they'll be super attentive . . .'

'We should go up there and dance around then, for real, definitely,' says Claire.

'In the nude,' says Mags.

'And take photos of ourselves,' says Claire.

'In the nude,' says Mags.

Alarm bells.

My mind flashes from witchery to life drawing. 'Let's not take photos,' I say.

Leave no trail.

'It's OK,' says Mags, 'we're not pervs or anything.'

Charlie will be searching.

'We must take photos,' says Claire.

'We're freaking Lexi out,' warns Mags.

'Well . . .' I try to make a joke of it. 'Don't take pictures of my hands.' Or my face, I add under my breath.

'Hey, Lexi, we're just joking!' says Mags.

I try hard to wipe the panic off my face. I don't mind dancing around in the nude, if my new friends want to do that. I don't mind photographs, but I definitely do mind anything that can identify me on any bit of camera or film or celluloid or cyber film or satellite or internet, anywhere in the entire universe.

'Don't worry,' says Mags. 'We're not going to strip off – that's just what they did in the olden days.'

'On the night before May Day, the witches would go and dance around and around, totally you-know.' Claire waves her ice cream above her head, giggles and pirouettes. 'And then they claimed the one who should be their true love and sent out bewitchments and curses on guys who stood in their way.' A lump of runny ice cream flies through the air and lands on the pavement.

'Ew!' screeches Mags.

'I'd totally love to be a witch!' cries Claire.

'Don't wish too hard,' warns Mags. 'Witches look real ugly.'

'Witches are cool,' counters Claire, 'and May Day is totally where it's at, with flowers and spells and stuff.' Claire bites into the remains of her soggy cone and licks her fingers. 'But you can't really do witchy things any more.' She lets out a long sigh like she wishes it was still the olden days. 'Because they kind of lock up the park at night and this town is filled with stiff disapproving old puritans. Plus, well . . . people think it's a little weird . . .' Claire sighs again and shrugs.

Like Auntie Gillian, I think.

'Like Mr Cook, our principal,' say Claire. 'His folks came right off the Mayflower and just got more conservative with every generation.'

'You're such a loser, letting the likes of Mr Cook spook you,' laughs Mags. 'You could pretend the gibbets were there, if you wanted, and dance up the sides of them and anywhere you liked.'

'But we couldn't ever, ever let anyone know at school,' warns Claire. 'Before we'd know it, we'd have the whole town sentencing us to hang!'

'It's not like witchcraft is real or anything,' snorts Mags. 'Magical powers are all phoney baloney.'

I say nothing. There is power in everything. I glance down at my hands. I see power in their scarred skin; each twist round each finger zings with dark energy.

Did I tell you I am probably a witch?

I didn't used to be, but Charlie called me a witch once too often, so I decided to become one.

Once after Charlie had boasted about how he'd deliberately run over a dog and left it squirming in the road, I made effigies in candle wax and found bits of his hair and mushed them into it. Then I coshed it over the head and cursed it and threw it under an intercity train.

It didn't work.

Spells can sometimes take time though.

So it will.

One day.

Plus I know about May Day. I know about Beltane's Eve. I know about curses and love spells. A sudden wild idea occurs to me.

My eyes zing.

Love spells.

But is there enough time?

I'll do it!

I'll have my heart's desire!

Why not?

Why not have that future promised in his smiles? That wide-open ocean of possibility. That freedom to be myself. To be his muse.

But only one week to make preparations?

I only have one week, because I know more than others. I know that the true power behind May Day starts on 27th April and that is actually only seven days away.

Seven days. Then Finn will be mine!

Perhaps you doubt this. Perhaps you have read only about the Wiccan religion and the Druids and witch trials and dancing the maypole and crowning the May Queen and you have never heard of Flora.

But you see, I have.

I know she is the true goddess of spring and the 27th April is the day when you can summon her powers.

Shall I tell you how I know this?

Well, when you are truly powerless, you have two options. You can turn to God or to Black Magic.

I tried God first, I prayed and prayed that God would save me and Mom. I prayed hard, every day and every night for years. All I got was burnt hands. So I turned to magic instead.

I set about learning all I could.

It's surprising how much you can learn when you put your mind and Google to it.

Magic is more like the lottery than a religion; it gives you hope. The hope that one day your prayers will be answered.

Plus you can't really pray to the Lord to kill someone.

So as Mags and Claire debate the exact site of the old gallows and what ceremonies we'll make, my mind races. There's so much to do. I think fast. I pull out my phone. I must consult Google.

And this is what Google tells me to do:

- I must find white blossom from a May tree.

- I must weave the face of the Green Man from the rough and prickly stems heavy with their flower.
- I must find a length of white linen that has belonged to a virgin for seven years.
- I must make it into strips for the handfasting.
- And I must start my preparations immediately! (Well, as soon as I've got home and been baptised by my mother's terrors. As soon as I've washed my hair free of salt sea and wild wind. As soon as I'm cleansed of ice cream and friendship.)

Mags and Claire have walked on ahead and they wave at me to catch up.

I'm pretty sure Aunt Gillian is totally a virgin. She definitely has that look about her. Not just virginal, maybe even man-hating.

A sudden rush of cold air whips up the headland. It seems to chill right through my flimsy jacket.

I clutch the cloth around me and shiver.

Tune in, I tell myself. *Tune in to the magic* . . .

The grass stirs as if invisible feet move over it. Salt breeze and the rustling of spring leaves. I stop. I look at the spot where they hanged Bridget Bishop.

I think of witchery and spells, of May Day and curses. Of God and unanswered prayers. I look back at the sea, at the dark horizon. My mind shoots out across the wide Atlantic Ocean.

Into the heart of England.

Straight to Charlie.

* * *

He is looking at a printout of a list of airline passengers. He has highlighted two names. The whiskey bottle next to him is three quarters empty.

He is chuckling and chuckling.

'I know where you've gone,' he whispers.

The computer beside him is open. Google has 'high schools in Massachusetts' typed into its search bar.

'You can't hide, my little pigeons.'

He drains the final quarter of the bottle into his glass. He swirls it around for a moment.

A list of high schools appears on the computer screen.

'Be very careful, witch child,' Charlie hisses. 'I'm coming and I'll find you.'

He tosses the whiskey back and swallows. 'It's only a matter of time, you'll see.'

He's enjoying it.

A breeze stirs through the room, rustling a pile of papers.

Charlie sets the glass down.

'You really can't hide, you know, however hard you try.'

14

I may be a witch, but I am not a thief, so I ask very politely if Gillian has an old tablecloth I can use for a project.

I also ask her if she has ever had a sweetheart.

She is happy to give me a choice of her linen. She is unhappy to tell me of her loveless past. I choose an ideal creamy white vintage cloth and take it to my room.

For the next seven nights, I'll let it sit upon my windowsill to soak up the strength of moonbeams.

Now to go out for a walk.

'Aunt Gillian,' I say, 'I've got to get out. I won't be long. I just need some exercise, a little fresh air.'

Her chin rises a little. It's enough. She approves.

I go into Mom's room, where she's hunched by the window staring into a laptop. The shine from the polished walnut table blinks up at me. The dark wooden parquet flooring is treacherous. Everything looms precariously towards me. Mom is deep in her fear zone. The smell of polish and the tick of an antique wall clock all warn me to tread carefully.

I lean over Mom's shoulder. She's changing her social media profiles again. She's been obsessed with this for a while. I kiss her cheek. Every day she changes her username or password. She's hiding her forty-two-year-old identity, laying false trails to confuse Charlie. There are a lot of sites that need expunging.

I think she's playing a dangerous game.

'Mom,' I say, 'maybe it's better to let it go, try to build a life here?'

'Hon,' she says, 'I will, I will.'

'You look so stressed,' I say. I give her a teeny shoulder rub.

She sighs. 'I'm just all nerves,' she says. 'I can't relax. I can't sleep. I should've been a better parent.'

'I love you,' I say.

'I can't forgive myself.'

'We're good now,' I say. 'You got us out of the UK, remember?'

'I'm just trying to keep us safe here too.'

'Yeah, like with this!' I laugh as I pull out a baseball bat from under her pillow.

She laughs too. 'I know, I know. I just keep it there in case.'

'You're cute,' I say.

'I'll never let him hurt you again, I promise.'

'We're safe,' I say, 'and stay offline.'

She nods and turns back to the laptop.

I kiss the top of her head and leave.

15

I turn my back on Aunt Gillian's house. Its tall, white-wooden, sharp-pointed gables reprimand me. I walk down the street. Spring comes more quickly here. I'm actually surrounded by May trees everywhere. The hedgerows burgeon with pale blossoms. Along the pavements, great boughs laden heavy with flowers sway over picket fences. Instantly I can tell these are a powerful species of May tree. From garden to garden, little plant identification labels announce their common and botanical names: Winter King Hawthorn, *Crataegus Viridis*, Green Man May Flower.

It could not suit my purpose better!

I collect sprigs in full flower. Tonight by moonlight, I will weave the mask of the Green Man. I will sit by my strips of white linen until it is done. And I will think of what I will do when I go dancing on Gallows Hill on the night of the 27th.

I think of Mags and Claire and the dancing and their talk of May Day.

The Festival of Flora must celebrate sexuality.

Yes, sexuality.

Somehow this sleepy, quiet, prim town with its disapproving spinsters and Bible groups makes me want to go wild.

Up ahead a huge Winter King tree is in full bloom. Mags and Claire were quite right when they said that we should dance naked. Though of course they were only joking. Just a game. They weren't serious. The tree dips temptingly over the sidewalk. The blossoms tremble as a passing train disturbs the air.

I am not sure I can actually dance in the nude in any case, not seriously.

Thinking it is one thing. Saying it – if only to myself – is another. Doing it requires you to be very gifted. Perhaps I can just take a nude photo of myself and then show it to the moon on the night of the 27th?

And erase it immediately.

Although something contradictory makes me actually want to get naked. Makes me want to do things that'll shock all these good people judging me from behind their net curtains.

As I reach the tree, I quickly scan around. Nobody's watching, hopefully. I snap off a sprig of milky-white hawthorn flower and add it to my bag. Blossom flutters down on to the sidewalk. I walk on a carpet of petals.

I imagine myself as the May Queen, bedecking an old, imaginary gibbet with the face of the Green Man. I imagine myself binding fast my hand with Finn's. He won't be there of course, but like Matilda, I will lay the magic finger on him and bind his soul to mine.

I step lightly on the shower of cream-white hawthorn confetti.

The magic will be done.

He will be mine for ever and ever.

It's really very simple when you've chosen to be with someone. However much they do or don't consent.

There is no escape for them.

I make the mistake of saying this to Mags during break the next day.

She sees me glancing at Finn in English. We're doing *Othello*. 'Don't even think it,' she says.

'Why not?'

'Jules Bridges is walking evil. If you make a move on Finn you'll pay for it with your soul.'

'I can have him if I want,' I say.

'In your dreams.'

'It may be in my dreams, but you can have whoever you want just by deciding it.'

'What if he doesn't want you?'

'It makes no difference.'

Mags looks at me as if I'm mad. 'Why would you want someone who doesn't want you?' she queries.

'I'm just saying you can.'

'That's messed up,' says Mags. 'Everybody should be free to choose whoever they want – you can't *have* someone like they're an object or something.'

I can feel all my defence mechanisms flare into an inferno. She's *so* wrong. She's never lived with a paranoid, disordered, jealous, violent, control-freak stalker, monster, mind-bender sadist. Obviously. She knows nothing about how you can be owned.

I suck in air slowly. 'Yeah, you're right about that. Everyone should be free to choose.' I pause. Beats pass. 'So how do you explain Jules, then, being so super possessive of Finn? Seems like he isn't free to choose anything,' I add.

Mags laughs. 'She's not human. She's demonic. You wouldn't wanna be like her.'

16

It is the 27th. I find my way along the coast. The moon is full. The dark promontory of the hill stands silhouetted against a light sea. In one hand I carry a plastic bag containing the strips of white linen, in the other the face of the Green Man all wrapped in paper. In my rucksack, I also have some handfuls of May blossom. After every marriage, the bride must be showered with confetti, don't you think?

It's quite a climb up Gallows Hill. It seems to take much longer than on the afternoon I strolled there with Mags and Claire.

If anyone looks out of their window right now, they'll think a ghost had passed, floating up the hillside, dressed entirely in white on her way to a phantom wedding.

For a second, I feel sad. I glimpse myself through a third eye, located somewhere in space. I'm a sad, unloved, damaged thing, going to a wedding all by myself.

Unloved and unlovable.

Resorting to fantasy.

And witchcraft.

And modelling myself on Charlie.

An overwhelming urge makes me stop, tells me to turn back. I wait until it passes.

Charlie would never give up.

I tell myself: you must be stronger than him. You must master his dark arts. You must be able to do what he does two times as bad. Only then will you be able to defeat him.

You must take what you want. You must defeat all enemies. You must possess what you love. You must be the predator, or you will end up the prey.

All prey is doomed.

After a few minutes, I continue. I reach the place Mags and Claire decided was the most likely gallows spot. The ghosts of long hanged, tortured and abused maidens smile at me and wave, invite me gracefully to dance. 'Wait, my sisters,' I say. I stand where I think the exact hanging spot would once have been. I hold the mask of the Green Man over my face. I turn towards the wide sea.

In my mind I erect my maypole, right here. I tie imaginary ribbons to the top of it. I imagine the Hanged Maidens as they should have been, bright beautiful girls, alive without twisted necks and twisted hands. *I will avenge you all*, I whisper. I begin to gently dance around my imaginary pole. Three times widdershins, and as I go I weave the spell and I croon my song: it's quite crude, but I know it will work.

> *By moon and stars and sea and sky,*
> *You are mine until you die.*
> *And if you try to undo this spell,*
> *By life and death and heaven and hell*

Your love for me will only swell,
For by moon and stars and sea and sky
You are mine until you die.

I take my one hand and I begin to wrap it carefully to Finn's with the sliced lengths of Auntie Gillian's tablecloth. In my mind I feel his warm palms, his strong grip, his encasing fingers. I wind and tie. I wrap and knot my real hand to his imaginary one.

I complete the handfasting. My hand with its burnt fingers closed fast upon his.

Then I raise my bound right hand. I crook my one free burnt digit and point it at the dark horizon. I show the sky my photo. I point my finger at the moon and I whisper:

'Mine.'

The blue-bright moon halo shimmers. A moonbeam fixes me in silver. My moon shadow darkens.

A grey cloud bulges up from the horizon.

The temperature drops. I shiver. A wild storm starts somewhere far out at sea.

The grey cloud sails up and up.

It turns the moonlight blood red.

TERRA ROSA

17

Venice Ward, Room 4

Auntie Gillian visited me this morning. I do not know why Auntie Gillian insists on being called auntie – it is so juvenile really. It doesn't convince anyone that we're related.

My mother never comes. Auntie Gillian tells me this is because of the accident and what happened. My mother is in God's hands now. Auntie Gillian says Mom loves me and is safe on the other side of something. Maybe she means the States. Safe on the West Coast? Perhaps she has to keep running and hiding. I try to hold on to the details, but like all things connected to the accident, they slip away.

The accident made substantial news, apparently. So no doubt Charlie is aware of it. I mean, he's still out there and listening for any kind of news of us, isn't he? By now he may have tracked Mom down to Massachusetts. That's what I've been thinking. Mom has had to go.

But I still want to know if she's all right, so I ask Auntie Gillian.

'She's in a safe place,' answers Auntie Gillian. 'We must pray for her.'

Her answer makes me uneasy. Something nags at me. I miss Mom so much. I wish I could hear her voice.

'Can't we call her?' I ask

But Auntie Gillian says we can't. There's no way to hear her voice. Nor can I be told anything more. Except that something dreadful happened and I should not be upset. That it will set my healing back. That it is God's will. That if I don't know anything, then I can't betray anything. And above all I must absolutely not get distressed.

When she says that, the nagging feeling gets much, much worse. And I instantly get mega-distressed. What does she mean? *Something dreadful happened? That it's God's will? That we must pray for her?*

Where is my mom?

Something unthinkable and unbearable starts to mushroom in my mind.

But Auntie Gillian is adamant and unashamedly ambiguous. She says, 'There is nothing we can do about it. We must take the long view on this. You must not get upset. And that's that.'

This is the kind of damage control that Auntie Gillian excels at. Not satisfied with exerting an iron grip over everything immediate, she pursues future distant events with vigour. 'If you get upset, you will not recover. And that may affect everything. Your mother is in a 'safe place'. And God is with her. Let His will be done. Amen.'

I don't know what Auntie Gillian means by betray anything. I have never betrayed anyone. I have done everything in my power to protect Mom and follow all the advice of the church.

But Auntie Gillian won't be swayed. I must just think of my mother as having gone for now. Perhaps for ever.

'That is the price you pay,' Auntie Gillian adds, 'for being foolish.'

I probably have been foolish. So I shut up.

I remember Auntie Gillian's face as being very white this morning. She is not known for smiling. She tried hard and pulled her mouth into something that I know was supposed to be a smile. I took a risk and asked her again what had happened. I asked her why the accident had made the national news.

I wanted to know. I wanted to see if I could remember.

Maybe she could bring in the newspapers, if she didn't want to talk about it?

My attempt to find out more was a failure. I don't remember her reply, even though it was only this morning. I'm sure she said something.

So I asked her about my mobile, instead. Could I have it? If I had it, I could call Finn. I could call Mags and Claire. I could research my accident. I could do so many things to put my mind at rest. I often ask her about my mobile. But she always answers that the police have it.

I don't know why.

She also thinks I should not have a replacement.

It has begun to dawn on me that I might have a really bad selective memory problem as well as general amnesia about the accident. I seem to forget some things as soon as they're mentioned. You see, I don't remember the reason she gave

71

for the police having my phone. I only remember what I said.

I replied, 'Oh, that.'

I wake in the night.

Blue lights flash.

'Run!' screams my mother. I will run but I'm so tired. I'm out of breath. He pounces. I fall backwards. I pull myself up. I grip the banister. I turn and race down the stairs. He's following. He's coming . . .

Blue flashing lights . . . police sirens . . . they can't help Mom. I must do something, find a phone . . . where is my phone?

WHERE IS MY PHONE?

Someone grabs my hands . . . I twist my hands free. I wrench them out of his grasp . . . the scar tissue tears, burns. If I am not here, he can't kill me. I race down the street. 'Stop,' he yells. I scream and scream and the screaming goes on and on . . .

And I'm alone racing away.

I will work harder on my memory. I will go over every event meticulously. I will make sense of each dream, each flashback. Like pieces in a jigsaw puzzle, I will slot each memory into its place until I have the whole picture.

I will not disappoint Aunt Gillian.

She has told me that they've set a date for the trial now and I must be able to take the witness stand.

I must be able to convince the jury that I'm trustworthy.

I can't seem to hold on to what the trial is about.

I hope I haven't done anything awful.

I set to work.

FLESH TINT

18

Massachusetts, Last Spring, April 28th

I'm settling into my new school well. I tot up my successes. Two new friends, a shared art project with Finn, a spell cast and no news of Charlie. I give thanks every day for no news of him. Studies going well. College applications being made. Future success on the horizon.

I wonder how my spell will work itself out. I think of Bridget Bishop and hanged maidens. I cross my twisted fingers.

I better be prepared. I wear my best, cutest hand-me-down blouse on the day after the spell-casting and sneak a bit of Mom's make-up on.

Fingers crossed Mr Cook won't notice.

There's an energy in the air. It feels like something is going to happen.

As soon as I'm in school, I'm sent to the office. It's right beside the photocopying room. That's where you have your fingerprints taken. You need that doing to access lots of things in the school. Up until now their system was confused, because my fingerprints were all scar tissue. So they've had me on a swipe card. Today hopefully they'll sort that out.

Someone else is there, waiting in the office, just out of view. I can hear them flicking the pages of a book or mag.

I can't help smiling to myself.

I know who it is.

I feel the breeze off Gallows Hill, light, heady and intoxicating. I see the eyes of the Green Man winking at me.

Thank you, Bridget.

I walk into the office and take the empty seat next to Finn. I'm right. I knew he'd be waiting for me, didn't I? I flex my fingers. I send up a prayer to the hanged maidens. I think of my spell. *Let it work.* I gaze at the floor.

A charge of electricity sizzles through the room.

Finn says, 'Oh, hi, Lexi!' Gone is the artistic absorption, the somewhat vague kindness, the light-hearted teasing comments about Janey Morris. He looks at me, opens his eyes, *really* looks at me. And I am seen.

Thank you, Hanged Maidens.

Noticed at last, just for myself.

As I want to be.

He draws in air and smiles. I smile back. The lady from the office opens her door and says, 'Next one?'

Finn nods at me. 'Go on,' he says, 'You first.'

I graciously assent. I smile a sweet thanks at him. Bravo for his gallantry. Then I point to my hands. I hold them up to the lady. 'I've come,' I say, 'and I hope your biometric fingerprint recog-system is going to like my prints today.'

The lady retreats into an inner section of the office, indicating I should follow.

I glance at Finn. His face blanches. He stares at my hands.
And this time he doesn't turn politely away.

They are ugly. I know they're ugly. I feel a fierce heat rush through my chest. I feel the urge to hide them. My hands must not betray me. My heart beats fast. A dark memory forms. Storm clouds gather.

Sweat dampens my forehead.

'I'm sorry,' I mumble.

I'm not sorry. Why did I say that? I want to shove my hands behind my back. My hands refuse to move.

My hands are more powerful than me. Instead of hiding themselves they flex and stretch and bend. They finger wave at him.

I see Finn's gaze travel from my burns to my wrists, up my arms. Back to my fingers. Back up my arms. But he is not recoiling.

His gaze reaches my face, my eyes. Mesmerised. Entranced. He stares at me and now it's my turn. I am bewitched by his pale hazel-flecked golden irises. I can't even blink. Snake eyes. Owl eyes.

Eyes that see into my secrets.

I blush.

I turn away.

My hands stay exposed. They remain stubbornly revealing everything, pointing to my secret.

With his hazel-flecked eyes watching, I follow the lady into the inner section. She presses my fingertips to screens and more screens. Twice. This hand. That hand. She taps keys, presses buttons. Then asks me to wait outside again where Finn is.

And he is still there staring.

'What happened?' he says. His face is white beneath its darkness.

How can I answer his question? I cannot tell the truth. *Charlie will find us.* So I'm new. I'm reborn. I have no past. I *have* to recreate myself. I am forever forbidden from truth telling. I am a lie. A deceitful being. A breathing falsehood. I am a liar not by choice, but by destiny.

I am forever damned.

I am a witch.

I hate you, Charlie.

But if I cannot escape this fate, then I must embrace it – otherwise I will live for ever in the shadow of my secrets, afraid to be this new Lexi.

I pause. I consider.

If I must become a lie, then it should be a brave one. A grand one. An expansive one! One that uplifts and elevates me; one that embraces my higher self; one that allows me to triumph over my past, become more meaningful, more generous, more noble.

Better.

A person Finn could love

The scarred hero of a heartbreaking disaster.

'I was burned,' I say; that bit certainly is true. 'By a fire.' That bit isn't – but at least it's believable. Plus I've already told Mags that.

'How?' he whispers, his voice hoarse, his eyes staring.

I quickly search my mind for viable and heroic scenarios with fires that would burn hands into a tangled mess of scar tissue.

House fire? Dangling from the burning sill of a second-storey window?

No. Not heroic enough.

Escaping with orphans through bush fires in Australia? Maybe not. Legs would be burnt too – although the orphan touch feels good.

But Australia? Please.

Orphans might not be believable anyway. And they're a bit *Rabbit-Proof Fence*.

Finn stares. He's gone a very sickly colour. I think he's holding his breath. Are my hands *that* ugly?

'Not a bonfire?' he whispers.

If he wants it to be a bonfire, I have no objection.

'Yes, a bonfire party,' I say. 'An accident . . .'

'Was there a boy . . . near the fire?'

If he wants a boy near the fire, so be it.

'Yes, how did you know?' I concur, all surprised. I *am* surprised. For it seems I hardly have to lie at all. 'There was this boy . . .'

Finn visibly jumps. His shoulders twitch and his breath comes out in a rush.

'It's you. Isn't it?' he says. 'I know it is!' Breathless. He seems in shock. His vocal cords stretched, raspy.

What does he mean?

I don't want to lose the moment. Here I am in the outer office of the school's finance section, all alone with Finn. Every girl in the school would give their best sexiest jeans to be here with Finn the Beautiful. And what is more, I have his fixed attention. He eyes superglued to mine. I occupy everything in his field of vision.

Right now he is mine.

If only for the moment.

My heart burns. Flora has heard me. The souls of the hanged maidens were listening. He waits breathless for my next words.

I withhold them.

His attention is like champagne, heady, intoxicating.

I must have more.

I drink it in.

'It is. Isn't it?' he says.

His tone is so yearning, so incredulous.

I nod. I have to. The ancient lore of magic demands it.

'It is. It is!' he repeats.

I haven't a clue what he means, but some soundless explosion has gone off somewhere inside him. He is all confusion and treacle and absence of balance.

A delicious feeling sweeps through me.

Power.

'Yes,' I whisper. And with that one word I seal my fate.

'Do you remember?' he says.

I know how to play this game. Finn desires me to be someone I am not. Charlie taught me all the moves. He taught me so well that I lost for ever the person I really was.

I am the chameleon, the shape-shifter, the changeling.

For a fleeting instant I wonder who she was, the real girl, the hero from his past, the one he's thinking of. Then I smile slowly and dissolve her in a bath of acid. I morph and change and subsume her. I take her place like a succubus.

'Of course,' I say. I narrow up my eyes, as if I can say a lot more, but I choose not to. I sip on the champagne. I wait to know his history.

'It's me,' he says, 'it's me, Finn.'

I must be careful. I must collide subtly into his mind and sift through his memories. I must extend a soft-paw hand, to tease out his story. I must learn and discover, claws retracted. Then – and only then – can I reshape my past.

I flex my burnt finger. I open the toolbox of my skills. I carefully access my agreeable touch.

First requirement: live the memory. Probe it. Insert distortion between lobe and cell and tissue of the facts. Curb impulse to respond. Blunt instinct to tell truth. I start with the sentence, 'Yes, of course, it's you.' Then, 'I know your name.'

Silently. The unspoken. *Every girl in the whole school knows your name.* I don't want to distract him.

'I never knew your name,' he said. 'I was visiting with my family in the UK when it happened. I'm so sorry, I just remember you standing there in that blue dress with that duffel coat on and then . . .' His voice trails off.

I smile at him. I cast my eyes down at my hands to prompt him to tell more of the story.

Let us remember.

'I never quite knew what happened. It was all so fast,' I say.

'A boy pushed me. He didn't mean to. I don't think so anyway; we were racing around with sparklers – I fell and then—'

I wish I could wipe a tear from my eye. It seems like a suitably sentimental, melodramatic motion to make, but I know it would shout fakery.

Any movement, any twitch out of place right now will spoil the flow of his delivery. He might stop, blink, see through the web.

Instead I rouse him gently. 'A game, yes, you fell,' I say, and I smile sadly. This time I open both hands, my palms glare out reproachfully at him. Knotted, fused flesh.

A sharp intake of breath.

'It is you,' he says. He stands up. He takes hold of my hands. He presses them between his own. He says, 'I'm so sorry. I am so, so sorry.'

And I understand that I saved him. When he was a boy, he fell into a fire. I pulled him out with my bare hands. I jumped into the abyss for him. I braved the furnace to rescue him from a torturous death. I am a hero.

The hero I've always wanted to be.

And why not?

If I must be forced to become a liar, then why not become a valiant liar? A noble liar? The winds blow down from Gallows Hill, carrying the breath of all the hanged witches. I will not betray the sisterhood.

Why not handcuff this beautiful boy to my own damnation?

He desires it.

'I've always wanted to find you,' he says. 'I don't remember much except the pain, but when I got better, I wanted to find you.'

'Did you scar too?' I ask.

He pulls up the trouser leg of his school uniform. Down one calf is a searing, livid mark. 'That's not all,' he says, 'but they're not like yours.'

I gasp. His leg so beautiful, like living sculpture.

'Tell me what you remember?' he pleads. 'I only have vague bits and pieces.'

I glance around the office. Brown industrial carpet, low square table, air freshener plugged into the wall socket.

Well, I'm so glad he doesn't recall any of the details, that is very convenient, isn't it?

I start my story. My imagination is endless. 'I don't think I saw you fall,' I say. That's the truth. 'But I heard screaming.' I'm sure I did. 'I can remember screaming, sometimes I wake at night and still hear screaming.'

Tears well up in my eyes. Always screaming and waking and more screaming.

'I can't believe it,' he says. 'I really can't; it's really you.'

Suddenly I no longer care whether he believes it's me or not. A rush of fear and loathing surges into my throat. The screaming and the boiling water pouring and pouring.

Charlie did this. Charlie is still burning me, forcing me to damn my soul with lies.

I blink.

'Oh my God,' says Finn.

I no longer care whether the girl in his history survived or perished miserably, or moved to Australia even. I don't care whether I'm being fair. Right now this is all we have. His yearning for some girl in some long-ago trauma and my lies and my pain. Nothing can wipe it away.

Oh God forgive me.

Charlie, you have taught me to be as twisted as you are.

A tiny voice inside warns me: *You go too far. Like the hanged witches you'll pay for it. You should stop it all right now.*

And inside I feel sick and ill with myself.

But right now I have ugly hands and he has a scarred leg and we share a common history of being burned. *Isn't that enough?*

I know it's not. I know lying like this will invite the Devil in.

I know it's wrong.

And I will be damned for ever.

I don't stop.

'I turned and all your clothing was on fire.'

I can't stop.

'I didn't know what to do. Everybody was screaming; I was the nearest. I just grabbed hold of you. I grabbed your coat and pulled.' And now I've started I can't go back. I must accept the consequences. 'The fabric of your coat melted and stuck to my hands and then one of the branches from the bonfire fell towards us, and I had to catch it or fend it off. So I did, but I wasn't very strong, so I couldn't pull you away or knock the branch aside and then it was just there, and the others came. And at first the branch felt just hot, but then it was on fire.' I relive the burning and the pain. 'I don't remember anything else. I was in hospital for a long time.'

There is silence.

'I thought,' he says, 'I thought – I didn't know – how could you have held out against that branch?'

'I don't know,' I say. 'I think when things like that happen you just do it. You don't really think about it. There is a time to think about things, but it's not while you're doing them, and somehow it didn't hurt – not until afterwards.'

'They wouldn't let me contact you,' he says.

'I wasn't there to contact,' I say.

He knows very little of this story. I'm on safe ground. I'm quite free to make up the rest. 'I didn't actually live in that area. I don't even remember where the bonfire was.' I let my eyes wander away from him. 'My uncle took us there, I was staying with my cousins. They ambulanced me to Bristol. They have a special burns clinic in Bristol. I stayed in Bristol for a very long time, then I went home.'

I know all about the Bristol burns unit.

'Ah,' says Finn, as if that explains everything.

The sound of a door bangs shut somewhere down the corridor.

'And now we've met up again, so weird.' Finn blinks. 'And we're working on my favourite ever art project together.' He runs a hand through his hair, messes the back of it up and blinks again. 'Like it's fate.'

I stare at the floor.

'I don't want you to think I never tried to find you,' he adds. 'Or that I forgot what you did.'

'You were only a kid,' I say, like I am now forever old. 'Both of us were kids.'

'I never knew your name.'

How doubly convenient.

'My name is and always was Alexia Clark,' I say, and with that, I put my hands out of sight.

The office lady comes back in. She hands me a new card. It's a swipe card.

'I've really tried,' she says, 'but they don't think that the finger scan will work for you at all, so we're giving you a fresh permanent swipe to use.' She smiles as if they have

83

everything under control in the entire universe. 'Any time you want to buy anything.' She nods to let me know she knows about access and printing stuff off the computer and buying things at school. 'We've preloaded the card with a gratuity allowance. You can top that up. We're really sorry that the system hasn't been able to work for you.'

'Don't worry,' I say, 'and thanks. I don't really mind if my fingerprints aren't on your system.'

She gives me a strange look, as if she's not sure whether that was a nice remark or not. She decides I must be far too embarrassed about my hands to be going around offering random insults. She pats my arm. She turns to Finn.

I put the swipe card in my bag.

'Finn,' she says, 'is this the third or the fourth time you've erased your prints since you've been here? Whatever are you doing to our system?'

But her voice is honey warm.

I suck in my cheeks.

OMG. Even *she* likes him.

She disappears into the inner office again. On my way to the door, I pass him. He holds out a hand, pauses, looks at me and whispers, 'Wait outside?'

I smile.

'Will you wait?'

I hover.

'I'd like to have your number?' he says.

Of course I'll wait!

I widen my eyes slightly at him to let him know that. I leave the office and stand in the corridor.

WEEK NINE

since the accident

O, beware, my lord, of jealousy;
It is the green-ey'd monster, which doth mock
The meat it feeds on.

William Shakespeare — Othello

PURPLE LAKE

19

Venice Ward, Room 4, The Shore Center for Medical Care
I hate this hospital. All they ever want me to do is talk.

However, I am getting better. I do not have drips attached to stands by the bed any more. And my memory is getting steadily clearer. But I do get bored. I just have to lie on my own until it's time for treatment.

Treatment means sitting somewhere and answering questions, like: How do you feel?

How do you think I feel?

Stuck in here, while the sun is shining outside? While Finn is waving to me from his long-legged, sea-splashed silhouette somewhere on a golden beach?

I ask a question back. 'When are you going to allow Finn to visit me? Why haven't you let him come in?'

Their faces grow solemn.

I don't want to hear their replies.

'I know he's been here demanding to see me,' I say. 'He's probably sitting outside, furious, waiting for you to let him in, *right now*.'

I blot out any other possibility.

They shake their heads, sadly.

Of course he wants to see me. Doesn't he?

'Why hasn't Mags or Claire come too?' I ask.

They'd come and see me. I know they would. We were friends. We never quarrelled.

Did we?

I can't remember. Did I quarrel with Mags and Claire? *Did Finn dump me?* My heart suddenly storms violently, like ice flakes in a snow globe. Shaken and shaken. *I can't remember.*

Did I do something terrible?

A trembling starts deep inside.

Why won't anyone tell me the truth?

Do all my friends hate me?

What did I do?

I'd call them, but I have no phone. I don't know their numbers. *The hospital won't give me my phone. They won't let my friends in.* My hands knot themselves into fists. My throat goes dry.

They let Auntie Gillian come in though.

And Crystal.

'I don't really like seeing Auntie Gillian every day. Please send her away,' I croak.

Surprised looks pass surreptitiously between them.

'No, I don't remember anything about what happened.'

Sly subliminal messaging.

Something terrible did happen. Not just the accident.

Last night's flashback threatens to repeat on me. I deliberately block out any thoughts of terrible things.

They watch me with their snake eyes to see if I understand. But I don't. I really *don't* understand. It's gone. I've blocked it. I can't remember any of it.

They probably like Auntie Gillian. She probably reports to them about every comment I make. Especially the snappy ones. She probably records and makes notes after every visit. She lurks around and adjusts the blankets and offers me fat-fuelling homemade cookies until it drives me mad. She watches me too. It's as if they are all waiting for something, some reaction that I haven't yet made.

The medics lean forward. The police officer leans forward. I'm not sure she is a police officer. She wears no uniform. I've seen her on guard outside my room. *Maybe Charlie found us? Maybe he is out there waiting to pounce as soon as I'm unprotected?*

'How do you feel today?' starts the nurse.

'Are you ready to work on the areas you need to focus on?' asks the psychiatrist.

'We would like as many details as you can remember,' says the police officer.

'When you accept the past, then perhaps we can move forward,' suggests the psych.

'How many young people were with you that night of the accident?' continues the police lady.

'I was alone.' I know that. The flashbacks are too vivid to lie.

'Just tell me what you know about the events that happened.'

I wish *they'd* tell *me*.

The sound of a tea trolley rattles down the corridor.

They never answer any questions. They are no good at answers. All they know how to do is ask more questions.

I get snarky. 'OK, if you must keep going over it again, saying that I need to accept things as they are and trying to make me tell you things I don't know about, I'm just going to sing this song in my head while you do.'

Lalalalalalala.

'Are you finished?' I mutter.

I block them out.

I indulge in the benefits of selective memory. They all lean in talking together. I close my eyes. I'm going to pretend to be asleep until they go away.

They will go.

It's very hard to wake up someone who is pretending to be asleep.

20

I'm lying here wondering.

What I wonder about is food.

Especially about all those cookies.

I do not see a nutritionist. Nobody checks that I am eating my vegetables. How can I heal if my diet is unhealthy?

If I get fat lying in bed all day, will you stop loving me, Finn?

I complain to Auntie Gillian. She is sitting bolt upright on a pleather-padded high-backed chair. Its pale wooden legs somehow look more important with her in it.

'How can they expect me to get better?' I say.

Auntie Gillian draws her eyebrows together. A medic passes by. He stops by the open door. He nods and smiles, a tight pressing of lips. Why do they approve so instantly of Auntie Gillian?

'You are under the supervision of the best doctors in the state,' says Auntie Gillian. 'It is a miracle you're still alive. You are very fortunate that our faith community agreed you should be treated under our group insurance plan. You should be thankful for that.'

She waves her hand, like a state official. The iodine-scented air doesn't stir.

'OK,' I say. 'I am thankful. But I would really like it if you could bring me a salad or something, or some fruit maybe?' I hesitate. I try a different tack. 'I just want to eat things that God provides for us,' I say, and raise my eyes. I think I'm putting on weight. I must be, lying here all day.

'Just a wonderful apple from somebody's orchard.' I hesitate; perhaps that was the wrong fruit to choose. Eve and the apple?

'Or anything,' I add hastily. 'Maybe some cherries? It might help me to remember.'

Aunt Gillian tilts her head to one side.

'I'm trying hard to remember,' I say.

Auntie Gillian laces her fingers together and folds her arms over her bosom. 'The trial is three weeks away. If you think fruit will help, I'll see what I can do.'

When Finn is finally allowed to visit me, I must look as lovely as I can.

She crosses to my bedside and lays her hands upon me. 'You are in need of God's mercy and must ask Him for forgiveness. Pray to Him. "For I will restore health to you, and your wounds I will heal, declares the Lord" – Jeremiah 30:17.'

I raise my eyebrows. I pull the corners of my mouth down.

What did I do that was so bad?

The next day Aunt Gillian brings in a basket of fruit. It has a pink gingham cloth tied over it. Attached to the handle is a card.

On the cards it reads:

You are in the thoughts and prayers of our faith community.

Auntie Gillian points to the basket of fruit. 'The elders have sent you this,' she says. 'I think you should write a letter of appreciation. I have brought a paper and pen.'

I hold out my hand. I actually am appreciative, and I will let them know. Then perhaps they may send me another basket in due course, and I won't have to live on graham crackers and chocolate spread.

'Thank you,' I murmur dutifully. 'Thank you, Auntie Gillian.'

'I'll leave you to write while I speak to the doctor.'

Then Auntie Gillian is gone.

I close my eyes. I don't want to write the thank-you note just this minute. I want to wind time backwards. I will try to relax. It might help my mind recover. I will fill it with happy thoughts, and not dwell on the darkness. I will remember a day when I was perfectly happy.

ALIZARIN CRIMSON

21

Massachusetts, Last Spring

It is early, early morning. Aunt Gillian has gone to her first call of the day and Mom is still asleep. Finn calls me.

'What's up?'

'What's up with you?'

'Been thinking about how weird it is that we've met up again and everything.'

I'd been thinking of how I climbed up to Gallows Hill. How I walked – three times widdershins around the gibbet spot. How I paced around until I found its power spot. How I stood under the full moon and pointed my magic finger up at the stars. My scarred, printless digit. How I exhorted it to bind Finn to me. How I released its power through the darkness of that coastal town and how it seems to be working. How all enchantments could not bar its way.

Those were the weird things I was thinking.

Was it wrong to claim him as my own?

For a moment, I think I know how Charlie feels.

That overwhelming need to possess. To beat down anything that opposes it. I shudder.

'Can I see you?'

The shuddering turns to a smile.

I yawn. 'I'm asleep.'

'Today?'

I want to stay asleep. I want that warmth in his voice to surround me.

'Now?'

You are unlovable.

I breathe out.

His interest is only the result of witchery and lies.

'Say yes.'

'Why?'

Please let him love me.

'I want to get down to the beach and clear my head. It's the math test next week.'

Just for me.

'Can't you do that by yourself, then?'

'But you're the thing I've got to clear from my head.'

I yawn again.

I bite my lip.

'It's not me you need to clear from your head, it's Jules,' I say. When you are unlovable sometimes you have to decide things for others.

'Yes,' he mumbles, 'yes, maybe that's true, but I can't do that without you.'

'Life isn't like that,' I say. 'You can't hedge your bets. I won't be used like an insurance policy. You must choose.'

'Just come,' he pleads.

22

It must have rained sometimes in that coastal town – a lot, probably. But my memories tell me it was forever sunny.

And I remember that morning so well.

My perfect day.

Absorbed warmth from iron rivets burning the back of my bare legs as I sit on that bench by the seafront over the boardwalk. Rounded pebbles sticking in the soles of my shoes, crunching on the concrete pavements as I walk with Finn.

We stroll down to the marina waterfront. Here we can have the sea all to ourselves.

We meander down the front alongside the tidy rows of boats in their safe little harbours. We pass cute bungalows and cut green lawns. We don't stop until we reach a little cove. We step down on to the beach. We hold hands.

I pull off my sandals. Finn pulls off his shoes too. We scrunch the sand barefoot, tiny grains lodging between toes. The sun is shining. The smell of salt. The slimy seaweed. Finn is wearing sunglasses. I stoop and collect bright lavender pink shells.

'Let's swim,' he says.

'You're mad.'

'I know,' he says. 'I feel mad. Maybe cold, cold sea is the only cure.'

'Go on then,' I say.

He peels off his jeans. A seagull squawks. His legs are awesome, Olympic. He rips his shirt up and over his head. His torso sculpted of marble. He stands there shivering with something more than cold. Skin and muscle. I gasp at how beautiful he is.

I think of my beauty. Hand-scarred on the outside. Soul-scarred inside.

'You gonna come too?'

'You're mad,' I repeat.

'OK.'

He turns and sprints down the sand, right to the water's edge. His legs blur. His silhouette darkens.

He scarcely makes a splash as he runs straight into the sea. Jumping long-legged over the waves. Deep turquoise water. He turns his head to make sure I'm watching. He waves.

I raise an arm.

I flex scarred fingers.

I am perfectly happy.

There is only one shadow to that perfect day.

Some instinct prompts me to turn around. Standing by the boardwalk. Watching from her own private thundercloud . . . is Jules Bridges.

MAGENTA

23

Venice Ward, Room 4

Today I am going for physical therapy. I sit in my wheelchair and wait to be ferried there. While I'm waiting, I look at my get-well cards. All three of them. One from Crystal. One from Aunt Gillian. One from her church. I think about getting well.

They say during the accident my hip was completely crushed. They rebuilt it using a new technology that actually prints out the body parts you need.

They used that and did a hip replacement. They said I was very lucky that so much technology was available. It meant I got the very best.

The very best in hip replacement allows your bone to grow into spaces in the material itself. It means that you fuse together with your prosthetic part. This, they tell me, is excellent for teenagers. This is because we have not finished growing and they would hate to have to do another hip replacement in five years' time.

'The little number you've been fitted with should last a lifetime,' boasts the consultant. 'You've been very lucky.'

PERMANENT CARMINE

24

Massachusetts, Last Spring

That evening Finn calls again.

'Can you come down to our cove?' he asks.

I don't know why he calls it 'our cove'. We have only strolled there once. But I like it. It sounds like I belong to him and he belongs to me. I don't care who the cove belongs to.

It is not hard to sneak out of the house. Auntie Gillian has gone to a church committee members' meeting. Mom has taken painkillers and sleeping pills and gone to bed. These days she has terrible headaches, which just get worse and worse. I think it is because she spends too much time on social media, trying to hide from Charlie.

In some strange warped way I almost think she wants him to find her. So that she can carry on dodging him. I guess hide-and-seek is no fun if you stay hidden and you never get found.

Or maybe she just can't let go. Maybe it's one of those till death doth part things.

The evening breeze coming off the sea is warm and cold and salty and fresh as I race down the hill. I am wearing a white dress. I know. I know. But I feel like wearing it.

Finn is waiting at the cove. The sea dances in shadows. We climb up on to a tiny headland. Just a few large boulders and some scratchy seagrass.

I am smiling. I am smiling so much the sides of my jaw hurt just below my ears.

The sun is setting over the sea and Finn puts his arm around me.

The sky darkens. Something is wrong.

'I've spoken to Jules,' he says.

'Ah,' I say.

The breeze drops and the day suddenly seems heavy around us.

'I cared about her once, you know.'

'What exactly did you speak to her about?'

'Us.'

'Oh.'

'She got really mad.'

I don't know what to say.

'I felt sorry and guilty and embarrassed and bad; it was not good.'

'Should I be worried?' I say.

'She saw us together at the beach.'

I don't say anything. I know she saw us.

'When you were clearing me from your mind?' I say.

He sighs. 'I can never clear you from my mind.'

I'm happy and worried and scared.

Don't go there, Lexi.

It's too late.

'She was hurt. She was upset. It was awful. She said she deserved better. She did deserve better. We've been together since tenth grade. She wasn't always as brittle as she is now.'

Brittle. That's a strangely forgiving word he chooses to describe her by. Maybe he still cares about her.

'She was funny and kind once. She helped me after my dad died. She was there for me and my mom.'

He still cares about the person she was.

I don't speak. I don't dare.

'She cried. I've never seen her cry like that. I couldn't really break it off cleanly.'

'How did you leave it?' I ask.

'I said that we needed space. That we'd have a break. I couldn't break everything off and leave her with no hope. She was hurting.'

I understand. Their relationship was deep. He is not free to be mine. He is on a sabbatical, a permission of leave granted by Jules to rethink how much he loves her.

'How long?' I ask.

'I asked for a few weeks.'

A few weeks to try me out?

'I'm sorry,' I say. I'd better make one thing clear. 'Is it because of me?' I ask.

'Yes and no,' says Finn. 'Maybe and maybe not. Everything is because of something.'

'Don't be obtuse,' I say.

'Well, everybody is affected by everything. '

'That's a cop-out,' I say.

'Yes, then. It's because of you.'

'Right.'

'You're so different from her,' he says. 'You're so different from everybody.

And everything.'

'Right,' I repeat.

'But you are. You're just different,' says Finn.

'I can't promise anything,' I say. I think of Mom and Charlie. How tomorrow we might have to leave. How can I let Finn rearrange his life and not warn him?

Finn doesn't move.

Tiny waves at the shore's edge lap in constant frills of foamy white.

'I *can* promise *everything*,' he says.

His arm is touching my arm. His skin is warm.

We sit there, as if we are waiting for some sign from the universe.

'Let's just enjoy the sunset,' Finn says.

A mackerel sky, tinted in blues and yellows with an underbelly of pink, dancing shadows and sparkles on the sea; I should be perfectly happy.

Finn closes his hand over mine.

The frill of waves and the boom of the ocean.

Our souls meet somewhere in its watery depths.

A breeze stirs.

Wisps of clouds.

Way beyond the horizon – over the Atlantic – a hurricane is brewing.

*   *   *

Over the Atlantic, in another country, a plane taxis down a runway, revs its engines. Suddenly there's the lurch and rush of take-off, thunder in the air, the gradient of the seating tilts upwards, the lights dim.

Fifth row from the back, in a window seat, Charlie reclines his chair. He ignores the woman behind, ignores her feeble, bleating complaints. Soon he calls to the flight attendant to bring him a whiskey. He rolls the ice cubes around the plastic cup. He unscrews the cap off the small bottle of bourbon. He peels back the opener on a can of soda.

'Ready or not, here I come,' he hums. 'Gonna find you and make you sorry.'

He raises his plastic cup. He sips the drink.

On his fold-down tray is a map of the east coast of America. There is a ring around one costal town drawn in black indelible felt-tip pen.

'I've figured you out,' Charlie gloats. 'I know exactly where you are. Thought you could get away from your old Charlie, did you? Thought you'd leave him behind, toss him away, after everything he's done for you.'

The hostess brings Charlie another small bottle.

'Such ingratitude. You'll have to learn to be more appreciative.'

The contents of the fresh mini bourbon drain over the ice cubes.

'Really, such unforgivable ingratitude,' he repeats in a low hiss. 'You can't treat old Charlie like that. Did you think I'd just let you go? Let you run away and forget all about me?'

'Foolish. Such foolishness. I'm going to have to teach you both some respect.'

He drains the cup in one go.

'Going to have to punish you. Teach you a lesson you won't ever forget.'

ROSE MADDER GENUINE

25

Venice Ward, Room 4

Unfortunately, the bones did not grow and fuse with the prosthesis as fast as my consultant would have liked. Apparently if I'd regained consciousness a little earlier I could have helped my hip heal at a preferential rate. It needed weight to be put on it, explains the physio. If you could've walked on it earlier that would have helped.

There is nothing I can do about that. I was in a coma for two weeks so unless there's a condition called coma-walking, it really isn't my fault. The physio manages to make me feel it is though. I recognise that he is just trying to tell me why his job as a physiotherapist is bound to fail in my case, but it still doesn't make me happy.

The physio has given me exercises to do. There is a little ramp I have to walk up and down. Then I must try to do steps. After that there are some stretching exercises.

At various times my physiotherapist monitors my pulse. He recommends a lot more weight-bearing exercise. He tells me to work a little harder.

I am not sure what working a little harder is. It takes all my energy to keep my balance. But as he is already on the defensive, I do not point this out.

After physiotherapy I go for my cognitive impairment reduction class. In this session my cognitive impairment doctor laments the fact that my hip is healing much more quickly than my brain. She recommends a lot more occupational therapy. I don't say anything. I haven't done any OT yet. I recognise that I can't win. There is always a very good reason why my prognosis is not as good as they'd like it to be.

And it's always going to be my fault.

After all, it's my body.

And Auntie Gillian is hot on my case, which doesn't make me feel any better.

However, something interesting did happen in physio. I was trying to work a little harder at the steps and lost my balance. Luckily the nurse caught me, but not before I bumped my chin on the ramp rail.

My teeth went straight into the soft flesh of my lower lip

It hurt.

A lot.

But the taste of blood made me remember something.

The party.

Crystal, Bobsy and Ethan's party.

And the fight.

ROSE DORÉ

26

Massachusetts, Last Spring

The evening is glorious. Big skies. Air full of heat and summer promise. And I'm so excited my blood is all bubbles and froth. Aunt Gillian has said I can stay out until 11.00 p.m. And Mom has said, 'Enjoy yourself, my baby. I'm so happy for you. Enjoy every minute! I so wish you could have been to a hundred such parties before. A girl should always be dancing!' She doesn't explain. She doesn't need to. Charlie never allowed Mom or me out.

Claire's dad comes with Mags and Claire to pick me up. He is soft-spoken and gentlemanly. Auntie Gillian knows him from church. I am in good hands.

'Wooee,' says Claire. 'Lexi, you look hot!'

'Nice dress,' says Mags.

I'm so happy they like it. Mom and I bought it at the store downtown especially for tonight. We don't have a lot of money. In fact, we live on charity. But Mom said, 'Every girl has to have a party dress.' It's modest and pretty, with a tiny sprigged print on it. Even Aunt Gillian approves.

I am wearing my new dress. I have two friends. I am going out to a party! I am dizzy with excitement. Finn will be there. I am all light-headedness and intoxication. Tonight opens up an infinite galaxy of opportunity!

'You are the bestest friends ever!' I say.

'Bring her back on time,' says Aunt Gillian. 'I can't abide tardiness. I'll be out all night at Mrs Proctor's, so I'm putting my trust in you, Dwayne.'

Aunt Gillian often stays out all night on vigils, always at a member of one or other of the congregation's house, praying for a sick husband or the suffering of the world. She is one of the most go-to, stalwart bastions of her church. I reach out and hug her. 'Thank you, Auntie,' I say, 'for everything.'

She looks a bit choked up and pats my arm.

I kiss Mom. She squeezes me tight.

We pile into Claire's dad's pickup and head off. An evening star is out. A lone blackbird sings his twilight song. The pickup backfires. Everything is perfection.

We drive for a few miles into some elegant suburbs, green hedges, high walls, rolling gardens, detached houses. We turn into a drive leading to a massive new-build clapboard house. Music greets us, comes crashing out. The night air shivers. Candles are strewn across immaculate lawns. I've heard there's a lake and hot tubs!

And I see him waiting. There silhouetted on a distant terrace, leaning against a pillar. Tall. Slender. Wired with tension.

No pushing through crowded dancers, no dodging cups and paper plates balanced on crossed knees and palms of raised hands, no elbows butting past me, no leery looks,

no cheesy remarks while I search for that one person I long
to be with.

Just

One

Cool

Handsome boy.

Waiting.

And I'm down from the pickup and excusing myself and
thanking Claire's dad and not listening to Mags, who's yelling
warnings, and I'm over the gravel drive, across the lawn,
round the shrubs and up the steps of the terrace round the
garden folly, and in his arms, where I've never been before.

And where I belong.

*We start to plan. Mom and I. Mom is convinced that Charlie may have wired
the house, may be recording all conversations. She is very paranoid. I don't
blame her.*

*Together we hang the washing out. Between the flapping dampness of
pillowcases and bed sheets we plot our futures. 'We will get away.' She says so.
I look at her. Worried.*

*If we're going to leave we should've done it long since. Before the bruising
and the scars. Before the warped hands. I look at my fingers as they struggle
to peg up the damp socks.*

'We will. We will. We have to,' she says.

*And perhaps, perhaps there is a different shade of dark in the rings
beneath her eyes. Perhaps the shadows are just a tinge more purple.*

*'I've written for help,' she says. I know she has no relatives left back in
America. I know before they all died they'd disowned her anyway. I wonder
who she has written to.*

'We will get away, my baby,' she says. 'We will.'

I peg out a tea towel.

'I've written to my church,' she says. 'They were the only people I could think of to turn to.'

I keep on hanging out laundry. Nobody must suspect us.

'I've asked for money. I've asked for any charity.'

I drop a white T-shirt on the grass. I can't imagine what that's cost Mom. To go back to the very people she fled from.

'They will help. They will.'

I pick up the T-shirt and shake the bits off it.

'If he thinks we're planning to go, he'll kill us,' I say.

In my head, I hear screaming. The slamming of doors. I feel a dark energy pause before it pours itself down my throat and petrifies me. 'Mom,' I say. 'Mom?'

'Just trust me,' says Mom, 'be strong for me.'

A cold wind wraps itself around my stomach. I can't breathe.

'I had a reply,' she continues. She hangs out his boxers, neatly with two pegs. One yellow, one blue.

I want it all to stop.

'Mom,' I say, 'if he finds out . . .'

She shakes her head just imperceptibly. 'I don't collect my messages here,' she whispers. 'I don't even sign into my email here.'

I don't ask how she's communicating with America then. He watches her all the time. He never lets her go out alone. He polices her every move. Maybe he has hidden mics in the house.

The laundry basket is nearly empty. We must go back inside. All discussions must cease.

There is one thing I must know, before I go back in.

'How long?' I say. 'How long before we go?'

'That's why I'm telling you, baby,' she whispers. 'It's nearly time. Our replacement passports have arrived. I need your help to get them.'

*   *   *

107

Finn wraps his arms around me. 'My God, you look beautiful,' he says. And I feel beautiful. I feel beautiful in a way I've never felt before. I do a silly twirl in front of him. Far away over the lawns, someone comes crashing out of the patio doors and screams: 'WHERE'S FINN?' I scarcely notice them.

All of a sudden Finn pulls me towards him.

'We haven't got long,' he whispers. 'I'm being missed already.'

I want to ask, by who? But I know who.

'I've been waiting for you to get here.'

He's been waiting for me to get here!

'So that I can do this,' and presses his lips against mine.

A jolt of electricity sears right through me.

My heart catapults and ricochets and jumps off a cliff.

I don't know what to do with my arms and then suddenly I'm kissing Finn back. And just as suddenly I'm not.

Finn pulls away, his face flushed. His chest heaving.

'I've been longing to kiss you for ever. But we can't, not here, or it'll be bad,' he says.

I am aghast and flailing and trying to catch my breath. I'm horribly out of control and a surge of something enormous and unavoidable is crashing down around us.

'Jules is here and she and her friends are watching me like a hawk,' he says.

I flounder and gasp. My knees are about to give way.

But I manage to step backwards.

'It's not that I can't be with you,' he says. 'It's not that I don't want to be with you. I'm just worried what Jules will do if she finds out. When she finds out. It's going to be bad.'

I don't think I really hear what he's saying. A magnetic field is dragging me forward.

'And I know I'm not really with her,' he says, 'I know we're taking some time to be apart . . .'

I'm crushed up against him again.

And.

He's kissing me.

And touching me.

And.

The moon spins and the lawns roll.

And.

Finn breathes at last.

'It's not fair to Crystal, Bobsy and Ethan . . . if something kicks off . . .'

I feel cold air where his skin was.

'Jules is going to go crazy.' He throws his head back and cracks it on the wall of the folly behind us. 'Ouch,' he says.

All thought of Jules or Crystal or Bobsy or Ethan or the party or fairness or distance or being with or without makes no sense. It's just Finn and me and an incredible, overwhelming sensation that us being together is more important than anything else in the world.

'What I'm trying to say is . . .' Finn pauses. 'I didn't really make a clean break of it with Jules at all . . . and I should have, and this could have been THE night that you and I could remember for ever and we'd look back and say, yes it all began then . . . but instead I'm going to have to go back inside, in a minute, to be with her.'

'Oh,' I say.

'She'll be looking for me, and I'm going to have to hang out with her and I'm going to have to look as if I'm trying to be with her, even though I am taking a break from her.' Finn steps away from me and waves his arms wide. 'It's messed up. It's so messed up. I don't even know how it will play out. I wish I hadn't come, but I knew you were coming . . . I had to come . . . and that's not fair on you and . . . I'll think of something.'

And he shakes his head and leaves.

I don't know anything. I've been hit so hard by something so powerful I can't think any more. I just go to the steps that lead to the lawns and sit down. I press my forehead against cold, cold stone and let the moonbeams soak into me until I know what to do next.

The patio doors swing open again. I whirl round, hoping he's come back. But it's not Finn. I drop my hands into my lap. A bunch of girls cascade out. I recognise them from school. Long legs. Short skirts. Glitzy tops. Fancy hairstyles. Heavy make-up. Shrill laughter.

Dogettes.

'There you are!' one of them screams. I jump. For an instant I think she means me.

'Jules is upset!'

Someone, a dark figure, hurries after them across the patio.

They're coming my way and I don't want to be seen. I slip down the stone steps around the back of some rose bushes. I sit there hidden in the shrubbery.

Away from the shrill voices, shrieking laughter, pounding music, Jules and the Dogettes cluster together on the terrace. I hold my heart steady.

'Poor baby,' says one.

I see she has her arms round Jules.

'Such an asshole.'

'We'll fix that bitch.'

'Don't cry, he's NOT worth it.'

'Don't get sad. GET MAD.'

A shiver runs through them. There are minutes of sighing and gulping, then Jules stand up. She tosses her head back. She sniffs. She draws herself together, brushes her hand over her eyes.

'Thank you, darlings,' she says. Her voice catches. 'I think I'm done here. I'm going home.'

There are some protestations, some wailing. A lot of hugging. They move off.

I come out of hiding.

Claire finds me and starts telling me off. 'Where were you? Where did you disappear to? You missed seeing Edson dancing. It was hilarious!'

She hands me something like a rum punch. I gulp it down. A different kind of intoxication swirls through me. Mags joins us.

'You should be real careful,' she says. 'You're way out there on a dangerous rock face, girlfriend; watch out you don't fall.'

I know she's right and I don't know how to get down from this dizzy height.

Therefore, I ask for another cup of punch. Claire giggles and says, 'You wanna be careful when you're drinking that stuff. Goes down like a cola, but boy it packs a punch.'

Mags giggles too and holds out her cup as well.

My phone pings. I flick it open, slide a finger across the screen. There is a picture of starbursts with a message underneath: Let's escape from the pack?

I text back: I can't really escape. I came with my friends. I am on strict orders to stay with them.

Just down on to the lawns then. Let's go out by the lake and catch up with ourselves?

I text back: OK

And Claire's back with another glass of punch and I drink it down and everything feels fuzzy and happy and scary and warm and Claire says, 'Are you going to sit on these steps all night?'

And I say, 'I don't know, but you go on in and have fun. I'll come in a minute.'

But in a minute, I am not going into the party. I'm walking down the lawn towards the boathouse, where I know Finn is waiting.

There he is, standing under the willows.

It's as if I walk through a portal into another dimension. Time stops. Or maybe it carries on without me.

And I'm in his arms. And I'm kissing him. I'm touching him. And we're holding each other, and he is whispering, 'Sorry, sorry, I can't stay away from you. Is this OK?'

I don't know what to answer. I have just seen Jules crying. I'm wearing the prettiest dress I've ever owned. I'm out at a party when I have no experience of parties. And I'm making out with the hottest, loveliest, sexiest boy in Coastal Town.

So I just say, 'Yes.' And when after a while he says, 'Let's go really wild?' And I just say, 'Yes.' Before I know what I am doing, I'm stripping off. We're both stripping off and we are laughing and shouting and skinny-dipping in the lake.

It is glorious and cool. Slippery and smooth.

I swim with long swift strokes out past the lake margins, into the deep chill centre. And I tread water in a pathway of moonlight.

Finn swims past, splashes me, laughs. I follow him. My hair is wet and plastered down my cheeks. The lake is mysterious and exciting. And suddenly I'm laughing and kissing him again and swallowing water and I know this is dangerous and I love it.

It's too deep to stand. We cling to each other. Cool slippery skin on cool slippery skin, touching underwater.

For a minute I am Michelangelo caressing my statue, feeling cold, cold marble and glorying in it. Everything excites. He is holding me close to him. Skin on skin. And at last we look into each other's eyes and we know that we are very close to a precipice.

'We have to go back,' he says.

We have to.

Back away from the edge. Back away from the cliffs. And the falling. And the danger.

27

Like seagulls swooping from our dizzy heights we must head for the shore and I must go back to Claire and Maggie. Back to Claire's dad. And the trust of Auntie Gillian and my prettiest dress which must not be crumpled or stained.

Back to Jules and hot tears on the steps. Back to the patio

and Crystal and Bob and Ethan and all the others. Back through the magic portal.

Back to the party, which will stretch on into the night. Tongues will wag and reputations will roll if they know. We cannot stay here. So we swim together to the shore and as I step out of the water he says, 'Hold it there. I want to imagine just for a minute that I am Botticelli and this is my first glimpse of my Venus. There, as she rises from the waves.'

And I stand there, ankle-deep in lake sludge with the moonlight blowing over my bare body, pale as bone and shining as stardust.

For a moment we are both poised there on the lake edge, then he says, 'You're shivering. I'll warm you up.' And together just for a moment we hold each other naked on the edge of the lake.

Before it becomes too late to stop, I pull away. 'Let's run to dry off,' I say, and we are running like Adam and Eve to the boathouse. We find our clothes, we dress again and the music rolls out over the lawns as we linger on our way back into the party.

Mags says, 'Where were you?'

Claire says, 'Your hair's all wet.' They both look at me and say, 'You're playing with a hand grenade, Little British Newbie.'

I laugh. I don't care how risky it is, because tonight I have kissed a shining god under the moonlight, by the side of a lake, and for me that is a moment I thought could never happen.

But I underestimate how hard it hits.

For later, I lie awake; I feel the cold marble of his body. In my mind I run my hands over his wet torso. I feel that hot fire upon my lips. I toss and turn in my bed and I am filled up with laughter and excitement. I am unable to sleep.

I am unable to think of anything except seeing Finn again.

QUINACRIDONE RED

28

Venice Ward, Room 4

I ask the doctor what's wrong.

'You had a nasty bang on your head, young lady,' he answers.

I ask him what things would make me forget.

He sits down on the side of my bed. 'Not everything,' he says, 'but some things. Possibly an hour or two before the injury – possibly more. Possibly all the chain of events connected to the genesis of the incident. The swelling has pretty much gone down now,' he says, 'but the mind has chasms and sinkholes all of its own and the brain needs time. You need time. Take things easy and enjoy the comfort of our clinic.'

He laughs. He pats the blanket when he stands up and says, 'Well, no rest for us doctors. I'll be checking on you tomorrow.'

I don't have time to take things easy. The trial is less than three weeks away now.

When he's gone, I call the nurse over. 'What does it

mean,' I ask her, 'if I can't remember a chain of certain things before the accident?'

She leans over and tucks in a stray bit of sheet. She takes her time. 'You'll remember soon enough, honey, when you want to,' she says. 'I've been a nurse on this ward for a long time and traumatic head injury or not – they all remember in the end, whatever they say – whether they want to or not.'

I look up at her. There is something ominous in the angle of her shoulder. 'I've been watching you,' she continues. 'It's very hard to wake up someone who is pretending to be asleep, you know that.' She smiles. 'Think about that. Think about why you do that. Maybe there are some things best left forgotten at the moment.'

She takes her time with some detail of the sheet. I put my head on one side, tighten my eyebrows. Why would I be pretending to be asleep? And why would it be hard to wake me up?

Carry on the pretence, whispers a voice from deep inside my mind. *Never wake up.*

Is this what I'm doing? Pretending to forget things?

The nurse tucks the sheet in tight.

'Don't look so worried, honey,' she says, 'you're not doing it on purpose. It's your brain, you see, your brain won't remember or hang on to anything it can't deal with. It will shut it off. It's protecting you.'

'Does everybody know that I can't remember?' I ask.

'Well, I should think so, honey,' she says.

I look at her.

'You keep asking them to tell you what happened, even though they weren't there. But they get tired of telling you

117

what they know, because you never hold on to it. You can't remember it from one minute to the next. Makes me think you're not ready to hear any of it, yet.'

Do they really tell me? How strange. I can't even remember that.

'Once, you were so distressed, I even lent you my phone, which I probably shouldn't have, and you Googled your accident, but it was just the same. You read all about it, and in it went and out it came.'

'So, I'm a bit lonely?' I say. I meant loopy, but lonely came out instead. 'I mean mentally ill, not functioning?'

The nurse gives the bed blanket a sharp tug and squeezes it in under the mattress. 'You can call it what you like,' she says kindly, 'you just won't remember anything until you're ready, and until then it's best not to overexcite yourself.'

She leaves the room. The summer sun cascades through the open window. It floods into the pale yellow curtains.

I sit there, hands clenched. So my brain has a secret life all of its own? It retreats away from me to a place I cannot go?

'Don't leave me out here so lost and lonely,' I whisper.

It doesn't answer. But I feel it waiting there, full of knowing, holding all my secrets safe. Guarding me. Staunch against the world.

Waiting for the right moment.

'Please let me in,' I whisper. 'I promise I'll be ready.'

CADMIUM RED

29

Massachusetts, Last Spring

Maggie runs towards me. I watch as the tarmac of the playground washes like a black river under her feet. I hear the smack of her trainers as she gets nearer.

'Lexi,' she gasps. She is wearing a very strange expression, a mixture of concern, relief and feral excitement.

'Lexi,' she gasps, 'you need to go home.'

'What?' I say. How absurd. I have an exam. You can't just leave school when you have an exam.

Maggie's shoulders are working themselves up and down. She bends over and places her hands on her knees. She seems to be struggling to breathe. 'It's Jules,' she says, 'Jules Bridges.'

'What?' I repeat.

I don't want to think about Jules Bridges. She is like a judgement hanging over me. I must pass my exams. Right now my whole future plan depends on passing them.

'Too late,' Maggie says, and points speechlessly over my shoulder to something happening behind me.

I wheel round. A group of girls are storming towards us. Some junior boy at the back is yelling, 'Fight! Fight! Fight!'

Fight?

'Jules Bridges,' screams Mags.

I'm not going to fight.

'Run!' screams Maggie.

Fights. Screaming. The crunch of knuckles.

I won't run.

The girls stamp nearer.

White bone. Red blood.

Out of the ether, from between the blades of grass, from between the leaves of the spindly trees that grow behind the basketball pole, students emerge, like damp rising. Seventh graders, eighth graders, tall, thin, raggedy, lumpy, and on every face is the same expression.

Eager. Vicious. Gleeful.

For a moment, I waver. *Run, my baby. Run for your life.*

There is nowhere to run to. And anyway I must not run. I must slap mosquitoes dead. Splatter them on the train tracks of my fingers. I will be the one to leave bloodstains behind me.

I don't believe in running from bullies any more.

My heart pounds.

If I am going to die, then I will die here, fighting.

'Fight! Fight!'

And anyway, you can't hide.

The air buzzes with a dark energy.

Jules Bridges is here, her pale blue eyes ice-cold. I indicate with one scarred digit that she should give ground.

But in front of her I feel my authority draining away.

Instead she leans forward. 'You're finished,' she spits. 'You're dead. Make your peace with your God right now. If you've got a brain, think about this, loser. *Nobody messes with me! Nobody messes with my boyfriend!*' Her voice rises to manic shrillness.

A few students titter.

I relax. So it's just going to be name-calling. Not real fighting. No broken bones.

Jules whirls round, all rage, all slicing razor blades. 'Nobody messes with me! Nobody messes with my stuff! Nobody! Nobody!'

Her stuff?

Weird.

It's almost funny. I even feel strangely sorry for her.

She whirls back again towards me. 'Did you get that? Loser?'

'I think I did,' I say.

She spins back around this time on a carefully poised heel. She pokes her finger out. Her pathetic untried, unscarred finger. She extends an arm. She draws a complete circle around her with her fingertips as she spins and spins in the air.

'Yes! All of you listen. You speak to her, you talk to her, you even look in her direction and you will get the same fate!'

What fate is that? I think.

Anonymity?

Somebody sniggers.

I look around the eager faces. I like anonymity. I prefer not to be talked to. That way I keep my secrets. Foolish girl. She has just given me my heart's desire.

And she's obviously not up for an actual fight. Just hot air and empty threats.

A few others snigger and there's a disappointed sighing as the thrill of a fight fades.

I have to get into my homeroom and revise.

She steps in closer. 'I don't know who you think you are!' She seems infuriated by the laughter. 'Or where you think you've come from!' She blocks my way past her. 'But here, this is how we deal with losers like you.' She raises her hand and before I have time to think, I raise mine back.

And on instinct I strike first, and I strike hard.

I didn't mean to. I miscalculated. I'm used to dodging punches. I'm used to dealing with deliberate cruelty. This girl's fury has called me off balance. I thought it was all just drama.

It's not just drama, a tiny voice in the back of my mind prompts. *You heard her weep. You felt her pain. You saw her broken.*

Have pity.

You've hurt her.

But before I have time to say sorry, she strikes back. Harder.

Eyes watering, I stagger sideways, rock on my feet and feel the stinging heat across my cheek.

Fight!

Fight!

Fight!

The chanting starts up again, excited, loud. Whistles blow. In the distance I see tall figures emerge and start winging their way towards us. But before the adults can reach us, a tall figure speeds forward, pushes through, dives between Jules and me. I taste blood.

'Back off her, Jules,' he orders. I squint forward. Images swim through blurred watery vision.

Finn. His face, dark, his eyes shooting sparks, the muscles of his cheek taut.

'I told you this had nothing to do with her.' His voice is all drawn steel.

'Nothing to do with her!' spits out Jules. 'You go down to the beach with her. You take her to *our* spot. You dump me. You arrange to meet her at the party. The party *WE* were supposed to go to TOGETHER. You sneak off with her and go skinny-dipping and start making out with her IN FRONT OF THE WHOLE SENIOR CLASS?

'Nothing to do with her.' Jules eyes flick lightning. A tornado of energy spirals around her.

My heart sinks.

Skinny-dipping? How did she know?

'Jules,' warns Finn.

'Are you saying that's a lie?' challenges Jules.

Everyone is listening.

'You all wanna see Finn and her making out, butt naked?' Jules shouts at the multitude of students now gathered.

Jules holds up a mobile and screening on it is Finn and me, wet and dripping by the lakeside.

My heart plummets. It drills an open wound into the tarmac. My blood pools out. The schoolyard rocks and won't steady itself.

My perfect moment, there as *The Birth of Venus*, becomes lurid and obscene before my eyes.

There's a resounding cheer.

A chant starts up.

'Show their butts!'

'Show their butts!'

'Show their butts!'

'It's only since she came here that everything's changed!' Jules raises her arm. Her voice is snarling tigers, her tone arsenic.

Inside me a silent scream builds like a tornado.

A hand shoots out, grasps her wrist. Its strong tan fingers hold firm. Jules twists in fury.

Finn steps in close. 'Please, Jules, this isn't how to deal with it. Just put that phone away and leave her alone.'

'Take your hands off me!' yells Jules.

Finn releases her hand. 'Just don't hit her again.'

'She hit me!' screams Jules.

'That isn't fair. You started this,' says Finn.

'It isn't fair? I started this?' Jules screeches.

'Whatever,' says Finn. 'I'm ending it right here and right now. Everything.'

'You wait,' warns Jules again, rubbing her wrist as if he's hurt her terribly.

'I'm sorry,' says Finn. 'But it's the way it is.'

It isn't her wrist that's hurting.

'I'll get you back,' she yells. 'I'll hurt you so much, you'll never recover.'

'This is not the way,' repeats Finn. His voice drops. He doesn't want everyone else to hear. He whispers fast and low. 'We're through. You're gonna have to deal with it, Jules. It'd be good if we could stay friends. Looks like you're about to blow that though. Showing everyone that video was stupid.' Finn hesitates. 'There's no easy way to say this.'

He looks like he's about to spell it out to her in short final sentences.

Even from where I stand, even with that horrific video playing in her hand, I feel kind of sorry for her.

The playground falls quiet. The students are mesmerised by this public break-up. Before he can speak, another whistle blows. The adults have finally arrived. Questions start.

'What's up?'

'Stand back.'

'Who started it?'

'What's going on?'

I turn my face away. I don't want attention. I hide my sting-slapped cheek, my bleeding lip.

Nobody says anything.

One kid mutters, 'Nothing, we're cool, sir.'

Nobody offers an explanation.

In the distance the bell sounds. The lead teacher checks his watch.

'We're good,' says another kid.

'Just messing around,' says someone.

'Make sure it stays that way,' concludes the teacher, clearly wanting to wrap this up. 'Now disperse. Get back to class.' He blows his whistle. When no one moves he looks around for backup. The deputy superintendent has already come out of the side entrance. He's blowing another whistle.

Whistles and bells.

'Get them into homerooms,' yells the deputy.

I turn to go. Finn catches my arm. Holds me. Gently, gently. Like handling a butterfly, he peels my scarred fingers away from my cheek. He cups my face with his hands.

'I'll post your butts EVERYWHERE,' screams Jules from the far side of the basketball court. She holds up the phone, waves it around. 'You're dead. You're finished. Both of you. I'll send it to the superintendent. You'll both be expelled! I'll post it on the internet! I'll teach you. BUTT-NAKED LOSERS. UGLY BITCH! I'll get both of you! I WILL!'

Finn cradles my cheek.

Internet?

'I'm sorry,' he says.

NO.

Finn runs his palm across the side of my face.

SHE CAN'T DO THAT.

Charlie!

He'll recognise me.

My cheek burns under his touch.

He will.

He will!

I MUST STOP HER. Race across the basketball court, snatch the phone, smash it.

'I'm sorry,' he repeats. 'She'll never touch you again. I'll make sure. Don't worry about the vid. She won't post it anywhere. She's just upset.'

Was it her phone or her friends? Snatch every phone?

SHE CAN'T POST ANYTHING ABOUT ME ON THE INTERNET. The panic rises and rises until I can barely breathe.

'I promise you.' He touches my lip, wipes away a drop of blood, his finger velvety smooth.

Jules and the Dogettes disappear into the school building.

'No,' I sob.

'I really do promise,' he says. 'It's my fault. I messed up. I should have broken up with her cleanly. I'm sorry.'

'You don't understand,' I say.

'It'll be OK,' Finn soothes. He put his arm around my shoulder. 'Please smile,' he says. 'I'm here now. I'll talk to her. If she touches you again . . .'

'It's not that,' I say.

'I'm here,' he says. 'I don't care what it is. If anyone threatens you, I'm here.'

I feel tears welling up in my eyes. I'm used to shouting. I am used to slapping. I know how to sacrifice. I can leave behind my most treasured childhood companion: my little Cubby, my darling teddy. The one who comforted me through the screaming nights, through the shouting and the darkness. I can walk away and leave Cubby to HIS scissors, to HIS trash bin. But I can't manage to stop this trembling. A tear slides down the side of my cheek and comes to a salty rest on my split lip.

SCARLET LAKE

30

Venice Ward, Room 4

I have to remember.

Aunt Gillian says everything depends on me remembering.

Remembering in time for the trial.

So I must try, although for the life of me I can't actually remember what the trial is all about.

Who is on trial? And for what?

I don't think it's me. Though I know I've done some awful things. I hope it's not me.

I hope it's Charlie.

But why would he be on trial?

Unless he'd found us and did something truly terrible. Something unthinkable.

I feel a cliff suddenly opening up inside my mind, as I begin to think the unthinkable. *Mom?* I feel myself slipping towards the edge.

Hang on, Lexi. Hang on.

Stay away from the cliff.

Mom? Where's Mom? Why doesn't she come to see me?

What has Charlie done to Mom?

Breathe.

Go over what you can remember.

I remember running away from the UK and Charlie.

I remember the walk on the beach. I remember telling Finn all about my childhood. But it was not my real childhood. It was the other childhood, the one where I'd gone to Mac's bonfire party with my fictitious uncle and imaginary cousins.

I remember the party. The swimming. The fireworks that exploded inside me. The cold smooth touch of marble. Botticelli's *Birth of Venus*.

And being so happy with Mags and Claire.

I remember Jules and the fight.

The smell of lunch brings me back to the here and now. I look around my hospital room, hoping its objects can help me remember more: solitary pleather chair, bed that looks as if it's come from some sort of Transformers movie, thin vertical blinds. I twist my head and see the massive toolbar strip over the bed. Its emergency light blinks and its digital patient number remains passively illuminated. To my right the laminated bedside table threatening to rock on its remaining three legs. And to my left, the turquoise monitor.

Beneath me, perilously tiled floors, squeaky bed wheels, handles and knobs and levers to raise me up and put me down – elevate my torso, my spirits, my soul – all this technology to help me recover.

But I haven't even got a clue what I'm recovering from.

WINDSOR ORANGE

31

Massachusetts, Last Spring

I can't get the video out of my mind. If Jules means business she'll upload it. My face will be out there for all to see. For Charlie to see. My body exposed for ever.

She'll post it online.

On every social media outlet

She'll add it everywhere.

That's exactly what she'll do.

Finn and me, making out, butt naked.

It'll go viral.

'Keep a low profile,' said Auntie Gillian.

'Just stay in the background,' said Mom.

'Keep your head down and your nose clean,' said the church elders.

The church elders!

'Just remember it's not only your safety that's at stake.'

'If Charlie finds out where you are, both of you will suffer.'

'Maybe others who have helped you too.'

'We can't protect you all the time.'

'So stay invisible. Stay safe.'

If that video goes viral. If it goes on to the internet. If everyone sees it. If it's flagged up in chat rooms.

Everyone at school will see it.

Including Mr Cook!

Charlie will see it. He'll find us.

He's looking for us.

The church will throw us out!

We'll have to go, move on. Leave school. Leave exams. Leave Mags and Claire.

Leave Finn.

Charlie's scouring the internet right now. He is stalking every teenage site, every school noticeboard. He has alerts on the words 'scar 'and 'fingers', alerts on everything.

He is so clever.

So, so clever.

A cyber genius.

Has magical vision.

Can read my mind.

Can read everybody's minds.

Can transport himself anywhere at will.

Calm down. Calm down.

CALM DOWN.

Check the facts: Mom's been monitoring his social media accounts. And it's true – he is actively looking. He knows I'm a teenager and I'll make a mistake and post something somewhere. When he gets a hit, he'll be on it like a tonne of bricks.

I bite the side of my lip. I twist my hands until the scar tissue catches against my nails. One place starts to break and bleed.

Who can I tell?

If I tell Mom, she'll panic. She'll say we have to go. Like yesterday. She's already totally paranoid, totally stressed. She has no money to go anywhere. She's a mess. If I tell Aunt Gillian, she'll be furious. There is only one thing I can do. I must speak to Jules. I must stop her posting the video.

Stop Jules.

Do whatever it takes.

Give up Finn?

32

The thought of giving up Finn makes my throat ache. *I can't give up Finn.* My eyes hurt. They well up. Because he's mine. *Mine.* He is the one that I conjured out of the gallows. He is the one I'm building my dreams around. *He is mine.* I have no future without him. No past unless he is in it. But I must speak to Jules. *How can you? You stole him from her?* I must see what I can do.

But I already know what her terms will be.

She'll demand I give Finn up.

Obviously.

And Charlie will find out if I don't.

So I must accept it.

A sudden fear.

What if Finn refuses to give *me* up? What if the spell is too strong?

How can I tell him about Charlie, the screaming, the nights in the shed? Mom's broken arm, my hands, the washing-up?

How can I tell him that everything I said about the bonfire was a lie?

I can't.

Ever.

At the end of the school day I wait outside. Maggie passes me. 'You look like you need company. Shall we go strolling on the beach again?' she asks.

I shake my head.

'What is it?' she says, 'You still upset about the fight and all?'

I nod. 'Yes. No,' I say. 'I need to speak to Jules.'

'You need to do *what*?' blasts Maggie.

'I need to speak to Jules. Tell her I'm sorry.'

'*Are you CRAZY?*' shrieks Claire. 'She should be the one saying sorry to you! Jeez, getting her minions to troll you and film you and everything. It's despicable!'

'Finn was her boyfriend. I would hate it if a new person came into my life and just took everything I loved most.'

Mags kisses her teeth.

'You're scared,' says Claire, rolling her eyes. 'Don't be, it's just a stupid video.'

'She was upset.' I shuffle uncomfortably. 'And Finn was her boyfriend. I don't want an argument. And I was really hoping that in this new school I could make friends and not get into any trouble. It's not really worth it.'

'You *have* made friends,' points out Mags.

'Not worth *what*?' joins in Claire.

'Or maybe *we* don't count?' they shout together.

'Do you realise that half of the known world would give everything, EVERYTHING, to be in your shoes? Finn in love with you! OMG.' Claire rolls her eyes at me.

But they don't understand. They don't know about the burning and the lies. They don't know about the fear and the stalking. They don't know anything, so I just shake my head. 'At least let me try and do it my way,' I say.

'You're nuts, girlfriend,' says Maggie. But there's a tone in her voice that says *no girlfriend of mine*.

They link arms and walk away. After a few metres, Maggie turns her head and glances back at me. The fire in her eyes is gone. Instead, a tide of worry is surging. 'Give us a call and tell us how it goes, you gopher,' she shouts.

Charlie knows something is up. A cloud settles over the house and even the fastened windows cannot keep the chill out. There are more than the usual bruises on Mom's arms. More doors slamming, more whispering, more shouting, more sobbing after dark.

I hide huddled beneath my duvet, shivering. What if Charlie can read my mind? What if tomorrow I go to my school office and collect the package, and he finds out?

I can't sleep.

Somehow he will know. Somehow he will storm into school and see two freshly printed passports have arrived, along with one credit card, two printouts of two tickets to America and a new cheap mobile phone.

The storm will break. The windows will shatter. An Arctic hurricane will blast us away and everything will be destroyed.

All night I lie there shivering.

In the morning I can't eat breakfast. Mom strokes my head and whispers in my ear, 'Act normal.'

But I don't know what normal is. Normal for us means living in terror, bruised and broken, shaken and silent.

Somehow I munch a piece of toast down. Somehow I endure the ordeal of his inspection. Somehow I make it to school. Somehow I collect the precious, precious secret package. Somehow I stow it in my school locker. Somehow I get home. Somehow I let Mom know our exodus is happening.

Tomorrow.

33

I see Jules long before she spots me. She is surrounded by her mean dream team, the Dogettes. They strut on long legs, like flamingos, pink shadows shimmering on the tarmac. Ponytails bob. Laughter shrieks. They link arms. They're down on me like the Roman army.

I do not shift ground. I am not afraid of them. They are only feathers. I must keep my purpose clear in my mind. I must visualise what it is that must happen. I flex my burnt fingers. I point them at the ground. I repeat to myself, gently tapping my foot, *No Video on the Internet*.

They march into my space. Some of them hesitate. But Jules is a true Caesar. Firm are her heels, strong her legs. Her eyes are all malice and venom. Her face is bone pale. Beneath her eyes are dark shadows. I see that they are going to try and walk straight past me, probably laughing and laughing. You know that laughter. One glance at me: spontaneous derision.

It hurts. But they will not get the chance.

This is my moment. I step into the stream. I confront the army.

No Video on the Internet. I stand firm. None of them shall pass. None of them can confront me. I send barriers of energy out across the gateway. The Dogettes come to a full stop.

'Loser,' shouts one.

'You've got nerve.' Another.

'What should we do? Say what you want us to do to her, Jules.'

I can hear the desire to punch, the thrill of kicking me to the ground swirling in the air behind the question.

'I need to speak to you,' I say. I point at Jules with my magic finger and all the others give us space. She stands there. The afternoon stirs. Leaves swirl. A hurricane is coming. Lava flows from between the cracks of the tarmac. I step across deserts and oceans and the Arctic. I stand in front of her. My purpose is clear in my mind.

My words have power.

'I would like to talk to you alone,' I say, 'without all of these' – I wave my hands – 'people.' My burnt, crooked finger points straight at her now. 'I have something to tell you.'

There is one way that you can always get somebody to run after you. For a brief period of time anyway. I use it now. I flex my voice. I infer that I know something about Jules that she doesn't.

'Something . . .' I let the word linger along the roof of my mouth. 'Something to tell you' – I drop my voice – 'that you won't want said in front of these . . .' I glance around again. '. . . people,' I finish.

She would like to slap my finger down. It's lucky for her that she doesn't.

A note in my voice lets her know it's a secret that is somehow shameful.

Nobody can touch the burnt finger and survive.

Jules's eyes quiver. She tries to thrust her shoulders back. Pathetic. Her will flickers. Her eyes swivel. She looks at the girls standing beside her and I know I've won.

For now.

'Meet me by the pier,' I say. 'At seven this evening. And don't bring them.' I spin on my heel, turn around and stalk off.

I can almost hear the silence, the bewilderment whirling behind me. Slowly a murmur starts. One of the girls, brave enough to speak, says something. A tone, confused, bristling with spite. Questions trail in the air. Then one cracks, breaks out a shrill laugh. After that their opinions fall like rain.

'Such a bitch!'

'We should shame her!'

'Harass her!'

'Expose her!'

'Ho.'

'Slut.'

'Tramp.'

But I have done my work. I shake off their evil words. My heart pounds. I don't listen to my spirit breaking. I know that Jules will be there on the pier at seven.

I just don't know at this stage what I'm going to say to her.

WEEK TEN

since the accident

The robb'd that smiles, steals something from the thief

William Shakespeare – Othello

CADMIUM ORANGE

34

Massachusetts Last Spring

Oh, Finn.

Let me keep trying to be honest with you.

It's so cold down by the sea.

I wrap my borrowed scarf tightly around my shoulders. My legs shiver. The breeze blows through my bones. The next few hours will decide everything. I'm ready. I curl my fingers into my palms. No magic must escape until I need it. I think of Finn. I hold him trapped in my fist.

If Jules releases the video, then I'll have to leave.

Though, I'll probably have to leave anyway. I'll have to cut all ties that link me to this place. And Mom will have to leave as well.

No Finn.

Because Charlie is clever.

And Charlie is coming.

And Charlie will never give up.

Until he finds us.

You can't hide for ever, not in the same place. Definitely not in Massachusetts. Not when Charlie knows Mom was raised here.

Charlie will check all of the high schools in the state. He'll trawl through every website. Find out everything. And even if I leave, he'll find out about Finn and stalk him until he finds me. For where there is love there is always a weak link.

And Finn will leave a trail that will blaze the way. Innocently.

Innocence is death.

So I will have to leave Finn. Anyway. Why not now?

I pull the scarf tighter. Either way, I will lose Finn for ever. But for Mom's sake and for mine too, I will still beg Jules. I will try not to leave this coastal town immediately. Not yet. Not until after the exams.

Even if I have to give Finn up, perhaps, sometimes we could still smile at each other across the canteen?

A huge gap opens up just over my heart. Perhaps he might wave at me and I might wave back? My throat goes dry, closes, sticks shut. I might be able sometimes to touch him. Sometimes our fingers might gently brush together. Maybe we could still sit beside each other in the art room and complete our project? Just a few weeks more. We might hold hands occasionally, meet in secret. Send texts . . . And then when the term ends and it's over, it will be over.

I do not cry.

My tears are sulphuric acid.

They dried on my cheeks when I was very small and left huge painful holes in my childhood. I have not dared to summon them again.

A flock of dark birds wheel in the air above me. They seem trapped by the same energy that holds me fast against these railings. The buildings opposite lean in and listen, waiting to hear the outcome of this evening's rendezvous. The rigging on the yachts tap-tap in the evening breeze. The boards of the pier shudder beneath my feet.

For a minute the horizon is lighter than the sky. Then the sun sinks behind a distant grey cloud. It falls and slips away, down into a deep dim night, down past Gallows Hill to the underside of the world.

And out of the grey night, the ghostly dark shape of Jules appears at the end of the seafront.

She glides eerily towards me.

YELLOW OCHRE

35

Venice Ward, Room 4

Have you ever been in hospital?

It's quite nice. I think I could get used to institutions. At first I didn't like waking up so early. The early-morning rounds are always the worst. The nurses are tired and snappy and they want to go home. They wake you up and shove pills at you and ask you questions in single monosyllabic sentences.

OK?

Need pills?

Got pain?

And as you roll over, sleepy, wondering why you're hearing the slap of a plastic pill cup on your bedside table: Can you sit up?

The head of the bed is cranked upwards.

A dagger is plunged into your hip bone. It winkles its tip between cup and ball joint. As the blade gets leverage against the bone, great force is applied to the hilt. The joint pops open, dislocates, a thunderstorm breaks outside the window. I close my eyes against the lightning strikes of pain.

I try again to sit up.

The nurse says, 'Need help?' She slides one arm behind my shoulders and eases me forward.

Nausea rises like a geyser, hot and irresistible, up through my gullet. I try to swallow. Sour. Acid. The nurse passes me water.

I flop back on the bed.

'Take these.' The slosh of water being poured into a plastic cup. All I want to do is curl back up in a ball and forget about today, forget about yesterday, forget about tomorrow.

I've been here for weeks and it's still the same.

As soon as the nurses have changed the shift, the nausea subsides. I hear the clank and rattle of the trolleys, the chink of spoons in china breakfast mugs, the smell of tea and pancakes. Sunlight streams through the window. The pills have begun to numb the pain. A new day has come. You can be anybody or anyone – just as you choose.

But it is hard to choose who you will be, when you do not know who you were.

Every day since the accident starts like this.

We left on a Tuesday. Tuesday was not a PE day.

We left everything behind. Especially the things we loved most. That is the only way to leave, without a trace.

We didn't want to attract Charlie's suspicion. We had to leave things a bit conspicuously lying around. Not too conspicuously, of course. I had to leave behind my most expensive pair of shoes. My laptop was abandoned wide open and running in my room.

We prayed for getaway time.

143

I left my books and my games, my make-up, my mirror, my PJs, my school books, my teddy and my cell phone. I had my school bag with my science homework and GCSE exam past papers. I went to school. I collected our passports and the package from my locker. I left school straight away before they closed the access gates. I told the teacher on duty that I'd forgotten my lunch. I caught the bus into town and went straight to the coach station and waited for Mom.

I waited and waited and prayed and prayed she'd be able to get there.

We bought two one-way tickets to Heathrow.

I didn't feel safe until the plane took off and I was sitting strapped in with Mom beside me.

We left on a Tuesday and I don't have PE on a Tuesday. So even my sports bra had to be deserted.

The doctors say my hip is mending. They say muscle heals faster than bone and bone heals faster than nerves. And nerves heal faster than brains. It'll take a long time for the brain to fully heal.

Nobody tells me why my brain must heal. During the car crash I don't even know if I hit my head. The place where I feel the most pain is actually in my chest. I did not get hit in my chest. The pain is like a thousand needles speaking their sharpness into my heart.

They cannot give me medicine for that. The doctors all agree there is nothing at all wrong with my heart.

It is only me who thinks it's broken.

INDIAN YELLOW

36

Massachusetts, Last Spring

Waves crash against the shore.

This is it.

Jules stands much further off than normal body space would require. She folds her arms over her chest. She looks like an Amazonian goddess. Her golden eyes have changed from fire to brimstone.

'Well,' she says, 'what is it you have to tell me?'

And I know there can be no charms, no spells, no manoeuvres any more.

She already knows far more in those arts than I do. So I simply look at her and raise up my chin and say, 'I'm new here. I didn't realise that you and Finn were such a unit. I thought you guys were pretty much through. I am sorry that I made out with him. I am sorry that it upset you. I didn't do it in order to upset you.'

'And?' She sticks her chin forward.

And, I hesitate.

Christ, how I hate eating shit.

'I just wanted to say, I had no intention of taking him away from you. If he's finished with you then it's really not my fault or my business. It's not because I've asked him to. I want you to know that. I don't know if that makes you feel happier.'

'And?' she says again.

Just keep sucking it up, I tell myself, pebbles and sand and seaweed and all. Think of Charlie and stick to your purpose.

'And that's all, really,' I stammer. I'm losing confidence. It's leaking down the sides of my legs and out through my shoes and seeping into the ground around me.

'*You think I'm stoopid?*' she says. 'You haven't asked me to meet you way down here just to tell me some lame-ass story like you don't want to upset me and that I can have Finn back if he wants to come. Girls like you would kill to have Finn. You really must think I'm totally stupid.'

I certainly do not think she's stupid. I think she's aggressive. I think she's venomous. I think she's duplicitous. I think she's manipulative. I think she's sad and I know she's angry. I think she's never going to stop hating me, but I do not think she's stupid.

'Yeah, well, not really,' I say. I take a deep breath. *Charlie*, I remind myself. 'I'm prepared to do a deal about Finn.' The words all come out wrong. '*You can't hide when you're in love.*' 'I won't compete against you,' I manage.

'Let me get this right,' says Jules. 'You won't compete against *me*?' She laughs derisively, as if nobody in the entire universe could stand a chance anyway.

Charlie and the hunting knife and the screaming.

I straighten up, take a sip of courage from the night air.

'I won't compete,' I say again.

She folds her arms and sits down on the bollard opposite. 'So?' she says 'You'll do that? Where's the deal in that?'

'So, well . . .' Now I must take charge. I must make this deal work. I flex my fingers. *Charlie is looking for us.* Be the predator. 'I want something in return.' I suck in energy from Gallows Hill. Power floods back. 'If you want Finn back, you need to make a deal with me. If you don't . . .' I pause. 'Finn and I will be in your face in every single corridor, down every single street, through every mall, in front of everybody – everywhere you go. I will personally tell the world how he threw you over in favour of me.'

Even through the night I can see her face flush. She stands up, takes a step back. Her hands ball into fists and her jaw tightens. 'Huh,' she says at last. 'Now I get it.'

I get it as well. I hit a raw spot. Briefly, I flick my eyelids shut. In my dreams I parade openly arm in arm with Finn. I imagine it . . . *along enchanted streets, down dreamy corridors* . . . I flick my eyelids back open. I look at Jules. She has turned to ice. I totally get it, the shame and the ignominy of being a dumped loser terrifies her.

Wind whistles down the pier. A cloud sails out across the face of the moon. I wait. If I am to exploit this weak link, I must follow through. *There's no way back.* I will have to give up Finn. Water slaps on the boards of the pier metres below us. But even as I decide to, I know I'm lying. *I can never truly give Finn up.* Not even if it means Charlie will find us.

Jules doesn't speak. I try to see things from her point of view. The hurt. The fury. The desire for revenge. The utter

147

sadness. How can she deal with this interloper, this British girl who cares nothing for her dominion?

How can she ever admit that someone like me could shame her so effortlessly?

I must help her accept the deal. Even if I am to double deal her later on.

'OK,' I say. I don't add any honey to my tone, any more. She's too smart for that. I make it as flat as the horizon. 'Here's the deal: I'll text him right now that we're through. I keep my hands off him. You erase that video from your phone the second I send my text. It does not go live. This deal remains a secret. If you break your word, I'll let everyone know about it, about what a loser you are.'

She sucks in air with a hiss. '*So that's it.*' She snorts. '*You don't want the video to run.*' She rests back a bit on her heels and nods her head. 'Give me one good reason why I shouldn't post it right now. Why do you care so much?'

Stay in charge. Suck up more sand, dirt, grit. Even dog shit.

'I need to make some friends,' I say. 'I'm going to be living here for ever, and I don't want to start my new life with that kinda impression. You don't need it either. It's a small community. Completely conservative. Once they know you posted the footage – and they will know – it'll make you look pretty pervy. Miss Peeping Tom Bridges.'

She laughs this time. 'Don't give me that trash,' she says. 'Don't you *dare* underestimate me. You've chosen your friends already and you don't seem to care what kind of "impression" you make. And don't patronise me! Or pretend to know what this "community" will think. I've lived here all my life and you just dropped in. No, there's some other reason and I want to know it.'

'What does it matter what the reason is?' I say, flailing. Power leaks away, drains into the paving underfoot. 'Does anyone ask somebody who buys a new car where they want to drive it to?'

She will never have Finn back. Not now. Never. Never.

'Well,' says Jules, 'if I don't get to know, then there's no deal.'

'I can't tell you.' I stammer. I'm losing the advantage so badly. It's haemorrhaging out of me.

'You tell me, or I walk away,' she says. 'The video will be live before you reach home.'

I see a glint in her eyes, a hungry fire licking dry leaves.

Will she swallow a story? Can I conjure one out of my magic fingertips? She is not stupid. Her mind is a laser. Her hold, talons of steel. She will scatter, scratch, dissect my words until she knows the truth.

'OK,' I say. My heart is a bird panicking in its cage. 'I'll tell you.'

I must say something that will be believed.

'You're afraid,' she says, 'I can smell it.'

I *am* afraid. She's like Charlie. She can smell an advantage.

She taunts. 'Why is the pretty little new British girl so afraid? Somebody's after you? Aren't they?'

She knows.

She knows.

There can be no lies now.

'It's the police, isn't it?'

At last, a break? An idea. A new deception!

'Yes,' I whisper.

Better the police than the truth.

'Maybe,' says Jules. She picks up a pebble and shoots it out in an arc over the edge of the pier. It hits the waves below with a killing splash.

'Yes,' I say, 'the police are after me.'

Too eager.

'No, it's not the police,' she says, in clear divine inspiration. 'It's somebody else, isn't it? You've done this before, haven't you? You've taken somebody else's boyfriend and you've been filmed doing the dirty deed with them and they're out to get you, aren't they?'

Now I don't know what to say. If I say yes to this, then I lied about the police. If I say no, she will not believe me. Either way I'm trapped.

'You'd better tell me, you slut,' she says. 'You'd better tell me everything.'

My mind turns cartwheels, climbs climbing frames, shimmies up ropes, runs along clifftops.

Until I find the answer.

The waves pound a rhythm on the struts of the pier far below. A seagull cries out.

'Yes,' I say, 'somebody is out to get me; it's not a girl – but it's something like that and the police are involved, but I can't tell you more, because it's a criminal case. And we had to be rehoused. We left, you see.'

And that is as much of the truth as I can manage. And I know that it's hopelessly inadequate and that it probably won't convince her of anything.

'I see,' she says.

Perhaps there is still some hope?

'It's not just me.' I start. 'It's my mom too. If you put that video on the internet then you'll be involving her.'

Her eyes flicker. Snake-like, she runs her tongue over her lips.

I've said far too much. But that is actually the truth. As much of it as I can tell. She would not have settled for less.

'I see,' she says again. 'You're here under some sort of witness protection scheme, are you?'

I nod. I cheer. That is so much better than I'd hoped. It gives me a basis to work on. 'Sort of,' I say. And it is true, sort of, isn't it?

'Well,' she says, 'I don't believe you. I think you're running scared because this video will be new evidence against you. You're not on any witness protection scheme, you're probably out on some sort of probation, some bail term and it's all about to get blown!' She laughs.

I know the subtext to that laugh. It reminds me of Charlie. It says: *I have you now. You are mine. You will do whatever I want.*

'So, here's the deal – my deal, not your trashy deal: you give up Finn. You never speak to him again without my permission or presence. I don't publish the video.'

'Oh,' I say. I can't keep the relief out of my voice.

'Don't thank me,' she says, 'not yet.'

More seagulls set up a midnight wailing. They sound like kittens mewing, small things in pain.

'I will not publish the video,' she repeats, '. . . yet. But I will not erase it either.'

151

I know what's coming. Suddenly I have a headache. I'm cold and I want to go home. The wind drives straight at me, tugs my hair and runs sharp fingers of pain across my skull.

She nods her head. 'Yes,' she says.

I sigh.

'When I say "back off", you back off. When I say "do my homework", you do my homework. When I say "buy me lunch", you buy me lunch.'

I take a step backwards.

'When I say "jump", you ask "how high?"'

'I see,' I say.

'You can take it, or you can leave it. It's entirely up to you. You have until midnight.'

At a quarter to midnight I text Jules.

I agree

She texts me back: Good. Tomorrow you will wait for me outside the school. Tomorrow I'm gonna let you know how high you're gonna jump.

CHROME YELLOW

37

Venice Ward, Room 4

All night I couldn't sleep.

I was in pain. Not my hip, something else, some weight on my chest. I begged Auntie Gillian when she came in the morning to ask them to do a chest X-ray to check that my heart is still working properly.

Finn never comes to see me.

I know there's something terribly wrong.

Did I really finish with him? Did I really make that deal with Jules?

The crushing pain is breaking my ribs. My heart is ruptured. My chest cavity is slowly filling with blood. But one part of me is not surprised he keeps away. I knew on that perfect afternoon, as I heard the seagulls calling, as I saw his torso in silhouette. That what we wish for always hurts us in the end.

I threw my wishes away.

Finn never comes to see me.

He will have good reason.

Jules must have told him how I bartered him away.

NAPLES YELLOW DEEP

38

Massachusetts, Last Spring

After I sent the text to Jules, for the longest time I curled up under my duvet. My heart beat so hard the bed shook. My legs felt like lead. My head ached. I could hardly breathe. At last I sat up. I found Finn's number on my phone.

Please forgive me, I wrote. I erased it. What was there to forgive? An evening swim? Slippery bodies brushing underwater? A kiss under the moon? Hands held? Skin on skin? But we had gone much further than that. Our souls had joined together somewhere out there in the depths of the lake.

I type: *You know it was fun at the party. But it looks like I kind of butted into your thing with Jules. And all that. So it's probably best we just stay friends? It was kind of nice to know you and . . .*

I want to mention the fire, how all of that was a lie. I want to be honest. But I'm handcuffed by my promises to Mom.

I erase the message. I cringe at the words *best we just stay friends.* I start again, poise my fingers and type nothing. How can I dump somebody who I'm not even really going out with?

Suddenly I get an idea. I go to the chest of drawers, pull open the top drawer and take out the strips of white handfasting linen.

I creep down to the kitchen: dark shadowy floors, a pale light coming in from the street. The creak of stairs. The touch of matting on my bare feet. The smell of freesias on the hall table. I find the kitchen scissors and pad back through the silent house over the wooden boards, up the creaky stairs, back to my room.

I sit by the window and throw the casement open. Then I cut the hand-fasting strips into pieces. I throw each piece out of the window. I let it go. I know I have to do this, even if I want to keep Finn. Mags is right. Charlie is wrong.

Love cannot be conjured. You cannot own people. Not Finn. He should be free to choose.

By tomorrow he may not even notice me. That would be easier, in some ways.

Easier on him anyway.

'You're free,' I whisper. I throw each snipped piece of linen out of the window. 'You are free to choose.'

> By moon and stars and sea and sky,
> You are free until you die.
> For love of you I undo this spell,
> By life and death and heaven and hell
> I release my hold and wish you well,
> For by moon and stars and sea and sky
> You are free until you die.

It is done. I turn my phone off. I get back into bed. I listen to the clock ticking. The last line of the spell stays stuck like an earworm in my head. *You are free until you die.*

You are free until you die.

I listen to the sound of my own blood pulsing in my ears. *Die. Die. Die*

BISMUTH YELLOW

39

Venice Ward, Room 4

Where is Mom, really?

Where are you, Finn?

I have nightmares.

I couldn't sleep last night because of this one nightmare. This is how it went . . .

I am cold.

I am standing beside a dark river. I am waiting for the ferry. It is the last ferry to leave, and I do not know when it will come. And there are wolves. I can hear them howling in the distance. These are dangerous shores to stand upon, in the dark. But I am not alone. Finn is with me. In my pocket I can feel the two pennies. They are the old, very heavy pennies from Victorian times – like the ones back in the UK, like the ones they lay on the eyes of the dead in horror movies. These pennies are going to pay our way across the river.

Finn removes his hand from mine and says he will be back, he's just going somewhere. And as I turn my head to ask where and why and don't leave me alone, he is gone, already disappearing into the mist. The wolves are howling and I do not know what to do. What if the ferry should come now and he is not here? Should I go? Should I wait? I have his penny. I am holding his fare. If I go, he will never get across. I search the darkness for him. But he is not there.

I call out to him. 'Finn!' I shout. 'Come back, I think the ferry will be here soon.'

There is no reply, only my voice echoing into the night.

'I'll wait for you,' I shout.

But if I do not get on the ferry and I stand here alone and he does not return, then the wolves will come.

I don't know what to do.

But if I leave with his penny then the wolves may come for him instead. They always come for the poor unfortunate souls who don't have a coin. Souls that are condemned to wander along the banks of the Cocytus, the river of lamentation, for all eternity.

I cannot protect him. Not unless he comes back and stays with me. And I do not know what to do.

I do not know what to do.

I DO NOT KNOW WHAT TO DO.

I stand there holding the two pennies in my hand.

The ferry arrives. 'All aboard,' the ferryman calls. 'All aboard for the final journey.'

JAUNE BRILLIANT

40

Massachusetts, Last Spring

I wait for Jules outside the school. She arrives late. This is my first punishment: she is late, therefore I must be late too and I must take the consequences of it.

She nods her head that I should fall into line with the Dogettes behind her. I fall into line. None of them talk to me. Whenever they can, they cast glances in my direction and then send out peals of laughter – as if they know all about my humiliation.

I hate you, Charlie. I hate what you've brought me to.

I keep my chin high. I smile a slightly enigmatic smile. Finn is standing by the basketball court with some of his friends. I wonder about the spell, whether he'll ignore me now. I hold my breath and keep on walking. I do not look in his direction.

He shouts across the playground.

'Lex-ie!'

Nobody looks in his direction.

My heart skips a beat. *He is free and still he calls out to me!*

Jules snorts. I see immediately that he is to be punished too.

I'm so sorry, Finn.

How can I ever explain?

After roll call, as I go to leave homeroom, Jules pokes me in the ribs. 'Sit down,' she says. 'It appears,' she continues, 'that you're doing a project with Finn. An art project?'

'Yes.'

'That is a pity,' she says. She pulls out her mobile and plays with it a little.

'I can't help it,' I say, 'it was the teacher who paired us up.'

'You will do every single joint part of that project with me supervising you,' she says.

I nod.

'What are you supposed to be doing?' she asks.

'We're doing life drawing – the human form in Renaissance art,' I say. 'We have to look at the old masters and do our own versions.'

She is not happy. A slight fever starts deep in my bones. My heartbeat sparks. 'What aspect of the project have you chosen to look at?' she says.

'The human form,' I say. 'Male and female perfection.'

She lets out a kiss of air between her teeth. 'If I were you,' she says, 'I would be *very, very* careful.'

'Well,' I say, 'that's the project, everyone has to do it . . .'

She looks at me. She plays with her mobile again. She smiles, a sudden smirk. 'You must earn my trust,' she says.

How I hate you, Charlie.

'If you want to do this art project with Finn then you must find a way of making me trust you.'

'Like?'

I hate you, Jules.

I hate you.

I hate you, Charlie.

I hate you, Mom, for getting me into all of this.

I hate you most of all, Jules.

You will never, never, never get Finn back.

All of them should just get out of my life and leave me and Finn alone.

'It's really not going to be such a big deal,' I say, trying to believe it. 'He has to produce a couple of pieces of art, and I have to produce a couple of pieces of art and then it's over.'

'Cool,' she says. 'I've just had a great idea for your art project. Give me your phone.'

I want to refuse. I want to turn on my heel and walk away. Instead I hand over my phone.

She slides across to messages. She taps in Finn's number. It comes up anyway. 'I'm gonna send him a text,' she says, 'to get your little art project started. Let me see, the perfect human form in Renaissance art . . .' A sly smile stretches over her upper lip.

She calls to Amy. Amy hops over with a simpering smile. 'You do art,' she says. 'Who is the most famous Renaissance artist ever?'

'Michelangelo,' says Amy.

'His most famous perfect human form piece?'

'Statue of David.' Amy shows her it on Google Images.

Jules hoots with laughter. She starts typing into my phone.

161

Amy looks over her shoulder. 'That's Michelangelo, spelt as one word,' prompts Amy.

They both start giggling. 'There you go, "boyfriend",' sneers Jules.

She hands the phone back to me. 'You can go now,' she says. 'Meet me at lunchtime. I like the salad with a cream cheese bagel. You get it for me. Then you can show me his response.'

Oh, Finn. How did I betray you like that?

She spins on her heel, bursts out laughing again, links arms with Amy and struts off.

TRANSPARENT YELLOW

41

Venice General Ward

They've moved me to a general ward.

I nibble on a muffin. I sip at coffee. I lie down, exhausted, fearing to move in case the needles and daggers return. Perhaps today they will force me to stand up and walk up and down steps and ramps for ever. Perhaps today they will move the IV or make me wash. My heart has been roasted and speared and spitted and braised like a carcass. It has been carved into neat slices. The lady in the bed opposite asks me what's the matter.

Finn doesn't come to see me.

I must have finished with him.

If my mobile were here, I could check to see if he'd sent a text. But I'm told repeatedly I have no mobile. I do not know what they mean. I always had a mobile. Am I not allowed to have a mobile? Or do they mean that my mobile is lost or locked up in some office on the upper floors, where I hear clicking and echoing footsteps, where trolleys are pushed to other beds?

Mobiles.

And now I remember: the mobiles and the Renaissance art project.

It started on mobiles.

I remember!

He returned so many texts to the one Jules sent.

Are you sure?

We could just copy the originals?

Not that I'm shy or anything.

I'm just thinking of you.

And that night at the party.

You don't have to model one yourself.

Absolutely not.

I mean, I'd sure like you to, but only if you want.

Heck! I guess I can.

After all, it's only an art project.

OK. I'm really cool about it.

It's our art project.

If you are?

Here goes.

The image came through with the caption: Imagine Florence and the rest.

When it arrived in my inbox, it felt like voltage in my chest. A wire of red-hot electricity enclosing my rib cage. A jolt somewhere near the solar plexus. It sent out a surge that stopped my heart.

And I thought of Finn in the dark in the lake.

Just as perfect as the statue of David in the square in Florence.

Because that was the first image.

Finn as David in the square in Florence.
I thought it was beautiful beyond words.
I believed it was art.
I died when I saw it.
I knew it was passion.
I just didn't know it was illegal.

CADMIUM LEMON

42

Massachusetts, Last Spring

It starts with the art project. But then it gets worse.

After school I wait as ordered in the middle of the schoolyard, so that everybody can see my humiliation.

I wait. And wait until all the lowerclassmen have passed and left. I wait while all the eleventh and twelfth graders file by. They snigger at my mortification and flick sardonic smiles at each other.

Just another dumbass Jules has put in her place.

'Not gonna let us see your butt, then?' hoots one of them.

At last Jules arrives. 'I'm so late. And so not sorry.' She breezes up to me. She cuffs me on my upper arm, cracking me around the shoulder, as if we are the best of buddies. I cringe and shrink away from her.

'You will never guess where I've been,' she says.

That is true. I will never guess.

'I've been in the art department,' she says. 'So, come on, guess what I've been doing already?'

I have no idea. I have no interest. I can't even pretend one.

Up until today, the art department has been, if not terra nullius, at least not part of her kingdom. It appears that will no longer be the case.

'Oh come on!' she says. 'After all, I'm the one who deserves to be upset: *you* stole *my* boyfriend.'

I don't bother to correct her.

'OK already, I'll tell you.' She seems to be brimming with excitement. She is all cartwheels and fireworks and energy.

'I switched!' she says. I freeze whilst she effortlessly levitates on a cloud of her own delight.

'Switched?'

'Yes,' she says. 'I switched my electives!'

'I've chosen art as my main one for the rest of this semester,' she says.

At last the penny drops.

'I've signed up for after-school life drawing class too, so that I can catch up,' she says. 'I'm a little behind on all that life drawing and old masters and whatever, whatever boring junk.'

I see. There will be no alone time with Finn. No more just him and me and our project.

No more us, even when there is no us.

Not unless we meet outside school.

I will meet him out of school then.

Out of sight.

I can't give him up.

For in school, I see that I will be watched and monitored. I will be judged and controlled. I will be told where to stand and what to say. I will be held to my bond.

I will meet him out of school.

In secret.

However dangerous that is.

I'll just have to make sure she doesn't find out.

That the deal has been broken.

In school I will be humiliated over and over and over in front of everyone, and Finn will not understand unless he understands.

I will meet him out of school for sure.

And he will understand.

'So, slut-head,' she says, 'if we have to have this little arrangement, let's make it work, shall we?'

I don't know what to say. I must not let my face give me away.

'Are you going to art club this evening?' she says.

'I can't go this evening,' I say. 'My mom's expecting me home.'

'Well, I'll be going,' she says, 'and Finn will be going, so you go on home to mommy.'

A conflict is sown inside me. It starts to burrow between tendon and bone.

A band of her Dogettes saunter over.

'Shoo, shoo, go on, butt-naked girl,' she says, way too loudly, and with a flick of her ponytail and a wave of her hand, I am dismissed.

WEEK ELEVEN

since the accident

And his unkindness may defeat my life,
But never taint my love.

William Shakespeare – Othello

OLIVE GREEN

43

Venice General Ward, Bed 3, The Shore Center for Medical Care

Do you think one of the purposes of a general ward is to accustom patients to the world outside the hospital? Perhaps to even get them ready for life beyond its walls.

That's the feeling I get.

Suddenly my days are full of conversation and visitors. Most of them are not visiting me, of course, but they bring with them shadows of the world again.

I have not got used to this yet.

I keep the curtains around my bed closed.

I focus on my task.

Remember before it's too late.

On the distant horizon of my subconscious, I sense a huge revelation edging towards me. It waits like a tyrant monster in the middle of its own dark kingdom. Over it a storm brews.

I am visited by Crystal more frequently these days. She is very attentive. I am so grateful to her. She encourages me in my quest to remember.

She has brought me lots of hopeful articles, about how blueberries reverse mental decline and rosemary helps to improve your memory. She tells me how even Shakespeare wrote: *There's rosemary, that's for remembrance.* Apparently those lines were spoken by Ophelia in one of his tragedies. Ophelia was a poor mad girl who committed suicide.

I try not to draw any parallels.

Crystal tells me about the powers of turmeric in helping dementia patients remember what they ate for breakfast. She brings me energy bites, which she calls brain bullets. She makes them from ginger, Brazil nuts, turmeric and dates, with a pinch of rosemary and salt in each bullet. '*Let food be thy medicine and medicine be thy food!*' she quotes from Hippocrates and orders me to bite the bullet.

She says, 'You can increase the number you eat on a daily basis.

'Just keep pumping yourself full of bullets,' she commands.

As if my brain is not already riddled with holes.

Today she arrived when the therapist was there. She placed a fresh supply of bullets on my bedside table. She spoke to the therapist across my bed, as if I wasn't there.

'How long do you think it will take for Lexi to remember everything?' she asked.

'That depends on many things,' said the therapist cautiously. 'I'm not clairvoyant, I can't see into the future.' She laughed at her own little joke with just her teeth.

Crystal fixed her with a look. 'But will she remember everything in the end?'

'Absolutely,' said the therapist, 'but only when she wants to.'

'I want to,' I said, reminding them I was actually there.

'She'll remember in her own time.' The therapist smiled with her eyes this time. 'You see, her brain is trying to protect her, and that's why it won't allow her to remember everything at once. Sometimes a memory can send you into shock.' She looked at me, this time with no smile. 'Which in her delicate state could be a setback.'

The therapist paused and settled her mouth into something ominous that was definitely not a smile. She was obviously not going to mention the exact nature of the 'setback'.

In case even the suggestion of it might unhinge me.

After Crystal and the therapist have gone, and the rounds of the day are finished, I eat three of the brain bullets. I hope they work. I want to remember. I want to wake up tomorrow and remember everything, however unhinging it is.

I dream of the hanged maidens. The moon is high and hazy and shines in an indigo sky. One by one they step down from hangman's scaffold. They are clothed in loose white gauze. Their hair flows freely; it swirls around them into the night air, like dark tentacles.

Out in the universe, comets blaze. Moonlight plays over the curves of the maiden's thighs. Like paintings of enigmas hidden behind smiles, they pause and look at me. A blackbird sings sharp, bittersweet notes into the swallowing dark. The hanged maidens hum a harmony, intoning the music of the spheres.

The first hanged maiden steps forward. It is Bridget Bishop.

She stands by the unmade stone by the vanished trees. I am not troubled, but I shiver.

Her eyes are wide and unfathomable. Her skin is as pale as bleached bone. And she says:

Sleep well, sister.

But be warned:

Those who choose to wake

Must

Beware.

I wake with a start.

I am still in the dream. For an instant everything makes sense. Then it slips away, in vanished trees and dark blackbirds.

I tell myself, whatever your subconscious throws up, don't dismiss it.

Find the truth.

Everything may be important.

Then I feel terribly ill. Dry mouth. Palpitating heart. I realise I'm drenched with sweat. Even the bed sheet is wet.

And my stomach is gurgling like a sewer.

Those brain bullets are lethal.

But a memory does surface.

SAP GREEN

44

Massachusetts, Last Spring.

Outside the school, I dawdle down the sidewalk. I pull bits of May blossom off the hedges. Stupid May blossom. At the corner I bump into Mags and Claire.

'What's going on?' says Mags. I look at her. I don't know what to say. I wish we could rewind the clock to the day we went up to Gallows Hill. The day we linked arms and ate cheap ice cream.

'Yeah, what is going on?' echoes Claire.

I shrug.

'Don't shrug me off,' says Mags, pointedly. 'I thought we were pals, but – hey, what do I know!'

'We are friends, I hope,' I say.

'Ha ha,' says Mags.

I play dumb.

'Don't you have any idea of what you've gotten yourself into?' Mags asks.

I shrug again.

'You're going to suffer, big time.'

Claire shushes Mags, then pushes her face forward and peers at me. 'What's wrong?' she asks.

I shrink away.

'You don't look very happy.'

I don't know what to do. If I move now, my bottom lip will betray me. My tear ducts might join in. I shrink back into myself. I remember all the times when I've had to pull on my armour. I can shrink and shrink until I am not here.

'It's nothing,' I say at last. 'It's just maybe, I feel a bit sorry for Jules.'

Mags hoots with laughter again. 'Good God, girlfriend, are you crazy? You've stolen her boyfriend and you think she needs your pity? You think she's gonna let you off the hook, because you're sorry for her? Oh my, that's handsome!'

Mags suddenly takes a step back, then just as quickly steps forward again. She puts both her hands on my shoulders and forces my face upwards.

'You're shooting all this trash because she's trying to bully you, isn't she?' says Mags, as if a lightning bolt of insight has gone off in her brain.

I have been so busy zipping my armour on and making sure my bottom lip is Botox rigid that I'm taken aback. I don't know what to say. I just freeze.

'That's what she does,' says Claire. 'She does that to everyone. Is it about the video?'

'Oh my God!' says Mags. 'She is, isn't she? She's got that video thing on you already and she's bullying the heck out of you!'

'She's done it before,' consoles Claire. 'You need us to help you sort her out.'

'Why didn't you tell us?' shouts Mags. 'You don't know what a bitch she is. She'll pretend to be so super cool, friendly even. It's all a performance; all the time she'll be planning to destroy you. I mean a-ni-hi-lation.'

I believe them. But it's too late. I jam my armoured helmet straight, pull the visor down over my treacherous tear ducts.

'You need to be careful,' agrees Claire. 'Remember Alice?' she asks Mags.

'Who's Alice?' I say.

'Who *was* Alice,' corrects Mags.

'Alice was nice,' says Claire. 'She was a bit like you' – Claire smiles at me – 'very pretty, but she came from Canada.'

'What happened to her?' I ask.

'She got catfished,' says Mags.

'What?' I say. 'How?'

'Like,' says Claire, 'when she started school, she was super popular. All the girls liked her. ALL. Her mom ran a beauty bar in town. It was awesome. They did everything from like facials to sauna and waxing to teeth whitening. So Alice got a lot of friends. LIKE EVERYONE. They wanted to go to her mom's salon and get free treatments.'

'Everyone liked her, which annoyed Jules,' adds Mags. 'And Alice didn't give Jules preferential treatment, which annoyed her even more. Alice was just nice to everyone, just generous and friendly.'

'So what happened?' I say. A cold wind finds its way inside my suit of armour.

'Messed-up-ery,' says Mags. 'Alice had a crush on one of the new teachers. In fact she was sizzling hot on him. A lot of us were. He was kind of IT.'

'So what happened?' I repeat.

'Well, nobody knew at the time,' says Mags.

'Alice got set up, basically,' says Claire. 'Jules told her that the teacher liked her back and had linked up a private online page so they could chat. Jules gave her the link, claimed the new teacher was some kind of cousin. Claimed it had to all be very hush-hush because teachers aren't supposed to link students. Made Alice promise not to tell anyone. Then Jules pretended to be Mr Arnold and got her to post all kinds of things that she wouldn't want known in general on the chat.'

'Like what?' I ask. The chill wind becomes an Arctic blast.

'Well, I guess, declarations of love, but then there were pics too,' says Claire.

'What kind?' I ask. I start shivering.

'Just ones you wouldn't want shared around,' says Mags. She looks away out towards the sea. I almost think she's biting her lip.

'Anyway, Alice kept posting, and Mr Arnold kept replying, and eventually set up a meeting with Alice, but he asked Alice to wear certain items of clothing that were a little – well, kind of weird.'

'And?' I ask.

Mags shakes her head. 'It was horrible.' She kicks out at the pavement.

'What happened?' I wrap my arms around myself.

'Well, everybody in the school got this intriguing invitation to this particular café,' says Claire, 'and then in walks Alice in this ridiculous laugh-out-loud outfit expecting to go on a date with Mr Arnold. Only to find herself being laughed off the planet. All Jules's mean crew were passing around printouts of all that stuff from the web page too – enlarged in super-huge type.'

'Then everyone took vids of her reaction,' says Mags. 'And those vids circulated for the longest time.'

'That's pretty horrible.' I blink rapidly. Ice caps shatter. Shards of ice slither down my back. My stomach clenches.

'Yep,' says Mags.

'Nobody could actually be sure it was Jules who did it, but the next day all the pictures and a transcript of some of the messages were sent to Mr Arnold. And circulated everywhere to everyone.'

'That was real bad,' says Claire.

'Poor Alice,' I say

'Yep, poor stupid Alice,' says Mags.

'She left the school, of course,' says Claire. 'And her mom had to close the beauty bar down. This town is real unforgiving.'

'And Mr Arnold left too,' says Mags. 'He was suspended, and there was an enquiry. He was totally innocent of course, but there was a lot of hate mail from some parents and he resigned.'

'Although,' says Claire, 'it actually had nothing to do with him. He didn't even know what was going on.'

'He left teaching,' says Mags. 'Other schools wouldn't touch him.'

'That's so unfair,' I say. The shards of ice turn into torrents of freezing water. 'How can you be sure it was Jules?'

Mags gives me a look, as if to say *girlfriend, you must be crazy to think it could be anyone else.*

And I know, deep in my heart, that it was Jules. I know she is capable of doing that. Capable of worse.

Forewarned is forearmed.

She won't get me with that trick anyway.

'Well, thanks,' I say, and I mean it. I truly do. I am *totally* grateful. Now I need to be doubly sure that nothing I do will lead me into a trap.

'That's not all there is,' says Mags. She peers even more intently at the horizon. 'There was another darker story, but no proof and it was a little – well – I don't know.'

'Tell me what happened?' I ask.

'Nuh-uh,' says Mags. 'I don't know if she'd actually go that far. It was never really confirmed it was her. And I'm no gossip. But if you want a heads-up: think Lucrezia Borgia.'

Lucrezia Borgia? 'What's that?'

'Look it up,' says Mags.

Claire gives me a teeny bitty baby finger wave. 'So, this is goodbye.'

'But can't we still be friends?' I ask. Though I know even as the words leave my mouth that's not going to happen.

'We don't buddy up with any of her crowd.' Mags shakes her head, pulls a sorry-about-that smile.

'If you break free of her, or need our help, we're still here,' adds Claire.

'Maybe,' says Mags.

'I still think you've got the cutest accent,' adds Claire.

'Anyways, we got things to do and places to go.'

They link arms, walk away in step.

Away.

I walk away too, in the other direction.

Out of the corner of my eye, I can see Jules leaving the schoolyard. A burning starts in my throat. I long so much to go and link arms with Mags and Claire. The burning sears through to my chest. We could all walk off down to the high street together and eat sloppy joes at Dina's Diner and drink bubble tea and munch on popcorn.

I glance behind me. Jules is watching.

I must be very, *very* careful. I must not give her any reason to set me up or play me out. The words of Auntie Gillian's church elders ring in my ears: *Just keep your head down.*

Do it. Keep it down. Keep your head so low you're licking gravel.

Play to win.

Use all you've learned from Charlie. Be the predator; act the prey. Stalk the beast and know its mind. Be ready to strike quick and strike hard.

Do your revision.

Pass your grades.

Keep faith with Finn.

Somehow.

In secret.

In hiding.

And then you can leave. Be free.

Free to be with Finn for ever.

PRUSSIAN GREEN

45

Venice General Ward, Bed 3

The medical staff are worried about me. It seems I am no longer making good progress. I've lost weight. I think that's good. They're not so sure. My blood pressure is too low. That's bad. I can hardly sit up without the room spinning.

My psychiatrist says it's psychological and just the sort of setback she feared.

My medic says it's physiological and is running new blood tests.

Aunt Gillian says it's because my conscience is not clear with God.

But I think it's to do with the memories. I know I won't get better until I remember everything.

For the trial is coming soon and apparently EVERYTHING depends on me.

WINSOR GREEN

46

Massachusetts, Last Spring

We meet. Finn and I.

He sees me with Jules. He texts me, asking me what's up. He waits for me in the mornings, early, before school, by the lone basketball pole, by the ancient alder tree. He asks me if I still want to be with him and what's going on with Jules.

I tell him that I will tell him.

Not here. Not now. Not by text.

We find a place, under the boardwalk, out of sight from the pier and the coastal strip. On the pebbles, with the ocean rolling in front of us.

I tell him that I just feel awkward at school. Since the video, since Jules and the fight.

I don't want another fight.

I'm keeping her happy.

Keeping him distant. Keeping her close.

Just for now. Just while the dust settles. I tell him it's kinder, its more dignified.

We hold hands. And he accepts my lies.

Sometimes we kiss.

But mostly we sit silent, trying to think our way past Jules.

Her shadow is heavy around us.

Finn keeps saying, 'It's weird, I think I'm closer to Jules now that we've split up. But not in a good way.'

'Explain?' I say.

'It's like she's always there. And even when she's not actually there in person she's in my head – hanging over me like a toxic raincloud waiting to drizzle poison down.'

My pulse races. What if she finds us out?

And posts the video.

My heart pounds with the madness of what I'm doing.

But all that good advice:

Keep your head down.

Don't attract attention.

Just get through the end of the year.

Doesn't stop me.

47

One day, at after-school art club, Finn catches me behind the stack of easels.

'I'm not a good person,' he says. He puts a hand on my shoulder.

Just the touch of his hand makes me ache to be in our special place together.

'I'm still feeling real bad about her. It won't go away.'

'Meet later,' I say. 'You know where? Nobody looking over our shoulders?'

His hand drops away. 'Every time I see her, I get these horrible thoughts.'

We stand inches apart.

'Like what?' I glance behind me. I don't want Jules to find us.

'It's like she's opened up something really nasty in me and I can't stop it leaking out.'

'Like how?'

'It's hard to explain.'

'Just try,' I whisper.

'It's kind of like *Othello*.'

'*Othello*?'

'Yep, *Othello*, it's that play by William Shakespeare. Aren't you studying it?'

I shake my head. I'm not in the same English group as Finn.

'Well, Othello's this cool alpha male guy who wins battles and gets everything he wants – including the girl he loves, right? But his so-called best friend, Iago, is playing him, setting him up.'

'She's not your best friend.'

'Well, she was.'

I'm edgy. *Can't we just meet later?*

'The play's about revenge, and control, and destroying anyone who you feel has gotten the better of you.'

Immediately I think of Charlie.

'You think Jules is planning to destroy us?'

'I think she's like Iago. Othello ends up falling for his trap and believing his wife, Desdemona, is unfaithful to him.'

I will never be unfaithful to Finn.

'It gets worse. Othello starts to go crazy believing it all.'

I reach out and touch him. His hand is cold. I feel him quivering.

'You're not mad,' I say, 'you're the sanest person I know.'

Finn shakes his head, shakes my hand off. 'But that's just it,' he says, 'I *am* going crazy. The poison has started.' He leans forward and stares at me. 'I'm having these horrible thoughts, Lexi. It's the way Jules is acting. It's the way you're acting. It's like there's some secret between you and her, it's like you're hiding something from me, and now that I've started thinking it, I can't shake it off.'

He grabs my shoulder again. His whole being seems to be sliding off some terrifying cliff.

'I can't even put my finger on it. I don't know if it was something she said, or did, or if it is you. *But I know there's something going on, Lexi.* You're hiding something. And now she's opened up this sinkhole in me and everything good and beautiful is slipping into it.'

My heart starts pounding.

'Please tell me you're not hiding something?'

I daren't reply.

'Just tell me. For Christ's sake! I want total honesty between us. A bond that is different from all the usual manipulative trash. Something real. Something Jules can't poison. I won't mind whatever it is you've done, but I must know.'

I think of Charlie, of the running, of the false names and the fake histories. I think of the pact with Jules and the fictitious bonfire story and the summoning spell and the hanged maidens.

I think of Charlie.

Where do I start?

'Tell me now, because I'm falling in love with you so hard. I can't stand it if it's not real.' Finn's eyes are ringed with fire.

I'll start with my promises to Auntie Gillian.

Keep your head down. Trust no one. Disclose nothing. The whole church community has gone out on a limb for you. Don't let us down. If you mess up, you're on your own. Don't ask me for help.

'I'm not hiding anything,' I say.

His eyes drop.

'You're not Othello.'

'Oh God, I hope not,' he says.

'What happens to him in the end anyway?'

Finn draws in a deep breath. He looks away from me.

'Othello kills Desdemona.'

VIRIDIAN

48

Venice General Ward, Bed 3

I have decided to go to occupational therapy today, to see if that can help me remember. I've joined the creative writing class. I am good at making up stories. All stories are just lies really, aren't they? I'm sure Shakespeare knew this. Othello was a big lie. Though perhaps Shakespeare used lies to reveal deeper truths.

Anyway, I am a liar.

And I need to know the deeper truth.

So, first assignment:

Write About a Time and a Place
When You Were Totally Happy

We started walking together. He and I. Out from our den under the boardwalk. We walked along the seafront. To one side, the waves crashed. The sea was rough. I liked it best when it was rough. It meant I did not have to consider swimming. I am not fond of swimming in rough water. I am not fond of waves. I don't like things that propel me. That push me around.

There was no reason to desire close contact between us. But on that sunny afternoon I desired it. I wanted to hold his hand. The previous day I had lied to him. I'd denied him a truth he'd begged for. It had scarred both of us.

I wanted him to put an arm round me now. I wanted us to be two parts of one whole. Two swans committed for life. So, obviously I walked at least half a metre apart from him and talked about exams and steered clear of lies. Closeness cannot be based on something false. All divides must be overcome by intention and honesty. So I talked about revision. About the grades we needed to hit to get into college. About the teachers we hated. And the ones we loved. About who was dating whom, and who we would date if we didn't have each other.

We talked about our favourite places and the weird locations we would go to in order to find true solace. He said he would go out on a boat until he couldn't see a speck of land, until he was surrounded by nothing but the wide, wide ocean. I said I would escape to a railway cutting where wild things are always allowed to express themselves – flowers and nettles, saplings and brambles, even wild souls could spray their hearts' desire in graffiti – endlessly repeating I ♥ U without fear for miles of track.

We laughed.

It was just as if I'd always been at school with him. And we'd never touched skin to skin.

There was a silence.

Then we talked of how everybody laughed at everybody else and how mixed up and pathetic and disingenuous everyone was. How the school was a training ground for hypocrites and bitches. And how we were not like that.

Along the beachfront the pebbles glistened like smiling eyes. They looked beautiful. And our hearts walked upon them, sucking those smiles into our souls with the crunch and rattle of each footstep. Alongside us the great ocean swelled, deep navy blue. It crashed torrid grey, all salt and tang and bittersweet.

I took a sidelong look at him. He looked like he belonged to me. As totally as my liver or lungs. I didn't have to look again. I knew his face by heart. It had always been there in the gallery of my innermost known things. I knew that, just as I knew if he was always beside me, I might have a chance at happiness. I was convinced that I'd met him before – in another life. My make-believe firework party was undoubtedly true. It was just that it happened maybe hundreds of lifetimes ago.

A sudden gust of salt sea air whipped my legs. A seagull squawked. A wave hit the side of the boardwalk and rose up in three metres of spray. In an instant we both jumped back and threw our arms out towards the sea, fending off the ocean. The spray broke hard upon the edge of the land.

We laughed in unison. Perfectly attuned.

And the air smelt of fishy things and salt.

And the ocean kissed the sky with smacking salty lips.

And in the distance the wail of the interstate railroad blared.

And the moment hit me so hard, I swayed a little with the dizziness of it.

That day the world was the most amazing place, just because he was in it. And I watched his T-shirt flap in the wind. I loved every strand of fibre in it. And along the line of his cheek, a single muscle twitched against his jawline.

I laugh. He catches my hand. 'Let's meet. Let's be together. In secret. In hiding. Wherever. Always.'

Behind him, the sun is shining on the horizon. The dark clouds are gathering over the land and my brain is somersaulting.

And I know there are no words I can offer him. Because no words can match this moment. And the moment runs and runs, seems caught for ever in the crash of the sea and the salt spray and the call of the gull. My words cannot contain this moment. So I simply lift my hand up and catch the sky and offer it to him.

You should never wish for anything too hard or too much. Wishes have power beyond this world, even beyond the sky. So, when I knew what my heart was wishing, I told it to be still. That such a wish would only bring misery.

I have never seen a relationship that worked out well. Love is something in a book or a film or a poem.

And even in those places it does not always end happily.

I picked up a hard pebble and held it tightly till it bruised my scarred palm and then I threw it as far away from me as I could, towards the open ocean. Take my wishes, I breathed.

That was the time and place when I was totally happy.

I put my pen down. I'm pleased with my efforts. I'm not sure if this perfect day ever happened. I hope it did. It feels like it did. I'd like to think Finn and I had perfect days.

My nausea has gone mostly, so tonight I'm going to go for the brain bullets again in a big way. I'm going to up the dosage. A lot.

I wait impatiently until lights out. Then I eat six of them. Double dose. I've got a feeling that tonight with the help of the bullets, I might remember what exactly the monster in the darkness is.

I send up a prayer to the hanged maiden: please let me remember.

I fall into a deep sleep.

I wake in the middle of the night, covered in sweat. The bed is drenched again. The bottom sheet slips and sticks to the plastic protector beneath it. The nausea is back.

I'm going to vomit.

I turn on my side.

I try to hold it in.

I spend most of the early hours vomiting.

But as I crouch over the toilet basin heaving up thin yellow gruel, a memory comes.

COBALT CHROMITE GREEN

49

Massachusetts, Last Spring

I am in the art room with Finn. We are concealed behind the stack of easels again.

'Just tell me what's going on, Lexi,' he whispers, 'I'm still getting this feeling that you're not being open with me.'

'I don't know what you mean.' I say.

'It's like Jules follows you around. Or always manages to show up where you are.'

'It's just coincidence,' I say.

'Please, Lexi,' Finn begs. 'If Othello had been open with Desdemona and she'd been open with him, Iago could never have divided them.'

I breathe in deeply. I want to tell him so much, about Charlie and the real reason my hands are ugly and the pact with Jules. I want to feel his arms around me, hear him tell me it'll be OK, tell me he's mine, tell me he knows her, tell me he knows how to find a way out of all this. Tell me. Tell me. Tell me.

But tell him?

That, I can't.

But Finn.

I wanted to tell you. I wanted to, so much. I wanted to give you a chance to protect me. But I'd sworn myself to secrecy with so many people. Forgive me. How can I explain? I must try. You need to really understand about Charlie.

Charlie lives on a different planet.

Planet Charlie is hostile to all life forms. To survive there, you must warp yourself into a monster, a liar, a cheat, an exploiter, a faithless, untrusting shape-shifter.

A witch.

And a liar.

Otherwise you are dead.

And I couldn't expose you to that.

Not you, Finn. My artist, my coolest, hottest, fittest boy in Coastal Town High School Academy. You had no survival skills for Planet Charlie. You lived for the truth. You breathed only naked open honesty.

I take a breath.

'Just tell me, Lexi.'

I swerve his request. 'I don't know,' I lie. 'Maybe Jules feels kind of lost. Maybe by following me about, she feels a bit nearer to you still.'

A flash of fire sears through Finn's eyes. 'I don't want to be near her. I don't want to say bad things about her but it was never really my choice to be with her . . . She has a way of . . . you know.' His voice trails off.

'Tell me,' I say. I believe him already.

'Well, she kind of . . . this is going to sound stupid and weak – but it's the truth and I've promised myself that I will always tell you the truth . . . she kind of bullied me into the relationship.'

'How?'

'She kept coming around to my house. Just turning up. My mom's real fragile. Needy to be truthful.' He shifts weight. A shadow passes over him. 'And before I knew what was going on, Jules was there, taking care of my mom and promising my mom all sorts of things and . . . yep, being lovely and . . .'

'I get it,' I say, 'you were the price.'

'It only seemed fair,' he says, 'to start walking her home, and one thing led to another.'

'That's normal,' I say.

The shadow lifts. 'You understand,' he says, as if nobody has ever really understood him on this point before.

I take his hand into mine.

Finn presses his lips together. 'I resisted, but not very hard, I guess. After all, she's cute. She can be fun to be with. And I was kind of scared too, I think.'

I'm glad he's honest. It rescues me. I have lived too long with twisted truths.

'Yes,' I say, 'she's cute.'

'But only on the outside,' he says.

I look at him. I angle my head, draw my brows together.

'Forget I said that. It was ungallant.'

'Ungallant?'

'It's bad enough – me having dumped her – without saying anything else.'

Again that breadth, that generosity of his. It saves me all over.

'I won't think you ungallant ever.'

But he shakes his head, declines to bad-mouth her. Though I already know.

I can look back in time and see his story. Jules worming her way into his mother's affections, manipulating subtly, tempting, guilt-tripping, bullying, minimising, becoming indispensable. Missed when not there, depended on when she was – until good-hearted Finn finds himself another fish reeled in.

The hanged maidens rotate on their gibbets.

Mags whispers: Remember the story of Alice.

A shudder runs through me. Jules actually reminds me of Charlie in a weird way.

I straighten up. 'You are not a bad person,' I say. 'I think you're the exact opposite. You're truthful and honourable and kind.'

Reeled in by Jules. No wonder he's scared.

Finn, my hottest, coolest, vulnerable, gallant god.

If he asks anything of me, right now, I will tell him.

I pray he won't.

Finn sees my fear. 'Look, I got an idea,' he says, throwing his arms up. 'Why don't we just forget it all.'

An Arctic tornado whistles down my spine. *What does he mean?*

Forget it all?

Forget what?

Us?

My throat tightens.

No more us?

I sway. Suddenly dizzy. An earthquake threatens.

I can't lose him.

I can't.

Not now. *Not ever.*

'Finn?'

'I got this figured out,' he says. 'We make a plan.' He nods towards the art room. 'We make a getaway.'

It takes a minute for this to soak in.

He ducks his head forward, and gives me a quick light kiss. 'This may sound crazy, but why not? Let's make a run for it.' His face lights up.

'A getaway?'

His smile becomes a wide grin. His eyes sparkle. He starts humming a retro tune: Tracy Chapman's *Fast Car*.

'Maybe, you know, like the song says, you and me could get away . . .' he grins. 'Somewhere . . . anywhere, I don't care . . .' Then he hums the tune some more and chips in with random lyrics. He grabs my hand. 'Why not?' He grins as he misquotes and is full of an irresistible exuberance.

The earthquake hits, but instead of falling, I fly.

Why not?

Why not run away with Finn!

Running away is something I totally know how to do!

'You can't hide, though,' I say, 'even if you run, you can't hide.' I just want him to know that.

'Wrong thinking,' he says. 'We run and keep on running, nobody needs to hide.'

I don't understand.

'You have to stop running and stay stopped in order to hide.' He picks me up and hugs me. 'It's a completely tactical about-face. We are never going to stop running.' He gives me a huge kiss. 'If we stop, it'll only be to rest and paint and not to hide, promise.'

And I'm blown away.

Why not?

Why not run away with Finn for ever?

'My mom won't care much. She's met a new man now that Jules isn't there to pamper her. Her new guy doesn't want me around either. He's totally taking care of her.'

'Are you sure?'

'Oh yeah – she keeps saying stuff like, "Soon you'll have to get out there and support yourself, start your own life." Or, "We all have to grow up," or "Life doesn't give us many second chances."'

I think about my mom, obsessed by social media, migraines and insomnia, just treading water until I'm safely through high school, just focused on us surviving. If I was off her hands and safe, maybe she'd like the freedom. Maybe she'd meet a new man, start to live again. I'd never thought of that.

'I think one day my mom will need some space too,' I say.

'So why don't we just go?' asks Finn. I try to ignore my lower self, which pulses out depressing thoughts like:

He doesn't mean it.

It's just-for-now talk.

Even if he does, he won't really leave his mom.

Even if he'll leave his mom, he doesn't have any money.

Neither do I.

But we could. *We really could.* It might solve everything. 'But where would we run to?' I say.

'Wrong question,' he says.

I shake my head, confused.

'That's a hider's question. We're not hiders. We are runners.'

I smile, laugh even.

'Better,' he says. 'We are artists and runners and Free to Live Our Dream is going to be our mission statement!' He is all colour and energy.

And I *do* feel better. I will run away with Finn. I won't have to worry about Jules ever again.

I'll let Mom know so she won't worry.

And then, I'm going to run and run and never hide.

50

Did we meet again in secret?

What did we plan?

Did we actually run away?

Was Jules always there in that art room?

I remember the smell of it: oil paint and clay; the streaks of colour on the floor. The tables taped with old newsprint and bits of peeled masking tape. I don't seem to remember that we ever had a real model. I know we were trying to complete our grade project. I think, since Jules joined, the other students had stopped coming. I can only ever remember just the three of us there.

Jules would insist that I stood straight in the likeness of

Venus de Milo (with arms). She'd get the overhead projector on and find a photograph of the original and project it on to me.

I clearly remember one Thursday after school.

'You stand still,' she says. 'We will do a complete life-size collage of you as the Venus.' She stretches a huge piece of sugar paper on the floor and gets charcoal, red and pink tissue paper. She puts a yellow filter over a spotlight and before I know what's happened, she's drawn around my shadow and I am lying there, outlined in charcoal with torn bits of pink tissue, like a dead body at a crime scene.

I remember posing as the Venus de Urbino too.

'It's art,' Jules says. 'If we are going to paint you as the Venus de Urbino you have to pose like she did.'

Does she mean naked?

Finn frowns. 'Lexi doesn't need to strip everything off.'

'Oh please!' says Jules.

'The Venus de Urbino is a bit rude,' I say, 'it looks like she's touching herself up.'

'It's art,' repeats Jules. 'Nobody ever touches themselves up in works of fine art.'

Finn shrugs.

'There's a difference,' says Jules, 'between art and porn.'

'Well,' says Finn, unsure.

'Pornography is lame. Art is awesome.' Jules tosses her head, rolls her eyes, and dares the world to disagree.

I'm not going to strip off anyway.

'OK, enough already,' says Jules, 'you're both so pathetic. I'll be the Venus de Urbino, then.' She strips off before I even realise what she's really up to.

Jules lies down on the makeshift couch (one tartan picnic blanket and two old stuffed cushions).

Her body is breathtaking. I catch myself staring and not breathing.

Finn freezes.

'Hurry already,' says Jules. 'It's cold.'

I grab a charcoal stick and start drawing. Finn does too.

We draw.

Jules complains.

We draw faster.

Jules complains more.

Finn looks at me. His face says *promise me we are going to get the heck out of this place very soon?*

I nod. This is torture.

'I'm colder than an iceberg,' says Jules. 'This was a bad idea. It's effing freezing. I'm done. I'm getting dressed.'

'Mine's not right yet,' I say.

'Take a photo,' says Jules, 'and you can work on your masterpiece whenever you like.'

Finn frowns.

Jules notices there's an energy in the room which she does not control. 'You guys are really something,' she says. 'Lexi, grab my phone and take a pic before I freeze my butt off.' Jules gives me *that* look. We Have an Arrangement.

I do as instructed. I can't see any way she can blackmail me further with a picture of her on her phone.

Finn sends me a text. I feel it buzz in my back jean's pocket.

Jules smiles for the camera.

'Next session,' I say, 'can we just draw still life?' Anything to stop this weird messed-up threesome, this voyeuristic staring at her flawless body. Jules just lying there. I can read her like a book. She's trying to arouse Finn, trying to show him exactly what he's missing. In a kind of perverse Look But Don't Touch weirdness. Plus trying to make me feel intimidated. Ugh.

'Next session?' scoffs Jules.

Jules is off the couch and pulling on her jeans. 'I'm not doing this again!' She snatches her phone from me 'I'll send that to you guys so you can finish your drawings on your own.' She forwards the image of her as the Venus de Urbino. 'Check your phones.'

I check my phone. I see the text from Finn.

I can't stand this. I'll get the car looked over, the brakes need to be fixed. As soon as they're done we leave. We just keep going.

Who cares about any next sessions?

Finn and I will be long gone.

WEEK TWELVE

since the accident

So will I turn her virtue into pitch,
And out of her own goodness make the net
That shall enmesh them all.

William Shakespeare – Othello

CHROME GREEN DEEP HUE

51

Venice General Ward, Bed 3, The Shore Center for Medical Care

I eat more brain bullets before I sleep. Twelve.

My night is filled with a patchwork of dreams and sweating and restlessness. I wake up feeling nauseous and stagger to the bathroom only to find I've got the serious runs. My mouth tastes awful, like I've been sucking on pennies.

But snatches of things come back. They flow in lumps that won't dissolve. I remember.

Upstairs a door slams. I freeze. Halfway over a front porch. I listen. The sound of a chair drags across the floor. A silence, hollow, unnerving.

'Please,' shrieks Mom.

A muffled sound like meat thumped down.

Shouting.

More shouting.

'Please.' Softer. Sobbing.

Something crashes. Low words. Then more shouting. The snap of something breaking.

Glass shatters.

I tell myself to run up the flight of stairs. Help her.

My fault.

My legs don't listen. Blood pounds against my temple.

I must stop him.

He may kill her.

My fault.

My fault.

My fingers brush across my face, smear wetness. I can hear him. Mom's room. A shriek cut short. Another kind of thud, like a hammer hitting soft wood.

A long, high-pitched scream.

Mom.

I feel sick and cold.

Run.

Hide.

Mom always said: If it gets bad, just run, baby girl. Run. And don't look back.

At first, I think it's a memory from the UK, but somehow I know it's not. It's from later. It's from the US.

Charlie must have found us.

I start to hyperventilate.

What happened?

My heart is a frightened rabbit.

Where's Mom?

More garbled memories come. I am not sure of their order. The past doesn't seem to have a timeline.

Finn is with me.

'Let's walk to our place down by the sea,' he says. He's

troubled. He hates this folie à trois at after-school art. The air is wild. The trees sway from side to side. A dark energy forms out over the ocean. He puts his arm around my shoulder. He pulls me close. Together we march tight against the wind down the seafront to the pier.

'I can't stand it,' he says.

'I can't stand it either.'

'I can't stand her being there all the time, even when she's not. She's totally gotten into my mind now. She won't leave me alone.'

I try not to sigh. We walk up under the boardwalk and sit close together on the pebbles.

'I must have you to myself.' He holds me close.

'The art class is a school club,' I say. 'We can't stop her from coming.' It doesn't comfort him. 'We need to complete our project as well,' I add. 'We have to put in the hours.'

I want so much to be rid of her – more than Finn will ever know. I want her to evaporate, disperse into a thousand particles. An image of her flashes across my mind: Jules scattered to the four winds, blown to tiny droplets, forever speeding away from me.

'Let's stop going, then,' suggests Finn. 'We can use the attic. My attic. Instead of skulking around in secret down here, let's meet there? For real.'

I think of her getting out her phone, running one beautifully polished fingernail over the screen. That veiled threat.

My lungs collapse. I gasp. I swallow air. 'Let's run away instead,' I whisper.

If I'm gone it won't matter what she posts. I can let Mom

know as soon as I'm far away. We are only staying here for me, so I can complete school. Mom will be OK. Mom only wants what's best for me.

Running with Finn is what's best for me.

And I hardly even care about school any more.

If we're running and running I'll never need qualifications.

I only care about being with Finn.

'I don't trust her,' says Finn, 'we must plan properly. And we must meet properly to plan.'

He's right. Something huge and dark is forming out there over the ocean. Soon it will lash the shores and everything will be destroyed and there will be no more running away.

'I must have you to myself,' he says.

'I'm here. There's just us and the sea and the wind.'

'I want you in another way,' he repeats. 'Something just for me. My muse.'

I'm not sure what he means.

'Tell me we can meet in my attic?'

Finn passes a hand across his face. He stares out to sea. I feel lost and alone even though I'm sitting so close with him. The windy shoreline shivers and the spray crashes on the dark sand.

OXIDE OF CHROMIUM

52

Massachusetts Last Spring

We meet at Finn's, after school, Finn and I.

He leaves school first. Alone.

I text him I'll be round later.

I wait until Jules is watching. She's always watching, so there's no need to wait long. But I do. I wait and faff around.

Then I walk home.

I dump my bags off. Kiss Mom. Tell her I have extra art class.

Then I leave by the side gate and run down the hill to the train tracks and take a shortcut over the old level crossing and keep running.

All the way to Finn's.

We lay out an old curtain over a stack of boxes in his attic and then over a chair. His attic is huge, all sloping beams and bright skylights. Finn and I are laughing, giggling, then picking up pieces of charcoal and pinning paper up on our easels. Sketching. Measuring angles of affection with thumbs and paintbrushes. We squeeze vibrant colours from little metal tubes. Their names enchant us. Permanent mauve. Mars violet deep. Renaissance gold.

And we make art.

He paints.

I model

At first I just sit in the chair with the projected light from a dormer window playing over me. Just like Janey Morris. Apparently. Later I show a bare shoulder and then an elegantly curved arm. A bare waist. Then somehow I am down to my underwear, reclining on the curtains, the cushions and the covered chair.

Where are those paintings?

What else did we do?

TERRA VERTE

53

Venice General Ward, Bed 3

I have decided to join art therapy.

I've been having a lot of flashbacks to those after school art sessions. It was all about the old masters. They must be important. Perhaps if I start drawing again, it'll jog my memory.

First therapeutic assignment:

1. **<u>Design a postcard you will never send.</u>**
   Are you still angry or upset with someone in your life? Create a postcard that expresses this, though you don't ever have to send it.

I set to work.

This will be a postcard to Jules, a postcard sent after I am well again, after Finn and I are long gone. I will get it printed up and send a copy from every rest stop I rest at. I will send it to her a hundred times. I will count every posting. By the hundredth posting, I think I will have worked all anger out of my system. I design a picture based not on the naked Venus de Urbino, but on another old master: Renoir.

I draw my version from a photo of the *Dance at Bougival*. I read somewhere that Renoir painted because he wanted his whole life and work to be a lesson in happiness. The painting I've chosen is of a girl and her man dancing. The lovers are not precious or pretentious. They are not trying to impress anyone. They are just happy. Plain happy. They are effortlessly together, in each other's arms, dancing their way through life.

I finish my postcard and lay it to dry. I imagine posting it when I am out of here and reunited with Finn.

I will write *Amor Vincit Omnia, Love Lexi & Finn* on it. Which is decidedly pretentious, but I don't care.

Its real message will be: You Blackmailed Us Now Eat Your Heart Out.

Where are you, Finn? Will we still be leaving?

An answer seems to come. *I'm here.* But it is not from Finn now.

It's from the past.

It's from a time when Finn and I made art out of oil paint and watercolours.

And charcoal.

And love.

And my throat goes dry.

And my heart pounds.

It's Charlie. He's walking the streets of a town that's so familiar. There is the seafront. There the waves roll up in frills of white foam. There the streets boast

211

proud white clapboard houses with white picket fences. There the gardens overflow with showy flowers. He climbs up a hill set back a little from the town. In the distance, the interstate railroad rattles its way across country. He looks down over the city.

'So, you're hidden here somewhere, are you, my little pigeons?'

Charlie takes his phone from his pocket and scrolls down through a host of numbers. He settles on one and calls.

'When can we meet up, my dear?' he asks.

A thousand shadows suddenly seem to race up the tree-lined street.

'Tomorrow it is, then.' Charlie puts the phone back in his pocket.

He surveys the city again, then murmurs, 'You can't hide for ever, you know.'

54

Art therapy is definitely working.

As they wheel me back from the occupational unit, another memory bubbles through. It *was about the photos.*

Me posing as the reclining Venus.

Finn smiling. Us watching Titanic together, promising each other our love was just as strong. I remember.

I lay down on cushions lined up together. There was no time. No time to draw each other at leisure. Time spent with Finn just evaporated. *Was it in Finn's attic?* I don't think the artwork ever got finished.

'You're so beautiful,' Finn said, stroking the length of my arm. 'I want to remember you like this for ever. Can I take a photo? Will you mind?'

I remember feeling a rush of sweetness.

And we took photos.

Him of me.

Me of him.

Me as the Venus. Finn as David. Me as Tom Wesselmann's *Great American Nude*.

Finn as Vitruvian Man.

And just him and me.

Me and him.

Just as we were.

Together.

It was glorious.

Wonderful.

Timeless.

It was so much more about desire than about the art project.

We laughed at our boldness. We held each other close.

Closer than close.

We became one.

We made art with photos.

And with our bodies.

And with our desire.

We promised each other we would create miniatures from the photos of each other and hang them in lockets around our necks. One day.

When we were far away, we would have more time.

Pictures just for us.

So we would always remember. That attic. Our youth. Our bodies. Our timeless acts of art.

And love.

For ever.

55

Crystal is waiting for me with a new tin of brain bullets. I'm so happy, I tell her how my memories are streaming in.

'Already?' she says.

'You were right,' I say. 'Those bullets really open up the mind.'

She looks a bit surprised, shocked even. I tell her everything I've remembered.

'Lexi, that's fantastic! Can you remember anything more?'

'No, but that's huge for me!' I smile my thanks at her. 'Can you help me do my walking?' I ask. I've stepped up my exercises since the physio told me all recovery is patient driven.

'God bless these little brain bullets then,' says Crystal, holding up the replacement tin.

I nod. Totally. Totally.

We walk. Today I will do half an hour. Each day I will increase it by three minutes.

I lean on Crystal. I tell her about joining my various therapy groups, how hopeful I am. How one thing I'm crossing my fingers about is the whole facial recognition thing. How I try to pin Finn's face down, how I long to see it, really clearly. How it morphs and blurs. How I'm really hoping art therapy will help.

I will try to draw it. And I won't stop until it comes clear.

We walk down an antiseptic corridor. Past the radiography unit. Obstetrics. Surgical. Coloured lines on the floor.

Gurneys. Medics in scrubs. Reception counters. Lifts and tired waiting faces.

And we walk back. Slowly. I rest a lot.

She asks if she can see the postcard and read my creative writing essay. I'm delighted to show her. She reads with close attention, her lips drawn back a little over her teeth.

'Very interesting,' she says when she's finished. 'I'll bring you more brain bullets.' Then she leaves a bit abruptly.

Did I say something to upset her?

I am tired. My hip hurts.

I reread through the essay.

Perhaps she's mad at me about something. Does My Perfect Day sound too cheesy? Did I talk too much all about me?

I start worrying.

I never ask her about what's going on in her life. That's not true – I have tried, but she always changes the subject or just says, 'I'm cool.' Maybe I should try harder. Maybe I'm not much of a friend. I must try to be a better friend.

Now I'm really worrying.

And being paranoid.

And now I've thought about being paranoid, the words of Mags bubble up and distort and get stuck my brain. Round and round they go, like a nasty broken record.

She's so cool.

But she'll pretend.

She'll pretend like she's a friend.

She'll pretend like she's a friend, but all the time she'll be planning.

Planning and planning.

Planning and hanging.
Plotting and garrotting.
Until you're rotting.
To destroy you.
To destroy you.

PERMANENT GREEN

56

Massachusetts, Last Spring

'I think I've moved on,' Jules says.

We are alone in the art room.

I try to read the subtext behind her words.

'I've got a basketball player in the NBA who's been texting me,' she announces. 'I really think I could learn how to be a cheerleader.' She grins at me.

I catch a sharpness behind her smiling incisors.

Methodically I lay my drawings out, one at a time on the table in front of me. 'I've really got to get this portfolio finished,' I say. I keep my communications with her to a minimum. I wonder why she's sought me out. Some new task. The old threat? I hold myself ready. 'I need to up my GPA.' I don't tell her about Running Away, my escape to my real future.

If only I could leave today.

Jules taps her phone with a perfectly manicured fingernail. A tiny gesture. Fear floods through me. I remember how Charlie used to tap his foot when Mom or I took too long to answer a question.

The old threat.

Here it comes.

She flicks through my drawings.

'What you need,' she says, 'is a proper life model. If you had more photographs to work from, it would be much easier. You could blow them up. That way all the proportions would be correct!' she smirks. 'Even those ones!'

I don't know whether to blush or not, but instead of blood rushing to my cheeks, it drains out of my face.

'You can't possibly copy an old master or get to know the feeling of the artist, unless you are inspired by the object, now can you?'

I know she's right. I remember reading how Michelangelo saw the form inside the marble and fell in love with it.

I remember our art teacher's words. 'True art has to come from what is being drawn, what is perceived; it's a dialogue between the object and the artist.'

'So,' she says, 'let's see the photo of Finn again.'

I hesitate.

She taps her phone.

Reluctantly I hold up my cell and show her the photo: Finn as David.

I feel a traitor. I feel unclean. I tell myself I have no choice, that after all there's probably nothing there that she hasn't seen already.

She takes my phone out of my hand.

'Hey!' I say.

'Don't forget who calls the shots,' she says.

'Give it me back!'

She starts to flick through my photo album.

Oh my God, she will see the photos.

She will call off the deal.

A sudden rush of fear makes me reckless. My *photos. Our photos.*

I stand up and grab her hand. I snatch my phone back.

'Stop that!' I holler.

She shrugs. A sudden crafty look. 'Calm down, dumbass,' she says, in that patronising voice she always uses with me. 'I just wanted to make sure you haven't got that photo of me still.'

With fumbling fingers I find the photo. 'Look,' I say. 'Gone.' I press delete.

She looks at me.

I wait for her to react. Cuss me out for having naked pictures of Finn. Tell me the deal's off. Threaten me. Expose me. I prepare myself to plead, beg, *anything.*

But she just sneers a bit, then just dismisses me with a flick of her wrist. *Thank God.* Relief floods in. She didn't scroll far enough up. *She didn't see the pics from the attic.*

'Sorry,' I say. *Do damage control.*

An icy shiver goes through me. I remember Mags's words. *All the time she'll be planning.*

Jules places her phone on the chair arm beside her and taps a rhythm across its surface.

'I'd be very careful if I was you,' she says. She runs a blue polished fingernail over the screen of her smartphone.

I breathe in. *Does that mean she saw the pics? No, surely not. If she saw them, she would be posting the video already.* I don't let my expression register a thing. *Play it safe.* She's just bullying me. *Keep your head down.*

'Sorry,' I say. 'Sorry, I snatched the phone out of your hand. You know — I just reacted. You have every right to demand your pic was deleted.' I watch carefully, trying to work her out.

'Good, I'm glad you're sorry.' She stretches me a plastic smile. 'I don't think it's appropriate any longer for you to have my pic, plus I was interested in checking Finn out one last time — just to be sure.'

I'm confused.

'Because I didn't come here to quarrel. Quite the opposite. I came to tell you that I am going to forget about everything, that I've moved on and I will erase that video that you're so scared I'll post.'

I gaze up at her. I don't understand.

'Here,' she says. 'I'll do it right now.' She finds the video of Finn and me making out on her phone. She holds it in front of my face. She presses delete.

For a moment I can't believe it.

Did she just do that?

Am I free?

And then immediately I wonder if she has made a backup copy. *Of course there are backups.* The video must still be on all her friends' phones for a start. But I feel hopeful that it's not. The two feelings compete in icy circles round my heart. They curl and clash. I don't know what to think. I am more caught than ever.

I don't know what to believe: to fear or to hope. The uncertainty is worse. Ten thousand times worse than the utter certainty of before.

Has she got a copy? Hasn't she?

She has.
She hasn't.
She has.
She hasn't.
Will she use it?
Won't she use it?

I'm caught. I'm a worm wriggling on a hook. She's reeled me in. Again.

I tell myself I don't care. I'm soon gone.

I hum Tracy Chapman's *Fast Car* to myself.

A plan and a car that's all we need.

Oh God, if only the car was fixed.

WINSOR EMERALD

57

I tell Crystal what I've remembered when she visits.

'Amazing.' She hands me a fresh tin.

'TBH,' I say, 'I think these brain bullets give me the runs.'

'Aw, heck,' she says, 'just when the memories were flowing.'

'Don't worry,' I say. 'I don't care if I have to go to the bathroom all night if it means I remember everything.'

'Are you sure?' she says. 'I'll help all I can. Like asking questions too. You don't have to eat the bullets.'

'OK, ask as well,' I say.

'So all the time Jules was telling you what to do, you never fought with her or rebelled?' she says.

I shake my head.

'Not even a little bit?' asks Crystal. 'Don't you think that's kinda weird?'

I can't remember what I thought.

I can vaguely remember some quarrels. They come with a dark shadow. Suddenly I feel really ill.

'Finn and I fought,' I say

'I'm not surprised,' she says. 'The whole thing seems really unhealthy.'

I lean forward and grab her hand. 'I can't remember what about, though.'

'Try to stay calm,' says Crystal.

My heart starts racing, a clammy sweat breaks out over my forehead. 'Is that why he hasn't visited me?'

'I don't really know,' says Crystal. She shuffles in her seat. 'Maybe.'

'Can you remember anything?' Maybe Crystal knows things too? 'Can you ask Mags or Claire? Can you find out what happened? Did we quarrel badly? Is that why he's not coming?' I stretch out my other hand and grasp her arm. Perhaps it really is true. Perhaps we broke up?

'I have absolutely no idea,' says Crystal, shaking her arm loose. 'You have to stay calm.'

'I could calm down if you'd find out.'

'Lexi,' says Crystal, her voice softening, 'Look, hon, school is out. The year is over. Everybody's gone. I hardly knew Mags and Claire even before. I've got no numbers for them – or Finn. Checking anything will take time. Folks go away for the summer, do summer school, go off to their new colleges. It's kinda embarrassing to stalk them down and bombard them with questions about hurtful things. You know how it is.'

I flop back on the pillow.

Maybe he's away with his mom. He said she was fragile. Maybe they travelled, went to Europe. He said he'd always wanted to go to Rome.

My heartbeat flutters and jumps. I break a sweat all down

223

my back. He didn't go anywhere with his mom. She had a new man friend. I feel really nauseous.

You quarrelled with him. You did.

And now I've got it into my head that he's mad at me, I can't get it out. That's it. He's mad at me. I did something unforgivable. I must have. I betrayed him in some terrible way. I try to rack my brains.

What was it?

Did he find out the truth?

The lies about the bonfire party?

I arrive at the edge of a precipice. I try to step forward. My foot slips. Sudden vertigo and I'm faced with an empty, bottomless void.

Please don't let him have found out I lied.

He must have.

He did.

He did.

He confronted me.

And there was no more running away.

I lean back on my pillow, exhausted.

'Take it easy,' says Crystal. 'You'll remember everything when you're ready, isn't that what the doc said?'

'I don't know,' I say. 'Sometimes I think I'll never know what happened.'

Crystal smiles and pats my twisted scarred fingers.

'Eat more brain bullets,' she says.

It's bedtime. I finish off the latest tin, masses of them.

I lay my head down and ignore the gurgling in my stomach. I ignore the erratic beat of my heart. Tonight I will remember everything.

I can't sleep any more. I lie awake, waiting for the next sortie to the bathroom. This latest batch of brain bullets has made me so weak, I don't think I can actually stand up to get to the toilet any more. I need help. My brain is all over the place.

Finn and I quarrelled.

He's holding my shoulders. Shaking me.

'Tell me the truth.'

Each memory like a damaged jigsaw piece. I can't put it together on my own. I feel so weak.

'Tell me the truth.'

The racing of my heart shakes the bed. The sheets are soaked again. My eyeballs ache. It hurts to turn them.

Shaking Mom.

Wake up.

Wake up.

A builder is hammering away inside my head. A whole demolition crew is attacking my forehead. They're in behind my eyes. My mouth is dry, tastes awful.

Charlie and the knife.

I'm going to vomit.

I try to get up, drag myself to the bathroom. I can't stand. I'm so dizzy. I go down on the floor. I'm vomiting, side heaving, gut wrenching. *I can't breathe.*

Someone says, 'Are you OK?'

I whimper.

'I'm gonna call the staff.'

The last thing I remember is someone shaking me. *Shaking, shaking.* A crushing pain in my arm. It radiates up to my jaw. The building collapses on my chest.

Then drips and green scrubs and a bright light.

WEEK THIRTEEN

since the accident

It is silliness to live when to live is torment, and then have
we a prescription to die when death is our physician.

William Shakespeare — Othello

PERMANENT GREEN DEEP

58

Intensive Care, The Shore Center for Medical Care

I'm not well.

I had a very bad turn.

I am hooked up to drips and monitors.

Apparently it was lucky I was in the hospital. They are running more tests than ever.

I will not be going to any occupational therapy for a while, it seems.

I am going to use the time to record my memories. A nurse has kindly brought me up my notebook.

I'm going to itemise each memory, and colour-code them. Colouring things in feels therapeutic and it's not too strenuous. It may help.

The earliest memories I will edge in black then like the dawn on to pink, the next red, then orange and so on like a rainbow. I'll progress slowly towards indigo. I shall label each strand of colour after the oil paints that Finn and I loved so much. The paints that every old master used when they were constructing their magnum opus.

Titanium white. Van Dyke brown. Payne's grey.

I spend all morning on it.

As I get closer, through blue and green, I have questions, there are gaps and events that seem to be missing.

Right now there are more questions than answers.

I've dedicated the whole of indigo just to the accident.

Indigo

The Facts:

- There was a hazy moon. (Although Crystal says not.)
- There was a railroad. A train. A car.
- I was badly injured.
- My hip was smashed.
- I hit my head. My memory was affected.
- My hands were badly hurt. (I don't remember hurting them. They'd healed by the time I came out of the coma. But I know they were damaged. The scarring is different.)

The Questions:

- When did it happen?
- Was there really a train?
- Was somebody else there?
- *Where was Finn? Where is Finn?* I think somehow Finn was there.

I write down the question in bright capitals in my indigo section.

- **WHERE WAS FINN?**

Aunt Gillian comes to visit. She brings in a drawing pad.

Aunt Gillian says, 'You used to love drawing. Maybe you can draw some pictures while you're recovering in the ICU. She puts down the drawing pad and picks up my coloured chart. She looks at it. 'Oh, Lexi,' she sighs. 'Everything depends on you remembering, but not at the expense of your recovery.'

I'm not sure what she means.

'You have to get well too.'

She almost looks kindly when she says that. I think I could get to like Auntie Gillian if she was not so stern.

And I will try to do some drawing. I will see if it helps.

'Hmm,' she says. 'Your hair has lost its shine. It looks very thin.'

I drag the drawing pad on to my bed and reach for my pencil case. I don't want to think about my hair. I know it's getting thin. My brush is full after a few strokes. My pillow is dark with loose strands. I rummage around inside my pencil case and find a 3B pencil with a charcoal, chalky, dark line, then I stare at the blank piece of paper.

'I'm going to make you a proper chicken soup,' says Auntie Gillian, 'as soon as I get home.'

I've been feeling so nauseous these days I'm not sure I'll be able to hold it down.

'We need to find out exactly why you're not doing so well.' She bustles off to find a medic.

I turn back to the drawing pad.

The paper is like my memory, empty and intimidating. I stare at it for a long time. I can see all the tiny ridges of it.

I must make a mark upon it. What were the things I need to think about: proportion, line, colour, shading?

I need to remember faces.

I think about Michelangelo and how inside every block of marble he saw living forms. I think about our art project. The proportions of the face, the shoulders, the chest, tanned marble flesh, veins and muscles.

The face.

Jules's smiling face stretched like a mask.

She never refers again to the video or to posting it online. She doesn't lord her power over me. But every now and then she takes out her phone and runs her beautifully polished fingernail over the screen. She taps it very gently and stretches her face into a smile.

My heart races. My blood drains away into the soil through concrete. I feel my insides disintegrate into dust.

And she simply smiles more.

But not at me.

She smiles at the face of the phone.

I snap out of the memory.

On the blank sheet, I quickly draw a face. But it's not the face of a phone. Or Jules's face.

It's Charlie's. His stubble. His grey eyebrows. I'm scared. I'm thrilled. I'm remembering a face! Ironic that it should be his.

I've remembered every detail of a face.

I'm healing.

And I see suddenly through a window in my mind.

Faces.

Charlie and Jules somehow together.

I remember.

Jules and Charlie.
Talking.

59

I am on the mend.

The doctors are puzzled. There is apparently nothing in the blood pathology which might have caused my collapse. I'm not allergic to nuts. Auntie Gillian spoke to them for the longest time, and said she was not taking any flimmel-flannel from them and would get to the bottom of it.

My arteries are all clear.

My BP and obs are fine. I'm on the mend.

Crystal has been in to see me with more brain bullets.

And I can go back to occupational therapy.

Deep breath. Today I am going to try and remember about Charlie and Jules.

Art Therapy

1. **Create a drawing that represents freedom.**
   The surrealists embraced automatic drawing as a way to incorporate randomness and the subconscious into their drawings, and to free themselves from artistic conventions and everyday thinking so as to access the inner mind. Draw with your eyes closed.

I select a thick crayon and an A3 sheet of paper. I close my eyes. I think of the surrealists. I access my inner mind. I am a bird. A seagull flying high above the sea. I can wheel and soar and dive. I can see the curved horizon and Gallows Hill. I can feel the cold blasts of air heading in from the Arctic. I pick up the crayon and draw the seagull as a storm of ice. I draw the north wind. I draw a hanged maiden with the rope around her neck cut. I draw a car driving fast towards the horizon.

And I remember.

CADMIUM GREEN PALE

60

Massachusetts, Last Spring

For some reason Jules seems to lose interest in the after-school art club. She comes sometimes, but not in the way she first did, peering over everything, her eyes following me every time I left the room, every time I looked at Finn.

Maybe she really doesn't care about Finn any more. Maybe she really did erase the video.

Maybe she ordered all her Dogettes to, as well.

Finn and I don't go to art club so often either.

Finn's car is still not fixed though. He's working on getting the money. I'm working on it too, but Mom is broke and Auntie Gillian is tight-fisted. Time becomes elastic, as if we are in a kind of limbo departure lounge waiting for our flight call to be announced.

Our artwork has become a secret language between us. When I pick up my pencil and trace an outline on paper, it is almost as if I am running my finger across his flesh. It is far too personal to hand in for a project. I tell him as much.

'I feel the same,' he says. 'The pictures I have of you are mine. All mine.'

It's a good job we're leaving.

We haven't yet set the date.

In the end, to get our final grades, we submit our pixelated, tissue-paper-covered, cut-out-collage versions of David and Venus de Milo. The artwork is good. The teacher praises it.

But it is not as good as the art we make in private.

We continue to meet in our secret attic.

Over and over.

We draw each other.

Over and over.

Repeatedly.

Passionately.

Over and over.

I am in Finn's attic again. His mom has travelled somewhere with the new boyfriend. They go away a lot. They don't like sharing their new lives with Finn.

'Let's work,' Finn says, 'one last time.'

The car is fixed. Tomorrow we leave.

Drawing each other is our special intimacy. We work from real life. Today, as always, I am his muse. I take off my clothes and arrange myself. Finn fixes up his easel.

He works with inspired energy. 'God,' he says, 'to draw you is divine.'

Tomorrow we will hit the highway and keep on driving.

No one will know.

'I think artists have a special responsibility to their art to prioritise it over every other bourgeois concern,' he says with a mischievous air.

Finn will not be missed for two weeks while his mom is away. That will give us a head start. We will tell our mothers, of course. But only from a safe distance.

'I never knew I could be so totally happy,' Finn continues. 'If only this moment could be stored for eternity. If only I could do that.'

'Just hurry up,' I say, teasing, 'I can't hold this pose for ever.'

'Drawing you,' he says, 'is even better than touching you.'

'By tomorrow we'll be gone,' I say.

'I must run my eyes over every curve until I have you by heart,' he says.

How I long to be gone. Even though Jules seems to have moved on, I'm all nerves. I can't forget Mags's warning. How can anyone ever get over Finn? And so quickly? It's ominous and scary. It doesn't add up. And I've been having vivid dreams too. Horrible nightmares of rabbits caught in traps. Of pigeons having their necks rung. I can feel a hurricane coming. The air is taught with it. Small things cry out and run before a storm hits.

'If only I can capture this moment,' repeats Finn, raising an eyebrow at me.

I try not to smile. I am so proud of my body. So proud it inspires him.

'As long as you don't capture me all distorted like a Matisse,' I say.

We do not get the picture finished. It gets late.

'I need to get home,' I say. 'I really do. If I get grounded for staying out late . . .'

Immediately Finn stops. He understands. We don't mention the plan. Suddenly the walls might hide hidden microphones. Some unexpected explosion might blow our escape sky high. My heart starts pounding. I cross my fingers, sending a prayer into the all-knowing universe of runaways.

Please let us get away.

'It would take a lifetime to paint you, anyway,' he says. 'And once we're gone I will study you for ever.'

'By that time, I should be old and wrinkly,' I say, 'and you would have to start all over.'

He laughs. 'No, I will capture you for ever, today, this moment just before we are free, and I will finish this painting – even when you're not here. I will run my charcoal over you and—' He laughs.

'Be uber-arty,' I say.

I do not object when he takes photos. I am learning to trust. I am unlearning Charlie.

'Now I have you for ever!' he teases. 'Even if you're not around.'

'I want to be around,' I say. Since Jules erased the video and has left us alone, I am growing in confidence.

I walk home alone from Finn's. He offers to accompany me – but it's easier to be invisible when you're alone. The impending storm disturbs me; tonight is not the night to be seen out.

I stick to the shadows. The wind whips my hair against my cheek, throws a salty kiss on my neck. Despite all ominous forebodings, I am perfectly happy.

The universe is kind.

I am in love with a passionate, vulnerable, uber-arty god.

Tomorrow I will be free to be at one with everything and totally myself.

Clouds scurry across the sky. The moon casts a shimmery road over the ocean. It's not late. Just an endless summer evening turning through pink and turquoise to darkest blue. It's certainly not eleven yet. I know. I have to be back before eleven. That is one of Auntie Gillian's rules.

I don't know what makes me take the long way home. I don't know what makes me stop under the boardwalk. Perhaps it is to catch one last sweet thrill of a perfect day. Perhaps it is to see the sea slaked in moonshine. To be in our first secret meeting place. To soak up its rapture. To watch each star twinkle awake. To lick the salty tang of sea spray on my lips. To kiss the night air. To think how lucky I am. Maybe to say goodbye to this strange haunted coastal town where I have met Finn.

Lovely, ghostly, terrifying town. I can love you now I know I'm leaving. You can keep your secrets and your lies. One day I will tell Finn everything.

Where might we go – California? Alaska? Will he draw me in Utah and Arizona? My geography of the USA is a bit shaky. Anywhere far away from here, far away from everywhere and everyone. I think about where roads might lead us to. Maybe to Italy. I know Finn wants to go abroad to Rome, to Venice, to Florence.

And my heart cries YES to it all.

Slowly soaking up the vitality of the evening, I curl up on the pebbles. Above the boardwalk, at my back the concrete front of the break wall. I have a little while before I need to be home. I look at the silver rays, gleaming through the timbers overhead.

Above the moon.

Below the earth.

Before the sea.

Behind the wind.

And I sit there cold on the pebbles, out of sight from everyone, feeling truly safe and blessed. I hear the crunch of footsteps overhead. I suck in my breath. I want to be alone. I want to hold this perfect moment to myself. All mine.

I hope whoever is walking overhead will pass soon. With a slight twinge of annoyance I recall that just above this patch of boardwalk are seats.

The footsteps stop overhead. I hear the creak of weight on iron. I sigh. Someone has sat down. Just my luck. I'll wait until they move. I'll slip home unseen.

Another set of footfalls. Lighter, quicker.

A man speaks.

My heart shuts down.

My limbs drop off.

A bullet spills my guts on to the pebbles.

I know that voice. I would recognise it through a thousand circles of hell. A cold sweat breaks out on my forehead. The size of my tongue swells to impossible. I feel it rise against my teeth and threaten to choke me. Nausea surges up the back of my throat. My hands turn hot and cold.

Charlie.

Here in this coastal town.

Right overhead.

Charlie has tracked us down.

Charlie who can smell whether you had fries or the Big Mac.
He is sniffing the night air. Right now.

Right above me.

61

With a thumping heart I listen, trying to be sure. Disbelieving. *Don't let it be Charlie.* But there's no doubt. His thin, reedy voice is unmistakable.

'Come on, who are you?' he says.

And then I hear a second voice. Another voice I have come to know and hate.

'It doesn't really matter who I am,' says Jules.

I can't quite believe it.

What?

Jules talking to Charlie?

I don't get it?

How?

When?

All this time?

No wonder she has 'moved on'. Mags was right

Jules hasn't moved on at all!

Charlie laughs. He's never liked non-compliance.

'Have you got what I want then?' he asks, his tone much deeper.

'I have everything you want,' she says.

'Fantastic, can you let me have it?'

'Oh, not so fast,' she laughs. 'You see I want something too. Have you forgotten the proofs I asked for?'

Through the dark space I can almost hear the blood pressure rising in Charlie's veins.

'You didn't think I set this all up for kicks, did ya?' adds Jules.

He snorts. I hear heavy feet shuffling. Warning shots firing out.

'Absolutely,' she says.

'Well?'

I must have missed something, although I am listening with every cell in my body.

'I want to know why you're looking for her.'

'It's a criminal investigation matter,' says Charlie.

'I like details,' says Jules.

'Undercover.'

'I'd still like the details.'

'Alright then.' His voice has gotten dangerously low. A cold sweat drenches me. It trickles into my eyes. I dare not wipe them. I dare not move. Charlie will smell me hidden beneath the boards. Charlie will hear every move I make.

'I'm conducting investigations into an international drugs ring.'

A what?

What on earth is Charlie up to?

'And?' says Jules.

My heart is beating so loudly it's going to give me away.

When Charlie doesn't answer, Jules continues. 'I contacted you, if you remember,' she says. 'And it took me a lot of googling to figure out you might be able to answer my questions. I want to know the answers to them before we go any further – who is this girl and why is she wanted in the UK?'

I close my eyes. *What is she thinking?* Doesn't she realise how stupid challenging him is? *The way she's talking.*

'The information you have is of particular interest to me,' Charlie says, ignoring her remarks. 'And I can't disclose matters that are still under investigation. Why don't you tell me exactly what you know, and I'll do my best to answer your questions after that.'

I'm confused. *What game is Charlie playing?*

'Hello, you definitely haven't heard of quid pro quo,' says Jules.

'I like to keep things simple. I'd appreciate it if you could cooperate with my investigation.'

I stuff my knuckles into my mouth.

'No,' she says, 'I want to know about her background in England, and, as I said in my email, I want, *especially*, to know how she got her hands burned. And I won't pass on any information I have about her until you disclose what you know.'

I squeeze my eyes tight, tight, tight. The stinging sweat burns into them, but I squeeze still tighter. I want to block my ears. Block out what he'll say.

Charlie laughs. It lasts a little too long.

Jules says nothing.

I bite into my knuckles, hold my breath. I realise my legs are cramping.

'I'd sure be mighty interested in your investigation as well,' she adds. 'Any details that you have on that would be swell.'

'Well,' says Charlie, 'I can tell you that from my research into her case that I believe she got her hands burned during an accident in a kitchen, with boiling water.'

Cigarette smoke wafts down between the boards. I press my hands over my nose. I find I have sunk my head into my arms and am all tangled up in them. I feel the roughness of my scars. I smell the twisted old skin. The smell they always have since the 'accident'.

'Nothing to do with a fire?' says Jules.

He laughs.

'Nothing to do with rescuing a boy?'

Out at sea, the horizon has gone dark. A storm is whipping up the waves. Soon the hurricane will hit.

Above me there's another silence.

I've missed something again.

Then Jules says, 'I see.'

'OK, so now, if you tell me where she lives, I can proceed with my investigation.' An appalling eagerness resonates in his demand.

I curl more tightly into myself.

'If you can also tell me her mobile number, where she goes to school, who she knows, who her friends are and where she might run to, that would be of help too.'

Jules laughs. 'Look, I like proof,' she says. 'I have to be totally sure what you're telling me is for real – that it was boiling water that messed up her hands and not some fireworks party.'

Charlie snorts. 'I don't understand. Is there some doubt?'

'Oh yeah! There is!' says Jules. 'And I'm gonna have to show hard evidence to be believed.'

'Why is it so important?' asks Charlie.

'Let's just say it's a vital part of the information exchange,' says Jules.

'You actually need the hospital records?' Charlie shuffles his feet. I hear the dense weight of him above me.

'Yep, I asked for them and I want them.'

There's a rustling. The sound of paper. The wind whips up sand. I can hear the rain starting to patter in the boards above.

'Well, let's hurry this up.' says Charlie. 'It looks like rain. I've given you those. They're copies of course. The doctors have retained the originals. Now it's your turn.'

My eyes seem to see circles of fire, Catherine wheels of light. I realise I'm holding my breath so hard I might faint.

'You haven't given me very much information, actually,' says Jules. 'The info about her burns was only part of the deal. You've certainly not answered anything about the reasons why she's under investigation.'

'Look, lady, you've got the records. Now, are you going to tell me where she lives or not?' His voice is dark with menace.

Jules ignores his question. 'Why did she leave England and how come she has a completely different name now?'

Charlie laughs his ugly laugh. 'Tell me where she lives first.'

'I can tell you this much,' says Jules. 'I have met her. And she is the one you are looking for. I absolutely know where she lives. I know everywhere she goes, the school, her friends. To tell you the truth, I'm mighty pleased to hear she's told us all a pack of lies about her hands. Still, I need some proof of her ID to go with this' – there's a rustle of paper. 'Then she can be exposed for the liar she is.' Jules's voice is full of righteousness.

'Well, I don't care about all that,' says Charlie carefully.

The rain starts to drum a determined rhythm on the boards overhead.

'I'd like to know the actual offence she's under investigation for,' says Jules, 'with proof.'

'I can't reveal that,' say Charlie.

'Pity,' Jules continues, 'because we can't stay out in this, but hey, I'll cut you some slack. If you'll give me your cell number, I'll tell you her address as soon as I get that information. I think that's fair.'

Thunder rumbles.

I start shivering.

There's a sharp intake of breath. He must be holding his temper in so hard. I grow cold. That bodes the worse for me and Mom.

There is some more creaking of planks, the tread of sneakers. The sound of a phone ringing. Some coughing. The click of a lighter. The smell of cigarette smoke again. I close my eyes and try to contain a fever spreading through me.

No one speaks. The ringing continues. There's no answer.

'That's my number,' she says. 'I've just rung you, so I have yours. We'll talk again. Look, this is a deal. You may be a special unit UK detective and all that, but we're here now, and if you want my info, then you have to give.'

So he's told her he's a detective?

Charlie mutters something.

There is a sound I can't quite make out. Then he says. 'I can get a phone number to you. You'll have to contact them and ask for the details yourself. It's the best I can do.'

'I guess that'll have to be OK then.'

So cheap. He can't even think on his feet. He's going to phone up a mate to set her up.

'If I get that to you tonight, can you tell me the address?'

I miss her reply.

The sound of footsteps walking away.

I don't believe I've been breathing.

I realise my top is soaking wet, right through to my T-shirt.

My legs are cramping in spasms.

I can't move.

It is a long time before I breathe normally. The storm rumbles away towards Gallows Hill. The moon hovers on the horizon. The sky turns from deep midnight blue to silvery grey. I know I'll be missed at home. I don't know what to do. I need to tell Mom. *I must escape with Finn.* Jules will tell Finn everything. I'll be grounded. Finn will never forgive me. *We must go before he finds out.* Charlie will find us. Jules has tricked me. She still has the video. She's going to reveal all at school. Finn asked me so often to be honest with him. And I've lied to him.

I don't know what to do.

If I tell Mom, we'll have to leave.

She'll insist we go tonight.

But I *must* leave with Finn. I *can't* leave without him. I don't want to leave without him. I want to explain to him. Tell him everything. All I want is to be with him.

Finn is everything: art and love and everything.

Go back to Finn's, then?

Tell him. Pray he'll forgive me?

Ask him to run with me, right now, tonight?

We can't wait another twenty-four hours.

I must tell Mom about Charlie.

What if Jules tells Charlie where we are tonight?

My heart rate shoots into overdrive.

I'll go home, tell Mom.

That's the best thing.

Perhaps I can talk to Jules, maybe I can persuade her not to tell Charlie? After all, she has all she needs now to disgrace me already. Perhaps I can still run away with Finn? Tell Mom everything. She'll be OK as long as she knows. Auntie Gillian will sort out something. Then go with Finn?

If Finn will still run away with someone who's not been open and nakedly honest with him.

It's not going to work.

I don't know what to do.

Tell Mom.

Now.

You can't hide.

You can never truly hide.

Taking only the shadiest back roads, I skirt around the town, nerves on edge, feet ready to jump picket fences, eyes peering into the darkest corners of the street, peering into the recesses of gardens, the thickest greenery.

Back to Aunt Gillian's house.

62

When I get home it's gone midnight. I try to think what to say. But Auntie Gillian's not there. She's gone to another all-night vigil.

I race up the stairs.

I creep into Mom's room.

Mom's in bed.

She's asleep.

'Mom?' I whisper.

No reply.

I shake her arm.

Nothing.

She won't wake up.

She must have taken a sleeping pill again.

She's not going to wake up, is she?

It's all my fault.

I shake her arm again.

I don't know what to do.

'Mom,' I hiss into the darkness.

'Umm?' she murmurs. Drugged. Groggy.

I take her hand in mine. It's limp. I slap the back of it. She scarcely registers anything. I shake and shake her. I can't wake her up.

'Mom?

'MOM.

'Charlie is in town, by tomorrow he'll find us!'

She doesn't respond. She throws off my hand.

'WAKE UP!'

It's all my fault.

He will find us.

A tornado will blossom right in the centre of this very room.

'MOM!

'MOM!' I screech.

Mom's not there. She's comatose. Her pill bottle is on her bedside table.

We have to go.

The tornado will rip us apart. I see a half-empty wine bottle on the floor too. Wine and pills? *Why does she do that every time Auntie Gillian stays out?*

Mom tosses and turns.

But it's no use.

She won't wake.

Find Auntie Gillian then? Tell her? What can she do tonight with Mom so out of it?

I don't know where Auntie Gillian is.

Good plans take time.

Our last escape plan took six years.

And what about running away with Finn?

I change out of my damp clothes. I go back downstairs, then rush back to Mom, trying again to wake her.

Upstairs, downstairs. Pacing. Panicking. Heart pounding.

I find a number for the church. It rings and rings. Nobody picks up. It's gone midnight. Nobody is there.

Try to calm down.

Charlie has not come. Charlie will not come until tomorrow. It's night-time. Jules will be asleep. No phone calls will be made tonight. She won't tell him till she knows everything. *Please don't let him come until tomorrow.* Plans can be made in the morning. *Where can we go to now?* No coaches. No trains. Auntie Gillian doesn't have a car.

Auntie Gillian isn't here.

Everywhere is as quiet as the grave. *He won't come till tomorrow, will he?* Think logically. Jules is planning a great denouement with me being arrested as her centrepiece. Probably. I check the front door is double locked. She won't want me arrested and removed to the UK before I can be publicly shamed at school. She'll be waiting until tomorrow. I hope.

Streetlight peeps through the skylight above the front door. I check the downstairs hall windows are closed and the shutters fastened. More gleams of orangey light. I keep my phone on me. I key in 911 so it will be there, immediately, if I need it.

I want to speak to Finn. But I can't. I have told too many lies. What if Jules has already let him know that I'm a fake, a fraud and a criminal?

What if he doesn't want to be with me?

I need to wait, wait until we are on the run together, then I can explain. Please let us still run away together.

I will sleep.

Make a plan.

At the crack of dawn tomorrow, I'll try and see if Mom will wake up.

Survival is all that matters.

I check the windows and shutters are tight. I can't take any more. I need to sit on my bed and rock myself like I used to back in the bad old days.

Rock and rock.

And cast myself into the hands of fate.

WEEK FOURTEEN

since the accident

O, now, for ever
Farewell the tranquil mind; farewell content.

William Shakespeare – Othello

COBALT TURQUOISE

63

Venice Ward, Room 4, The Shore Center for Medical Care

I've been moved out of intensive care, but not back to the general ward. I'm in Room 4 again.

I return to my colour chart.

<u>In Violet</u>

The Arrival of Charlie

- *Did Jules tell Charlie where I lived?*
- *Did Jules tell Finn everything?*
- *Is this why he no longer comes to see me?*
- *Where is my phone, what happened to it?*
- *Did Charlie come to the house?*
- *Did Charlie break my hip?*
- *Did he hit me on the head?*
- *Why did I leave Aunt Gillian's house?*
- *Was I running away from Charlie?*
- *Is Mom OK?*
- *WHERE IS MOM?*
- *WHERE IS CHARLIE?*

- Is he still here?
- Will he try to get into this hospital?

I tell myself to calm down. Aunt Gillian said I'm safe now. And Mom is at peace and safe too. Aunt Gillian would never lie. *Calm down.*

I must remember.

What happened that last night at Aunt Gillian's after I'd overheard Jules and Charlie? After I'd gone to bed?

Breathe deep.

Go back. You are safe now. Just try . . .

PHTHALO TURQUOISE

64

Massachusetts, Last Spring

I don't sleep. I tidy Mom's room and pack her a bag. She still won't wake up. I tidy my room too. I go through everything I own. I pack my stuff into two bags; one of them has things I can never leave behind again.

I put that bag beside my bed. I lie down with my shoes on.

The second bag is filled with things that if I have to, if I *am forced to*, I will leave. I lie there in the darkened room fully dressed. The wall clock ticks. I've put on a pair of jeans that I could go to school in, *and run away in. Why did Auntie Gillian have to be out tonight?* I imagine the street outside. Charlie prowling, putting two and two together until he works out which house is ours. I hear him click the gate at least ten times. *He's in the yard.* I check the window. Nothing. He's not in the yard. There's only the stars. They twinkle in an indigo sky.

I breathe on the glass until it's all steamed up. I draw a hazy moon and rub out the centre of it and peer through.

I watch the shadows on the front lawn, just in case Charlie has come into the garden after all. *Is he hidden out there behind the shrubbery?* Did I check all the windows? What will we eat when we run away?

I creep down to the kitchen and find a Ziploc plastic bag. I check all the windows again. Inside the bag I put dried fruit, some figs and dates from the big stone jars that Aunt Gillian keeps on the side board.

I take a packet of hazelnuts and two tangerines. Tangerines are heavy but they don't go bad easily. I take a bottle of water. I pack everything into a small rucksack. I hear a noise. A click. *Is it the front door?*

I freeze.

Nothing.

At last I creep into the hall. The front door's locked. Finn and I can survive on nuts and dried fruit till we are clear of Massachusetts.

Make a plan.

This is what I'll do.

Go to school really, really early and confront Jules. Spoil her 'surprise'. Tell her who Charlie actually is. Tell her he's not a detective. *Will she care?* Record the conversation. *Yes, she'll care about looking an idiot.* Make her stop before she calls Charlie. If she doesn't call Charlie, he won't know where we live. Mom will be safe. Then call Mom – she'll be awake by then, hopefully – tell her I've packed her a bag and she should leave. Tell her I'm leaving town straight away too, tell her not to worry, that I'd slow her down, what with factoring in school and everything, that it's all my fault, that I'm a liability. Tell her to get out NOW.

Then call Finn.

Tell him we must go straight away.

If he hasn't spoken to Jules, I'll tell him everything after we've left. If he has, I'll beg him to forgive me. *He has to forgive me.*

Everything will be OK. I feel better now that I have a plan.

I go back upstairs. I lie down on the bed and draw the duvet up to my neck.

Should I call the police?

When have they ever helped?

They'll probably turn up, ruin the quiet of the street, ruin everyone's sleep, ruin Auntie Gillian's reputation.

Then leave, saying they can't do anything until a crime has been committed.

Then should I call Jules?

No. Don't call Jules. It'd be counterproductive. Confrontation will be much better. She'd just be forewarned. *She's not going to be answering phone calls now anyway.* Not from me or Charlie. My heart pounds. It makes the bed shake. The crashing sea comes tumbling in through the window and splashes round and around the room in cold waves.

I think about Iraq. I think about Siberia. I wonder which of them is the more remote, the place least likely that Charlie will track me to. I think about dyeing my hair, changing my style, using make-up.

I wonder if Finn would like Siberia and orange hair.

I can never change my scarred hands.

Despite the warm duvet, I shiver. I open up my laptop and find out the train times into central New York. If Finn's car lets us down, we can take the train. It will be easier to lose ourselves in a big city.

We will run.

Mom will run. Auntie Gillian will help her.

Why did Mom have to knock herself out tonight?

This coastal town was too small. It was a bad choice. Maybe it seemed like a good idea to disappear into a little nowhere place. But it just means we stick out like sore thumbs. And everyone here is so nosy and interfering and judgemental. Charlie was bound to find us. It's impossible to lie low and keep your head down in such a small self-righteous place.

There are three trains a day into New York.

The last one is at 9.21 p.m.

I go into Mom's room again and try and try to wake her.

She rolls over, drowsy and incoherent. She mumbles and bats me off.

I go back to bed and lie there shivering again.

I try to imagine what Charlie might be thinking.

Forewarned is forearmed.

He sits in his motel. He's smiling to himself. A bottle of whiskey stands open on the cheap chipboard desk. He's put a plastic tray out and on it is an array of hunting knives. Each one is laid out carefully. He picks up the first one and tests its sharpness against the coarse skin of his thumb, singing a little nonsense song to himself.

He forms a fist with his right hand and tests his strength, flexes his biceps.

A tuneless whistle hisses out, from between the gap in his teeth. He removes a mobile from his pocket and scrolls down his contacts until it rests on a phone number. He smiles. He swigs the whiskey.

He calls the number.

'*Ask you a favour, mate? Yeah, if some American bird calls you, just tell her, the case she's interested in is gang related. A number of robberies, a honey trap and a drugs ring. Improvise. Yeah? The girl she's interested in, Lexi Clarke, was involved and is needed for questioning in the UK. That's all. No more till I call, OK? Got it? Thanks, mate. Owe you one.*'

Charlie pours a fresh drink from the bottle.

'*Oh, my little pigeons,*' he hisses, '*tuck your little heads under your little wings tonight. Tomorrow we will see what we will see.*'

He opens his phone again and this time he sends a text.

Then he opens his photos. Pictures of me and Finn by the lake. He studies them, smiling all the while.

65

I sit bolt upright in bed.

Shadows slip up the walls.

I reach for my mobile. I must *speak* to Finn. Warn him that our getaway is in danger. That I'm sorry I lied. That everything is crashing down around me and I need his love.

That we have to run before it's too late.

That if it's too late he should go anyway. And not look back. And remember me as I was before all this.

I start a text. The text that I will not send unless all is lost.

Dear Finn,

This is a difficult text to write.

Then I erase it.

I want you to promise me one thing.

I'm not actually sure what I want him to promise me.

Remember that I am still the person who went down to the beach with you. We are still the same people who created the most beautiful art ever done in any coastal town on the planet. We had a dream. We were going to escape, to be with each other for ever. To be free to be artists together. If my name is not really Lexi – a rose by any other name would smell as sweet, wouldn't it? Romeo and Juliet, not Othello? Please smile. I'm trying to be uber-literary. I know that story didn't end happily either. Please forgive me.

If I'm not the girl who pulled you from the fire, does that make a difference? I need you to trust me. Deep down I'm not a liar. Deep down I long to share the naked truth with you. There are many reasons for everything. Please trust me. If I don't turn up tomorrow, go without me. As soon as I can, and if I am still alive, I will tell you where I am. I'll join you and we can be together, but until then do not let my silence deceive you. I will be thinking of you with every breath I take. This side of the grave and beyond.

Even though the end bit sounds clichéd, it is the truth.

Always and always

Your Lexi

I close my phone. I won't send the text unless I have to.

I pray I'll never have to.

MANGANESE BLUE

66

Venice Ward, Room 4
2:30 a.m.

I try to stay awake. I know if I sleep now there will be the worst of nightmares. I can feel the dark shape of the monster hovering over my bed. I can feel the lash of the storm as it swirls around me. I have come this far and now I'm too afraid to go any further.

I know I can't hold out against sleep for ever. I want to know everything. And yet I don't want to. But I can't stop now.

I will know.

I will.

I sit up and find the tin of brain bullets. They're probably going to make me sick again, but there can't be anything that much wrong with dates and nuts and spices – and it's worth it for the memories they prompt, isn't it? I know it is. I'll risk it. I eat as many as my tired teeth will chew. I wait. I swallow. I chew again. I stuff every final crumb into my mouth and wipe round the tin with my finger.

Then I just lie there and shiver. So scared.

And the dreams come.

But it is not the great revelation I was expecting. Nothing of Charlie, nor the accident.

It is instead of the first hanged maiden, Bridget Bishop. She is transformed into an angel. With storm-filled eyes and bone-bleached skin, she stands at the end of my hospital bed.

Around her the cloth of gauze floats, as if blown carelessly by some preternatural wind. She looks at me and raises her hand and points her fingers at me.

I am frozen. I cannot move. A numb paralysis comes over me. I cannot blink. I must meet her eyes.

And I must understand.

Not in cautions nor in counsels but in images her warning comes. From her outstretched fingers snakes emerge. They slither and uncoil in sickening slipperiness.

And I cannot move.

And they slither across me.

And whisper in my ear.

And I lose consciousness.

COBALT BLUE

67

Massachusetts, Last Spring

It's 6:00 a.m.

I try again to wake Mom.

Shaking.

Cold water.

Shaking and shaking.

'MOM!'

'Leave me, 'lone.' Thick mumbles.

'MOM!'

'Love you.' Heavy head. Eyes don't open. Incoherent.

Shaking. More water. Slapping back of her hands.

Nothing.

Oh God.

I leave a note pinned on to the front of her PJs.

Please leave, Mom. Charlie is here. He knows where we are. Love you.
I'll call. XXX

I can't stay.

I can't leave.

What should I do?

I've got to go. I need to catch Jules early.

Please wake up, Mom.

I don't want to leave you.

I don't know what to do.

Think clearly. Charlie doesn't know *yet* where we live. You are sure of this, because he would have been here by now and done his worst.

So you have to go. You have to stop Jules.

I kiss Mom. I leave the house and run as fast as I can to school. *I'll come back. I'll phone you as soon as you're awake. I'll stick to my plan.*

I can't describe the running and the ache in my lungs and the terrified fast beat of my blood or the high whine inside my bones.

I can't.

Oh, Mom.

If I even think about anything going wrong, I'll become a pulsing mass. I'll feel the voltage of pain, and it'll destroy me.

I didn't get a chance to tell you, Mom.

I should have somehow.

I'll make a chance. I'll make Jules back off.

Then I'll phone. And I'll come home. I'll make a chance for us. I will. We'll have the whole day to get far away. Auntie Gillian will be told. Auntie Gillian is never cross with Mom. Auntie Gillian will organise everything. I hope they'll find a way to forgive me. I'll leave either way. With Finn or with Mom.

I'll wait for Jules and challenge her. She'll have to understand. Charlie isn't a detective. He's not. He's going to hurt us. She'd be aiding a crime if she tells him. That's a criminal offence. He's made a fool of her. She'll look an idiot. She can do what she likes with the video. Tell the school. Show me and Finn butt naked. I don't care.

But she can't tell Charlie where we are.

Then I'll speak to Finn.

CERULEAN BLUE

68

Venice Ward, Room 4
6:00 a.m.

There are ambulances wailing outside my room. Somehow they have gotten into my dreams.

Police cars outside.

Sirens.

Ambulances. Police.

Mom on the sofa. 'Run, my baby.'

Charlie bends over her.

Blood. Bone white. Her arm weirdly misshapen.

The police. Ambulances. Sirens.

I race to the door and Mom screams and screams. Race down the stairs.

Blue lights flash.

Sirens wail.

Police at the front door.

'My mom,' I whisper. 'You must stop him.'

I point upstairs.

Calm down. Just a dream. Try to remember.

FRENCH ULTRAMARINE

69

Massachusetts, Last Spring

From the school yard, I look eastward. The sun lifts above the horizon. I imagine the sea shining. A crystal path reaching out to the land. A path of sunshine stretching a golden ribbon straight to me. I open up my arteries and let it in.

Think positive.

I don't know why my heartbeat doesn't slacken.

Dear God protect me.

God of Aunt Gillian.

God of the hanged maidens.

Don't let Charlie find us.

Students start to arrive. Cars pull up where they shouldn't and drop off kids. Students loaded with bags emerge, engines rev.

No Jules.

I'm suddenly terrified she won't come. *She'll skip school and call Charlie.* I pull out my phone. *But what about her great planned denouement?* I don't want to let her know how desperate I am.

She'd just love that. I've held off contacting her, but I can't wait much longer.

Maybe I've read her all wrong?

I scan the streets. Nothing.

I wait.

No Jules.

More cars arrive. Has she hitched a ride in with one of the Dogettes?

No.

I've got to do something.

I dial her number. It rings. Each ring is an eternity. Between each note an abyss yawns. Surely she must answer?

She picks up. 'Hello.'

I open my throat and like a dying fish gasp wordlessly into the phone.

'Yes, Lexi?' she says impatiently.

'We need to talk,' I croak. I want to beg and fawn and whimper. I want to shout and scream until she listens. I want to shake my agony into every bone she has, so that she can see how she's killing me.

I hear her sigh. For a minute my butterfly mind realises that she too was hurt. Does she ache still? When I took Finn from her, did she die as well? As I'm now dying? I want to say something to make it all better, but instead I gasp and choke.

Then I remember Mags.

Everything is a performance. All the time she'll be planning.

'OK, OK,' says Jules. 'Where are you, anyway?'

'Waiting for you,' I manage. 'At the school gate.'

'I'll be there in a minute,' she says. Like it's just any other ordinary day.

'We definitely need to talk,' I say again.

'I'll be there, already.' Her voice suddenly has an icy breeze blowing through it.

I wait. I shuffle my feet, roll my shoulders. The last of the cars pull off. I shiver. She still hasn't come. Then suddenly she is here, right in front of me.

'Well, what is it you need to talk about?' Her voice is Coca-Cola on ice.

Even though I've been waiting for her, I don't know what to say. My voice is caught in a mousetrap deep in my throat. It hurts.

I think my face is going red.

'Well? Come on,' she says.

I take a deep breath. My top lip trembles. *Just when I need to be eloquent.* I can feel my lungs exploding. My eyes feel sticky. My chest is shivering like jelly.

Just confront her.

'I saw you,' I say. 'I heard you,' I say.

Why can't I seem to find the right words?

She rocks back on her heels, pulls her brows together.

'You what?' she says, confused.

'I heard you talking to Charlie.'

There, I've said it.

Her chin comes up. Her mouth goes down. Her eyes pop wide. 'I don't think I actually know what you're talking about,' she says.

I suck in another breath of air. The jelly in my chest shivers and shivers.

'Yes, you do,' I say.

The ocean drops fathoms in a split second.

'You met Charlie. He told you he was an undercover detective. You sold me out. You broke our deal.'

Her tongue protrudes slightly. She taps the tarmac of the schoolyard with one toe of her pointed shoe. I see her fingers flex, and suddenly I know she's arsenic.

Worse.

'You're sailing in dangerous waters,' she says. Her voice is thin like razorblades and cold as ice.

I don't know how to continue. Am I supposed to beg her to protect me? Tell her about my broken past? Explain the thousand abuses I've lived through? I can see immediately that I might as well try flying.

I must find some leverage.

I look deep inside myself and see nothing but a great empty pit.

'I think you broke our little deal, first,' she says.

'He's not a detective,' I say. 'This is serious. He might kill us.'

She rolls her eyes and exhales. 'So melo-dram-atic!' Her voice is snide contempt.

She thinks I'm making it up.

I try to buy time. 'Please don't tell him where I live. You'd be aiding and abetting a crime. He's violent. He'll hurt us.' She's not buying it. What do I do?

Already she is glancing across the tarmac towards the school doors. In a minute she'll swing on her heels and leave.

'*What do you want?*' I scream at her.

'You do not have anything that I want,' she says. 'There is nothing that I have ever wanted from a train crash like you.'

And she is right. What she wants is to see me crushed, obliterated.

Mags and Claire were right. I've always known it.

She's always wanted that.

I'm defeated.

'And frankly,' she says, 'I don't believe you. I know what a liar you are. That guy definitely is a detective and you need to face the charges you're running from. You've skipped bail and are wanted for something really serious. Don't think I don't know! And far from aiding and abetting a crime, I'm acting like an upright citizen. I'm reporting on you, so that you can be brought to justice!'

So that's what she's been told. I've skipped bail and am on the run!

'In addition, I'm going to give the school a copy of that abominable and lewd and disgusting video of you and Finn McKenzie by the lake. Parents should know the kind of students who are sitting alongside their kids. The school should have a chance to act in their interests.' She holds her head up high and breathes in her own self-righteousness.

A cauldron starts to boil inside me.

I'm all played out. A stupid helpless thing washed up on the beach like some stranded whale, dying. And I thought I was so clever, so tough.

The boiling brew spurts out. Acid splashes.

What do I do?

Run home. Wake up Mom. Now. Pack and leave. Run. Run. Keep on running. Leave no trace behind.

Forget Finn.

He will slow you up. He will leave a trail a mile wide. He doesn't understand. Jules will have told him by now anyway.

No. I *must see him. He has to know the truth.*

But Jules is just a girl like me. I can stop her. *I must stop her.* I'm still sure Charlie doesn't yet know where we live. Jules doesn't seem to be very clear about my so-called crimes. She won't tell him anything until she's had every last detail she can get out of him. And Charlie *didn't* turn up at the house. And I'm still alive. *Yes, I'm alive.* I know Charlie. He can plan and scheme, but from the moment he knows where to strike, he won't wait – not if he doesn't have to.

He wouldn't risk us flying the nest again.

He'll be waiting, but we still have a small window of time.

I will make it wider. I will get her phone. I will smash it. Then let's see if she can call him!

And before I can think of anything else, I am on her. Punching, slapping, scratching through banned make-up and lipstick. 'You can't tell him!' I scream it. I grab her hair. I yank. 'I won't let you.'

I feel the cauldron bubble over inside me. The rage of all those years of Charlie seethes in my backbone, streams out through my mighty hands right down to my scarred fingers.

She screams and screams.

But I don't stop. Her hold over me is gone. She can do nothing else to me. And I think I will kill her. I think it's a good idea. I will stand over her bloody mess on the tarmac of the schoolyard and I will stamp and stamp until she and her foul phone are dead. I will.

I want to.

Strong hands are pulling at me.

They won't let me.

I scream and tear at their grip.

I must stop her.

She is down on the tarmac. All I have to do is stamp.

And I realise they are my hands. I am stopping myself.

I can't do it. I can't stamp.

She has won.

I dive for her bag instead.

Get the phone.

Suddenly there is a circle of people around me. Her bag is snatched to safety. *A stupid, stupid Dogette.* No way to get her phone now. *Then I must go.* There is shouting and bells are ringing. Tall black shadows are rushing out towards me. *Run home now.* The skies, white and blue, rain down on the tarmac: black, dark tarmac.

Arms grab me. I struggle. *I must go.*

I am sobbing and shaking and Finn is there too. He's holding me. He's shouting at me. I can't hear what he's saying.

'Let me go!' I scream.

'Tell me it's not true?' he says.

'Let go,' I sob.

'Tell me, please, Lexi, that everything we are isn't built on lies?' His voice is broken.

His arms are replaced by an official grip. They hold me tight. They lift Jules off the tarmac. They fuss over her. They hold me fast.

'Lexi?' shouts Finn. *'I don't want to believe her.'*

I am marched into school.

I am ordered to sit down in the principal's office.

I am trembling and shouting and trembling. There is blood on my hands. It smells. *I need to run.*

I need to get out.

I need to tell Mom. I pull out my phone. We're not allowed phones in school. I don't care. I've got to call Mom.

'I'll have that, young lady,' says the principal. He marches in through the door.

'No!' I scream. 'I'm calling my mom.'

His hand closes over my wrist. The phone is wrenched from my grasp. 'Your mother will be called,' he says, 'when we've figured what's going on. Now you need to calm down, and tell me what happened.'

My chest drains out. 'Give me my phone,' I sob.

'I'll send the counsellor in,' he says, 'and when you're ready, you can enlighten us as to what all this is about.'

I can't tell anyone what 'all this is about'.

'I don't want the counsellor.' He doesn't understand. 'I need to call Mom.'

Now.

I lunge for my phone, but he is too quick. He grabs my fingers and twists.

'If you don't want to tell us now, then you will sit here until you're ready to explain yourself,' he says. And as he goes out, he shuts the door behind him in a way that tells me: You Cannot Leave This Room. If You Do There Will Be Somebody Who Will Stop You.

The white walls stare at me. I try to stop heaving. I'm a mess. *This has all gone wrong.* My fingers burn. I tear and shred the edges of my nails.

The door opens. The counsellor, Mrs Francis, walks in. She sits down. 'Lexi,' she says gently, in that I-so-totally-understand-where-you-are-coming-from voice that has just a whiff of all-the-feelings—that-you-have-have-happened-before-and-I-understand-you.

I stare at her.

I don't even know what I'm looking at. Her face is pale and large like a plate and flaccid like lumps of dough.

Does she really think she can help me?

What use is counselling against kitchen knives? Broken bones? Boiling water? She doesn't have a clue. This is not about my 'feelings', this is about me and Mom.

My mom.

'Lexi,' she says, 'you must tell, what happened? Why did you attack Jules?'

'I can't,' I say.

'Then you will stay here until you can,' she says. 'I can tell you, they've got the security camera footage and it looks like you entirely instigated this. It appears that you waited at the gate, you psyched yourself up. You blocked her in and then you attacked her.'

'Can you call my mom?' I ask. Maybe she will call, maybe I can just get one moment to say something.

'I'm afraid I can't,' she says. 'Not until the superintendent has spoken to her.'

A tide of dark water washes through me.

The counsellor sees me drowning.

'Try and tell me what you're feeling?' she says. Trained kindness beams out.

I say nothing. There's no point. It'll all take too long. Jules will call Charlie as soon as she can. If she hasn't already. They'll be interviewing her now. It won't be long.

But Charlie will still have to *get* to Auntie Gillian's.

I've got a few minutes.

The counsellor is talking. I don't hear her. I catch only the end of her kind little homily. '. . . I'm afraid that we must investigate. Your very future at the school depends upon it. It's very, very serious, Lexi. I don't know at this point that the school will be ready to keep your place for you . . . if you don't cooperate . . . but if you can give me anything . . . I'll fight your corner . . .'

If I can get out of the school now and run as fast as the wind back to Auntie Gillian's, we might have a chance. I look around and try to guess if the door is locked.

'Try to tell me why you did this and I'll truly try to intercede on your behalf.'

If I can warn Mom, we can still run. I'm not going to think about Finn. Not now.

'I don't care,' I shout. 'It doesn't matter any more. You must let me out.' On an impulse I spring out of my seat and bound to the door.

It's locked.

An avalanche crashes down on me. 'Why is it locked?' My arms fall limply to my sides.

Surely they can't lock me in?

'We have a duty of care,' says the counsellor, 'and the state you're in makes me think that you're not safe to yourself or anyone else, just at this moment.'

So calm down. *Calm down.* Do it. You can. Put on a facade. You know how. You were trained for that. Don't alert her to the fact you want to run. *Imagine she is Charlie.* You must navigate her like she's a tiger.

'You must stay here until you can calm down and explain yourself.'

She's my only hope. Calm. Count to ten. Breathe in slowly. Breathe out slowly. Maybe if I disclose just enough, I'll get her to phone Mom.

'OK,' I say. 'Please listen. There's a reason why, which I can tell you about later, but my mom's in danger,'

The counsellor's eyebrows twist up. Like she is thinking: This Is Some Story That She Is Making Up.

'Please just call my mom and just tell her these three words: "Charlie is here." That's all. Just say I told her. She'll understand.'

'Ah, but you see, I don't,' says the counsellor, 'and I can't pass anything on until I do.' She sees my face. Her eyes widen. She gives me a nervous smile. 'It'd be like carrying a suitcase on to a plane that I hadn't packed myself, wouldn't it?'

What is she on about?

'You don't have to understand,' I sob. 'Just tell her.'

Calm down.

I can't. I can't.

I keep shouting, 'YOU DON'T HAVE TO UNDERSTAND.'

'Lexi,' Mrs Francis says again, 'you are obviously very upset and you're obviously very angry; these emotions are related to the way in which you're thinking and feeling and experiencing events. I need you to let me in. We do not have a lot of time. There have been other developments in this matter, which the head will come in and inform you of in a minute. I want to be able to talk to him on your behalf. I'm happy to call your mother once we know more, after the head has spoken to her. And with his permission. But he's told me not to let you contact anyone. It's possibly a police matter now, and definitely a child protection issue for the school, so I'm limited in what I can do.'

Other developments? The police? What is she talking about?

The video of Finn and me?

The stupid story of me out on bail?

What's happened?

Mom?

'So I do need you to be very honest with me. I need you to trust me. I need to know ...' She pauses, choosing her words carefully. 'I need to know if as a girl you've felt pressured into doing anything by any boy at this school?'

I look at her. *What planet is she on?*

'Or is there anything you'd like to tell me about your past?'

I take deep ragged breaths. They seem to tear down through my throat and inflate my chest. They burn and slice.

What does she mean?

'Anything Jules has told you isn't true.' *My tongue is so dry.*

I draw in the next ragged breath and my voice is ragged too.

'It's no use,' I squeeze out. 'Please, if you can help me at all, make that one phone call.'

'It's out of my hands,' says the counsellor. Her voice is suddenly much cooler. 'We must wait for the police to advise now, Lexi.'

I look at her, aghast. I don't understand.

'I'm not on the run, you have to believe me.'

The counsellor crosses her arms as if I'm entirely off track.

It must be the video then. This narrow-minded school community are outraged by the video?

But how can the video be a police matter?

Or has Charlie already hurt Mom?

'Do you mean that video of Finn and me at a party?'

'I'm not at liberty to discuss anything with you,' she says, exactly as if she liked me in some previous lifetime, but has had to rapidly revise her opinion.

I look down at my hands. Why is she talking to me like this? Have I evolved overnight into a monster?

The head walks into the office. 'I would like you to stay.' He smiles politely at Mrs Francis.

'This is confidential,' he says. 'This will be a difficult conversation.'

Behind him stalks a police officer.

My eyes dart from the police officer to the head to the counsellor. White. Serious. Scared. My heartbeat is already tachycardic. Now, it shoots past the sound barrier. The clogging dryness closes off my throat.

Are they going to tell me Mom's dead?

'Where's my mom?' I whisper.

'We will call your mother in due course,' the head says.

Breathe.

Mom's still alive?

There's hope.

I breathe out. I must get to her.

'We need to establish a few basic facts first.'

I stare at him.

'Can you tell us what happened at the gate?'

'Yes,' I say. Calculate. Navigate. *They are all tigers. Just get out. Get to Mom. Say anything. Agree to everything. It doesn't matter. Speed this up.* 'I attacked Jules.' I speak quickly. 'It's OK, I admit it. I had my reasons. I'm not going to go into them right now, unless you can let me speak to my mom. I'm not sorry about attacking her. I'm sorry to be wasting your time. You can expel me. That's OK. I'm happy to go right now. Or you can call my mom to collect me. Just let me speak to her.'

'All in good time,' the head says. 'Now, I want you to answer my questions just with yes or no. Then we can call your mother.'

I bite my lip. 'OK,' I say. Pain in my chest is radiating right round me in bands of steel. I can't catch my breath. Each band tightens and is red hot.

'Is this your phone?' he says. He holds up my phone.

'Yes,' I say.

I'm puzzled. I glance at the officer and at the counsellor, but everything about them is glancing away from me.

'Look at it carefully,' he says, 'and tell me again, just to be sure. Is this your phone?'

Immediately I suspect that it might not be. I take the phone and have a look at it, but it is my phone. It's got the cover I put on it, and my home screen picture.

'Guess it's mine,' I say.

'Good,' he says. He nods at the policeman, who notes something down in a pad. 'Do you realise that everything that has been downloaded or uploaded on to this phone is your responsibility?'

I'm confused. I don't understand. Is there some copyright stuff on it? My music?

'Answer yes or no,' hisses the head.

'Yes, I suppose so,' I say. *This is wasting so much time. Why can't they just accept I attacked Jules and let me out?* 'I mean, phones can be hacked, can't they?' I shrug. I'm sure they can be hacked. 'Maybe it's been hacked,' I say.

'I do not think this is a case of phone hacking,' says the head with a rather satirical, horrid voice.

'What is it?' I say, suddenly panicking with new unknown fear.

The police officer takes the phone, opens up a page, and then turns it around and shows me an image.

Oh my God.

I gulp. I blush.

How dare they look at my photos!

Exposed on the screen is Finn as the statue of David. All his kit off. Totally nude.

Then one of him as Vitruvian Man.

And of him as naked Achilles by Gumery.

Of Finn as Adam on the ceiling of the Sistine Chapel.

Of me as the Venus, as the muse, as the life model . . .

The police officer runs his finger across the screen to the next image.

Me as the Great American Nude.

And more.

And again.

All the tiny hairs all over me curl up and wither.

'These are your photographs?' he says. It's not a question, though he asks it that way.

'Give me my phone!' I say. My face is burning and hot. *This is crazy.* They can't do that. That's my personal phone. 'You have no right.'

The head interrupts. 'Yes or no, Lexi,' he says. There is a sternness in his voice, like he's some kind of high court judge. Some kind of founding father. All judgement. All condemnation. Some kind of the Pilgrim from Plymouth. All puritanical. All outrage.

This religious bigoted little town has poured itself into him and filled him up.

'Yes,' I say. *How dare they go into my phone and look at pictures of me and Finn!*

I'm sure there's a law against them doing that. We are both over sixteen and those photos are for an art project. We can get married and legally have babies if we want.

The police officer scrolls through more of my pictures, then hands the phone to the head.

The officer looks at me. He says: 'Young lady, I'm going to read you your rights. You have the right to remain silent. You have the right to ask for counsel, but under the circumstances in the presence of Mr Cook, the headmaster, and Mrs Francis, the school counsellor, who can act in loco parentis . . .'

'I don't understand,' I butt in.

'You should know that the possession of indecent images of a juvenile is a federal offence,' he says. 'I am prepared to give you the opportunity to explain yourself. But up to this point you have not been able to do so.'

Indecent pictures?

A juvenile?

A federal offence?

He looks at the counsellor. 'Has Lexi told you anything?' he says.

I'm confused.

I interrupt. 'I thought this was about the fight?'

A federal offence?

'That is another matter,' says the head. 'The illegal possession of these images is far more serious.'

'The video?'

'We are currently looking at an internet posting as well,' he concurs.

The penny drops.

Illegal images.

Not the video.

All along this is what she was planning. When she first prompted Finn to pose as David, sent us her photo, demanded to see my phone.

This was her plan all along.

They must have Jules in another room. She must be playing milk and honey and injured innocence. She is playing dewdrops from heaven with bells on. She has told them about the images on my phone.

Illegal images.

I didn't even know they were illegal!

So clever.

Images which she knew were there.

She's told them.

She planned all this.

My heartbeat shoots past the speed of light. If she's told them about me, she'll have told them about Finn. *They're on his phone too.*

I start to shiver. I look at the headmaster. I can see Jules *has* told him about Finn's phone too. My insides curdle.

'Is the boy in question at this school?' asks the police officer.

'Yes,' says the head.

Mags and Claire always said: She'll pretend, she'll perform, but all the time she'll be planning.

'We will need to question him as well,' says the officer.

And I know now there is no hope.

My world implodes. *I'm never going to get out of here.*

Federal offence? What does that actually mean anyway? *Can they really arrest me?* The images were mostly started for the art project. *An art project the school asked us to do!*

Charlie will find Mom. I might as well be dead.

Before I die, if I can, I must warn Mom. I owe her that.

'There's something I need to tell you,' I say.

The room goes quiet.

This is hard. But it must be done. I will be brave now like I should have been all along. I draw in breath. 'I'm not who you think I am. My real name's not Lexi and my mom and I are in hiding from someone who's trying to kill us.'

The head looks at the officer. The officer looks at the counsellor, who shakes her head.

Oh my God, they think this is some story I'm spinning to get myself out of trouble.

I can hear the pitch in my voice getting higher. 'He's just arrived in town. And he's violent and my mom doesn't know. And Jules is going to tell him where to get us. That's why I attacked her.' *DON'T YOU SEE?* 'I need to call my mom and warn her that he's here. *He may kill her.*' My voice is rising and rising, and dissipating, like steam through cold air.

'Really,' says the counsellor, 'try to stay calm, Lexi. Making up dramas isn't going to help anything. We have already been told that you're wanted in the UK by the police, and they've sent a detective out to work with our guys here. It's already being looked into.'

Oh My God.

'Get Lexi's mother on the phone, please,' the head orders into his walkie-talkie. 'Tell her that I'd like to talk to her myself and to await my call very shortly.'

'*Please,*' I sob, '*don't tell her to wait, tell her to run.*'

It's no use. He's not going to.

I go cold.

I've told them and they still won't do anything. *Think. Think.* If they're questioning Jules, they'll have her in some room somewhere with someone. *Calm down. Think.* I have a little bit of time before she calls Charlie and tells him where to go. Don't I? *Please let there be time.* She won't dare use her phone during the interview. I look at the three faces in front of me. If I ask to leave now, they won't let me. I must play everything very cleverly from now on.

Calculate.

I must take charge.

Step this up a gear.

I must make an opportunity and get out of the school.

Get home.

They are not going to give me my phone back. They will not deliver my message.

All the jelly inside me suddenly stops trembling. My ribs stop expanding and contracting. I breathe in slowly. I let the breaths hold me strong.

I have only one purpose. I must give my mom that one chance. I must think.

'It was an art project,' I say.

'So I've heard,' says that headmaster.

'Really?' mutters the police officer.

'It's true,' I say. I can see immediately that this officer has never heard of the statue of David or Rubens or the Venus de Urbino or Michelangelo, or any of the old masters. He has never been inside an art gallery in his life. He has no understanding of any of it.

'Continue, Lexi,' says the counsellor, 'try to explain yourself, if you can; anything will help.'

'We were doing a project on the old masters,' I say. 'We had to give our own versions. That was the instruction from the art department. These photos are just for sketching; they are not indecent, they're art.'

The three adults stare at me.

'That was the task. You can ask Mr de Nero,' I say, 'the art teacher.'

Nobody says a word.

'We were told to put our own stamp on the old masters; that was part of the project. It was the artists themselves: Leonardo da Vinci and Titian, who created the pictures. They are studies in the human form. Not pornography.'

The policeman snorts in laughter. 'I don't think that's a very good defence, young lady,' he says, 'for having indecent images on your phone.'

I stare back at him. Don't bother to justify. Don't question or defend.

'Get Mr de Nero up here, please,' bellows the head into his walkie-talkie.

I can think only one thing: get out.

I look at them. 'It's Jules, isn't it?' I say. 'She told you about this.'

The principal looks at me. I can see that he's angry. This is going to bring his school into disrepute. He's going to have to deal with the press, with possible court cases. This is going to blow this religious little community sky high. It was not something that he'd wanted on his watch.

National news.

Nude students.

Dodgy art projects.

Kinky art teacher.

Indecent images.

Illegal pornography.

'Miss Julia Bridges has behaved perfectly correctly,' he says. 'She has reported a crime. She has reported *you*, despite being attacked. She has been a valued pupil at the school since she started here.'

Yeah. Yeah. I rack my brains. *How can I get out?* The school is surrounded by tarmac. It stretches down to the basketball pole. The whole campus has wire netting and high fences around it.

The basketball pole.

Behind the basketball pole is the alder tree! It's not covered by security cameras and though the tree is outside the campus, its branches poke through the fence. They will hold your weight. You can scramble over.

If only I can get there.

I estimate how long it would take me to run down to the basketball pole and get to that corner of the schoolyard. If I run like the wind, and my legs can hold up – perhaps four minutes?

'I need the bathroom,' I say.

The head looks annoyed. The policeman looks suspicious. They both look at the counsellor.

'You'll just have to wait,' she says.

I crook my magic finger. I create the sad dead faces of the hanged maidens in my mind. I speak to them.

Help me.

Help me in my hour of need.

I clear my throat. A strange low thrum resonates in my voice. 'I need to go to the bathroom,' I repeat slowly.

'Please take her to the girls' bathroom.' The head sighs and looks again at the policeman, as if to say *we have to.*

'You'll need to accompany her,' the officer says. 'She can't be allowed to go into the bathrooms on her own.'

Thank you, I whisper to the hanged ones.

Thank you, my sisters. Stay with me. Help me.

Next problem: how to get from the bathroom out of the school building itself. *I should have asked my hanged sisters for help long since.* And how to escape from the counsellor? I wonder if I give Mrs Francis a punch on the head, will it knock her out?

I've never really hit anyone before, not in a cold-blooded way, not to really hurt them. But I have to do this. I have to save Mom. I am in so much trouble now – what is one more thing?

I smile, but I do not let the smile reach my eyes. I know how to do that. I look at the counsellor. She is not a large woman. She's one of those weak skinny types that look like they're total junk-food vegans. Dry thin hair, pasty-faced.

I look around for a weapon.

There's a handy kind of paperweight on the desk, but I know I won't be able to take that with me. I think about what there might be in any of the bathrooms, something I could cosh her with on the way back. It's all rather funny really.

It's not funny actually. I'm going to have to punch her with my bare knuckles. I try to fix a fist. Ever since the accident, I have not been able to make a fist properly. The best I can achieve is a kind of loose grasp.

I suppose I could swing broadside with my forearm — that might do it. But it's not as if she is going to stand still and let me, is it?

My mind jumps to solutions, at a thousand times the speed of light. Maybe I don't have to knock her out. Maybe I just need to give her the slip, just need enough time to get away, to get a head start before she realises. In the bathroom maybe I could get out of a window?

Think.

The office we're in is two storeys up. Even if there's a window in a bathroom — and I seem to remember that all the bathrooms do have a window right at the back, in the furthest cubicle from the door — a two-storey drop? It would be too far. If I broke a leg, I wouldn't be able to run. I flex the muscles of my calf.

What about a toilet on the ground floor?

I don't think they've got windows; that was clever of the architect, wasn't it? Making sure that nobody could squeeze out of a bathroom window anywhere in the building.

Then I remember something.

The girls' changing room in the gym area has a toilet, *and* it has a window, *and* it's on ground level.

Students use that window to pass bits of gym equipment through.

That's it.

I shall have to convince Mrs Francis those are the toilets I need to use. Faster than the speed of the universe, my brain clicks through a compendium of possible lies.

I could say I'm cold?

I am shivery.

I start to shiver to give verisimilitude to my future lie.

I need to get my jacket, which I have sadly left in those changing rooms, obviously.

She might say: don't worry, you can sit nearer to the radiator/borrow a scarf/have a hot drink.

I stop shivering.

I could say nothing. I could just go there. Quickly and make her play catch-up.

I think that's the best plan.

I will say nothing and just head off, fast. Then wait until she challenges me; at least by then, we might have gotten down to the ground floor.

I put my plan into action. The counsellor stands up and opens the door. She signals for me to follow.

I stand up. I straighten my back. I tilt my chin up. I narrow my eyes. I hold up my head with as much attitude as I can.

And I am out of the room.

70

I head off down the corridor fast.

'Lexi,' the counsellor shouts after me. I quicken my pace. I reach the central staircase and slam through the swing doors. I take the stairs going down. Two at a time.

'Where are you going?' yells Mrs Francis. She's followed me down the stairs. She's walking fast. I guess she's not sure if this is a crisis or not.

I cast one contemptuous look over my shoulder and yell, 'Bathrooms.'

'Lexi,' she calls, 'there was a bathroom on the second floor.'

But by now she's lost the advantage. She's running to catch up.

I don't need to say anything else, just stay ahead of her, not too much to panic her, but enough to get to the changing rooms.

'I had hoped . . .' she gasps, as she tries to gain ground, 'that you would be more contrite.'

'I'm going to the bathroom on the ground floor, where it doesn't smell,' I say. On the spur of the moment.

'I'm going to . . .' she pants, 'I'm warning you. I'm going to call the office right now.'

That's where she makes a big mistake. Instead of threatening and manipulating and trying to play the nice guy, she should have used her walkie-talkie straight away without all the preamble. I know now she's not going to use it. Not just because I'm walking quickly to the ground-floor toilets. She just doesn't want to look weak. She wants to play Ms Capability Nice-Knickers People-Pleaser.

The counsellor gets out her walkie-talkie. She waves it at me.

I carry on jogging, 'I can't wait,' I yell, 'I'm bursting.'

'I'm going to let them know,' warns the counsellor.

I stop. OK, I'll play along now. We're already on the ground floor. Plus, one call from her can actually have backup summoned as quick as a flash. Not that she's serious. She's just pleading in a bullying way.

Anyway, I need to convince her now.

Plan B.

I look back at her. 'You don't understand,' I say.

'Oh, I think I do,' she says.

'No, you don't,' I say. 'Imagine what it'll be like for me to be walking around on those upper floors where every classroom has a window that opens up on to the corridor.'

I send a prayer up to the hanged ones. I play the pity card with just the right mix of pathos and despair. 'Everyone will see me.'

As predicted, she says, 'You should have thought of that before getting yourself into this mess.'

Sanctimonious cow.

I simply swallow. 'I didn't actually know it was a mess,' I say. 'I thought I was doing an art project.'

She hesitates. Her liberal open-minded personality script kicks in. I can almost hear it saying, *She's right. It was just an art project, perhaps she's a true victim. You need to explore that possibility . . .*

'I appreciate,' she starts, 'that the photos may have been innocent.' She pauses as another thought seems to strike her.

'But your attack on Julia was not innocent, Lexi, and you have to accept that.'

I hang my head and jiggle a bit. 'Can I get to the toilet, please, miss?' I say, all submission and contriteness.

'And that dreadful story about your mom being in danger. That was truly unnecessary. What on earth were you hoping to achieve?'

'Please, miss?' I jiggle.

But she's going to get her pennyworth in, now she has the lead. 'Since you came to the school, this is the second fight you've had with Jules, and now all of this has come to light; it's not looking good.'

She seems to have forgotten about using the walkie-talkie. I need to focus on convincing her to allow me to use the toilets by the changing room.

With a bit of luck she'll never have been in them and will have no idea about the window at the back. She'll wait for me, stuck in the small vestibule between the showers and the loos.

'You still need to use the toilets upstairs.' She points to the upper levels.

Suddenly an idea occurs to me. She's a member of staff. She has probably never tried to use the girls' toilets. She has her own designated staff facilities. But she must know about the lockdown system. All student toilets are locked during lesson times.

Oh, fabulous idea! Why didn't I think of you before!

It would have saved time.

Now I must play this carefully, for actually, I've an idea that some toilets may be left open, and it is only on the third and upper floors they're locked, but hopefully she doesn't know this.

I hang my head. 'Please, miss,' I say as I shift dramatically from foot to foot. 'I'm desperate and the toilets may be locked on the upper floors. Because it's during class, you know, the lockdown system?'

She hesitates. She looks unsure.

Oh, sisters in witchcraft. Oh, hanged maidens. Aid me now!

'Believe me,' I say with that deep thrum in my voice again. 'If we want to use the toilets during lesson times, the only ones we can be sure to access are in the changing rooms in the gym department.'

I arrange my face as if to say *that is a school policy, you guys put it in place.*

Perhaps she sees my logic. Perhaps she knows the photos were innocent. Perhaps the hanged maidens hear me.

Whatever it is, she decides to do me a good turn.

Stupid her.

'OK,' she says. 'It's not a big deal, Lexi, we can use the toilets on the ground floor, but I do need you to think a little bit about the way you're coming across.'

I flash her a bright, brief sunny smile. 'Thanks,' I say.

Thanks to you, my maidens.

Then I literally run down the rest of the steps, out across the main promenade and through into the PE department. I can hear her footsteps behind me. I barge through swing doors, race down a darkened corridor. Moments pass. Lights flicker on. I wait just briefly, pivoting on my heel, and then say, 'I'm going in here. I can't hold it any more.' I make my voice break and tears come.

'Go, go, go,' she says.

71

I open the door to the girls' bathroom. I turn around and click the lock behind me. I'm in a small, open changing area which can take about ten to fifteen girls. There are bigger changing rooms, but this one is reserved for those who have issues – they're being bullied or have some religious or health reason for using them.

The space is not well designed. It feels like an architectural afterthought. The lockers are too big and the aisles between the benches too small.

At the back of the changing area are three toilets. Actually one is a shower. I make for the far-end toilet.

I lock the door behind me. I stand on the closed toilet seat and then the cistern. I push open the window. It's one of those steel-framed catch windows that swings upwards and outwards. The glass is frosted. I turn my back to the window, sit on the windowsill, then pull my knees up to my chest, swivel around and dunk them out through the open window. Then, I slither out behind, legs first, watching my back so that it does not scrape the catch.

As soon as my feet hit the ground, I'm on fire. Heart pounding, I race like the wind, down the side of the gym block, round the back of some extension buildings, across the green turf, over to the tarmac walkways.

I head for the basketball pole. Sweat breaks out everywhere. My neck and back and armpits. I do not hear anybody shouting behind me, though my hearing is on fire. My eardrums throb, waiting for that whistle or sign that I've been spotted.

None comes.

I imagine the counsellor standing, waiting outside the toilets. I wonder how long I've got. Will she give me a little bit of extra time if she thinks I'm weeping?

In under two and a half minutes, I'm at the far end of the schoolyard. I reach where the old tree stands. The tree does not grow inside the school compound. The school has been trying to get it cut to stop students escaping, but, as it's not theirs, they've failed so far.

- Their problem: its branches poke nearly through the chain-link fence and form a perfect step ladder for truants.
- Our solution: stick the toe of your sneaker through the gaps in the fence, balance them on the edge of the branches. They give that extra bit of leverage. Then step up and access your FREEDOM.

Like a squirrel, I am up the fence and over.

Handhold over toehold.

There is no barbed wire or other barrier at the very top of the fence, but it is quite high, a good three metres up, and there's a lot of foliage. Heights don't bother me. In the hierarchy of fears they don't even rate. I'd scale El Capitan in Yosemite if it meant evading Charlie. Quick as lightning, I'm over the top, pushing through the greenery and coming down the other side. With the tree to manoeuvre against, it's real easy. I love that tree. I hope they never cut it.

In a flash, I am down on the grass and running. Scratched but winning. I don't care whether they raise the alarm now; I have enough of a head start to get home.

I burst out of the nearby street and hit the highway.

Mom, just don't open the door until I get there.

72

Down the street. Running. About two kilometres to go. The pavements are slick with last night's rainfall. Paving slabs try to trip me. Picket fences lean at odd angles. Rows of trees threaten to fall. My chest hurts.

In the distance the interstate railroad threatens to leave its tracks and mow me down. Somewhere an ache starts at my waist. My hips feel stiff, my legs heavy. I try to extend my stride. Go faster. A stitch stabs into me. I suck in great draughts of air.

Run.

Faster.

They took my phone.

If she dies I'll never forgive them. Never forgive myself.

This is what Jules planned all along. Those pictures.

Finn.

What have they said to him? Have they arrested him? Poor Finn. He didn't deserve this.

Please, God. I pray to the hanged maidens on Gallows Hill, to the sacred gods of the sea and sky, to the one true

God of Auntie Gillian: Please don't let them find images on Finn's phone. Please let him have deleted them.

Please, dear God. Protect him.

Protect my mom.

The uphill incline of the street feels like a mountainside.

Run faster.

Past fences and driveways, gates and garages, gardens and front doors, huge detached clapboard houses, elegant porticos, clipped hedges, super-green lawns, semi-detached bungalows, wrap-around verandas.

Run.

A seagull cries eerily like a newborn child, mewing and squealing and wheeling around overhead. A truck passes, horns wail out a distant call.

Run.

Parked cars. An old lady with a dog. City trees. The sweet-sick smell of frying chicken. Candy wrappers twirling. Breeze. Borders of flowers. Sweat starts to trickle down my face, the fabric of my shirt clings to me, thin, drenched. Sweat in my eyes. Stinging.

Up ahead I see the tall gables of Auntie Gillian's house. The weathervane at the front is spinning in the breeze. The house looks quiet. Perhaps I am in time.

Oh God, let me be in time.

Only another few metres. My breath comes in seizures. In hurricanes. In blasts that knock me sideways and explode in my chest.

There is no screaming coming from house. *Perhaps I am in time.* I open the gate in the picket fence. For a moment I bend double to get my breath back.

It's going to be OK.
It's going to be OK.

I unlock the door. A blast of air catches it. I hear it slam against the wall. I wince. I need to be quiet just in case. I step into the house. At first the air smells empty. Void of anything, but there's a strange energy.

And then I hear it.

Sobbing.

He's here.

Oh God.

I need a phone.

I have to call 911. I race to the hall, pick up the house phone – but there's no dial tone.

The house phone line has been cut. Not cut, yanked. Wiring hangs from the wall, from broken trunking.

I have no mobile. There is no house phone. How angry Auntie Gillian will be. A knot forms at the back of my throat. I can't swallow. I can't swallow. *I don't know what to do.*

What shall I do?

Race outside to a neighbour? That will take far too long. It might already be too late.

Instead I dash to the kitchen. I pull a knife out of a drawer. I have no idea how to use it. That is a stupid solution. I put it back. If he hasn't got a knife already he'll get this one off me. More sobbing. The sound of a thump on the floor. *He's upstairs in her room.*

I take the stairs two at a time. I think I must be breathing through every pore in my body – though I feel like I'm breathless and exploding. My lungs split and scream. I ignore them. I throw open the door.

It's him.

I knew it would be him.

I knew.

But actually seeing him. It's different. Him. Here. Here in our refuge. In our home. Our own safe place.

I can't take it in. I freeze.

So familiar. So alien.

So inescapable.

Everything has been leading to this. How can he still have this hold over me? His thick dark hair swept back from his sloping brow. His eyebrows. That nauseous smell of stale him.

That two-day-old stubble.

Those same old shoes, worn down on one side of the heel. His energy filling up the room. My fear filling up my body. Huge, uncontainable. I stop short at the doorway.

'Lexi!' screams my mom. 'Run, my baby! Run!'

73

But I can't. I never could. How can I leave her now, when this time it's all my fault? She looks so frail. Her face is already swollen and dark with bruises. She's bleeding. Leaning against the bed frame and bleeding. My mouth goes dry. Throat closes up. My heart can't bear it. I must draw him off. I must try to give her a chance to get out of the room.

I can't believe I have no phone.

Just when I need one.

Perhaps she thinks I've phoned the police. She's hoping they'll come.

'So.' Charlie whips his head round and I see the full force of his ugliness. 'There you are, witch.' Charlie turns away from Mom. 'You won't escape me now.'

He steps menacingly towards me.

Steel glints in his right hand. *Oh, Mom. We can't hide any more.*

'Mom! I scream.

'RUN,' screams my mom.

Shining steel waves through the air towards me.

I back up to the doorway. I stumble on to the landing.

He has chosen his time well. Auntie Gillian will be out all day. *No one is coming to help us.*

'Run!' screams my mother.

Run. Leave her? I can't. And I'm already gasping and out of breath. I can barely breathe. My legs are jelly.

He pounces. I skate backwards. I slip. Stumble. I pull myself up with the banister and turn and race down the stairs to the bottom. I pause and check behind me.

He is following. He must follow. I need to draw him away from Mom. Mom screams, 'Leave her alone. Leave her alone!' He is coming.

He seems to stop. Hesitate.

'You'll never get me,' I taunt. 'You're nothing but a loser.'
Run, Mom. Run.

That spurs him on. He comes charging down the stairs. At the bottom I turn and run through the front hall. I don't slam the front door behind me. I don't want to give him any reason to go back inside.

Get him away from Mom.

I race down the driveway to the wicket gate. I turn. I do not see him on the porch. I hesitate. He's gone back upstairs.

I must go back too.

I must try to get him out.

But it's no good. I can't. I try to put one foot in front of the other to go back into the house again. But I can't. I'm stuck. My legs threaten to give way. I simply can't.

How did it come to this?

INDANTHRENE BLUE

74

Venice Ward, Room 4
8:00 a.m.

I wake up groggy. Two nurses are standing over me. A doctor is seated beside me. A medic in scrubs is waiting.

My face is gently sponged. 'Try and wake up, Lexi.' My arm is stretched out.

'Sodium chloride 0.9 per cent,' says the doctor.

Someone has taken a sledgehammer to my skull. Every movement brings the hammer down. 'I want to get her hydrated fast.'

'Can I change the bed yet?' says someone.

I realise I'm lying in a mess.

'What's the matter with me?' I try and say. The words won't come out. A grey cloud buzzes everywhere. My brain pounds. My mouth is dry. The nurse rolls me to one side and strips out the bottom bed sheet. I try to sit up. Lightning sears through me. I flop back against a pillow.

'Stay awake, Lexi,' says the nurse. She slaps the back of my hand. 'Doctor wants to talk to you.'

'Lexi,' says the doctor. 'Can you hear me?'

I try and nod. I stop when lightning strikes through my head.

'Just squeeze my hand if you can hear me.'

I squeeze her hand.

'Squeeze once for yes, twice for no. Did you get that?'

I squeeze once.

The nurse lifts my hips and bum, slides a sheet under it.

'Good. Lexi, your potassium levels are very high. They're dangerously high. We need to know what you've been eating. Have you been eating anything other than hospital food?'

I squeeze once.

The nurse very gently rolls me on to my back. 'Sorry,' she whispers.

'Can you tell me what you've been eating?' says the doctor.

I squeeze once.

'Was it some kind of supplement or pill?'

The nurse tugs and adjusts. I moan. 'Sorry,' she whispers again.

I squeeze twice.

'Was it this?'

I open my eyes a little. The light is brutally bright. The doctor is holding up the tub of chicken soup Aunt Gillian brought in and left in the kitchens with the nurses.

I squeeze once.

'Take a sample.' The doctor passes the tub to a medic.

I squeeze twice.

'Did you mean no? Not the chicken soup?' asks the doctor.

I squeeze once. I open my mouth to speak, but my tongue is too huge. It's swollen up and fills my dry mouth and I can't seem to get words past it.

'Take your time,' says the doctor. She turns to the medic. 'Take a sample anyway, it could be the chicken.'

I squeeze twice.

The doctor peers at me. Oh God, the lights are so bright. I struggle to pull my hand out of hers. 'What is it, Lexi?' she asks.

I point at the tin.

The nurse passes the tin to the doctor. She opens it. 'This tin is empty, Lexi. Was there something in it?' She takes my hand.

I squeeze once.

'I see,' says the doctor. She passes the tin to the medic. 'Can we get a sample out of this?'

The medic shakes the tin. 'Not really. Nothing in there.'

I close my eyes. The doctor pats my hand. 'Don't worry, Lexi, we're going to get you sorted out. You just rest.'

I seem to be slipping into a thick fog.

'We'll give you something for the pain and the diarrhoea.'

The fog is laced with spears that stick into my head.

'Give her morphine; let's start with 2.5 milligrams with the ORS and see how she does.'

The doctor takes my hand again. 'Did the contents of the tin contain any dates or salty nuts?' she asks.

I feel a gentle tug on my arm. I feel the nurse roll me sideways as she finishes tucking in my bottom sheet.

I slip into the fog. The spears dissolve. The memories start. I forget to squeeze the doctor's hand.

PRUSSIAN BLUE

75

Massachusetts, Last Spring

I should never have let it come to this.

I should have stayed away from Finn.

I should have outsmarted Jules.

I hear a police siren at the end of the street. The school will have called the police. Thank God for Mr Cook. The police will come here. I can tell them. *Oh, come quickly.* I step out, back down the garden path, on to the street to hail them down. My legs so heavy and wobbly. I hope the police won't just focus on arresting me. I need them to go into the house.

I have confused everything. I must make the police understand. I must tell them. *They have to believe me.* They have to.

The police sirens die away.

They have not come for me.

They have not come to help Mom. A sickening lurch tears through my stomach. I must find a phone. *I must do something.* I try to rack my brains. A neighbour. That old woman who lives across the street? I race across the street. I bang on the door.

I bang and I bang.

Nobody comes.

I'm wasting time.

Nobody's coming.

Another neighbour? They're probably at work, at school, at the shops, out the back, in the shower. I race back across the street again. Another neighbour. And another.

Banging on doors.

Banging and banging.

No one comes.

Finally an old man comes to one door. *At last.* He's leaning on a metal frame.

'Please call the police!' I say. 'There's a madman in my house attacking my mom!' He takes one look at my face. His eyes know. He believes me.

'Please,' I scream.

'Please don't come into my house,' he says. He shuts the door in my face, but I can see through the frosted glass that he's calling someone. He's telling them. Or he's reporting me. Either way, the police will come. Surely. Won't they?

Mad girl banging on my door.

I should go back now. I should try to help Mom. I could try. I could find a way. I turn. I lurch back to Auntie Gillian's house.

Inside the front door, I start screaming, '*The police are coming, get out, get out, get out.*'

He must get out.

My shouts echo up the hall.

Screaming coming from the room. Thank God there's screaming. I hear my Mom again.

'Run. Run. Lexi, run.'

My legs free up. The police are coming. They must be. I race up the stairs again, but he has locked the bedroom door now, jammed something against it I think. I can't get at him. *I can't help Mom.* I rush to Auntie Gillian's room. I don't know what I'm doing. She doesn't use a mobile phone. She doesn't believe in them. I hear the police sirens.

Thank God. Thank God. Thank God.

The police are coming.

Thank God.

76

Down the stairs.

Out.

I race to the front drive. A police car. At last, a police car. Two policemen get out. Blue lights flash. They do not look in a hurry. They've got armed bulletproof vests on, but no visors or extra gear. *They won't be able to stop him. They'll have to wait for backup.*

'Please help,' I scream. 'He's in the house. He's attacking my mom. You must help. Upstairs. The front room. Upstairs.'

'Now young lady, please explain.'

'He's up there. He's got a knife.'

'It's Lexi, isn't it?' one of them says. 'We've come to take you back to school. Please don't be difficult. Just come along quietly with us. There are questions to answer and if you don't want more trouble, we suggest you get into the back of the police car.'

'No!' This is RUBBISH! This isn't helping. 'You must save my mom. You must help her.' I twist my hands. I step away from them. The twisting hurts my scarred skin. 'YOU'RE WASTING TIME,' I scream.

'Now, relax, Lexi. We don't want to have to put you on the floor.'

'YOU MUST HELP MY MOM!' Why won't they understand? The two policemen step towards me.

'He's in there! My stepdad. He's got a knife!'

A muffled scream sounds out from the first floor. Dark. Low. Guttural.

Something flickers across the face of one of them.

'You stay here with the girl, I'll check it out,' one officer says. Then he bounds into the house and up the stairs.

'What's going on?' asks the other officer, like all my yelling was for effect.

He gets his walkie-talkie out. '453 here. We're gonna need some help. Back up at number three, 47th Street.' He's looking up at the window. Now that he's heard the screaming he believes me.

'Go and help her,' I shriek. 'She is being attacked and here you are, wasting your time on a teenager.' He takes one look at me and looks back towards the house.

Suddenly there's a really loud high-pitched scream.

Mom.

In agony.

Dying?

I need to get out of here. He's guarding me. If I wasn't here, maybe he'd go in and help Mom. I'm always doing the wrong thing.

Another scream. Loud. Urgent.

'Maybe that's your partner,' I say. 'Maybe he's being attacked too.'

Please go in and help.

Hanged maidens, hear me.

'NEED BACKUP! GOT A POSSIBLE FATALITY HERE. CALL FOR AN AMBULANCE URGENTLY!' yells the policeman from inside.

'You stay here, young lady,' he says. He turns, enters the house.

Oh, Mom.

A possible fatality.

She needs help.

Save her. Get her an ambulance. Arrest Charlie.

If I hadn't been here that second policeman would have gone in.

Give emergency first aid.

Oh help her, hanged maidens.

I'm just a distraction.

They must focus on Mom.

When the police backup comes, they'll be occupied with arresting me. When they could be saving her life.

If she is still alive.

Then leave. That way you won't be a problem any more.

Mom always said: If it gets bad, just run, baby girl. Run. And don't look back.

Quick as a flash, before the other policeman can come out again and be distracted by arresting me, I race off down the street.

A fatality.

It's Mom. She's dying.

She's dead.

Please don't let Mom die.

I can't think.

I don't know where to go.

Don't be a distraction.

Down the next street, down the avenue.

Down towards Finn's.

Down towards the railroad.

WEEK FIFTEEN

since the accident

I kissed thee ere I killed thee. No way but this,
Killing myself, to die upon a kiss.

William Shakespeare – Othello

DIOXAZINE VIOLET

77

Venice Ward, Room 4, The Shore Center for Medical Care
Crystal stands over my bed. She has yet another tin of brain bullets. She smooths back my hair. My forehead is clammy.

'I'm so sorry,' she says.

'Don't worry,' I whisper.

'Was it the brain bullets?'

'I think so.' I smile. I can't talk much. My tongue is still swollen. My mouth dry.

'Can you tell me what you've remembered?' she asks.

I shake my head. I'm still too weak. I want to tell her, but I don't want to. I don't want to go back there. 'Later,' I whisper.

'Did you remember everything?' she asks.

'Not everything.' I try to sit up. 'Not what happened at the railway.'

She breathes out and sits down beside me, holds my hand. 'Well, I won't bring you any more brain bullets,' she says. 'I'll take this new batch away too. You've remembered most of it, I guess? It won't matter too much, will it, if you never know the rest?'

I blink. I try to work out if it will matter or not.

'You must stop eating them, if they upset you.'

Mom.

Mom's dead, isn't she?

Of course it matters. I have to know.

'It can't actually be the brain bullets that are upsetting you, though,' she says. 'They're all just natural stuff. Organic, even. I've got a theory that it's the memories themselves that are upsetting. That's what is happening. The mind is so powerful. Maybe just believing you're eating something that will help you remember is all it takes. Like a mental placebo effect.'

She could be right.

'But the brain can work in the opposite way too,' she says. 'I think it's called the nocebo effect. If you don't take the brain bullets maybe your brain will shut down on those memories for ever; you'll never get sick, but you'll also never remember anything else either.'

My sides ache. I feel so ill. After all this I don't want a nocebo effect.

'It's kind of like a choice,' muses Crystal, stroking my hand. 'Choice A: take the brain bullets and remember it all, BUT risk dying – or B: don't take them and live, BUT accept that you'll never know.'

Choices.

From some children's book I seem to remember the lines:

'Make your choice, adventurous Stranger,
Strike the bell and bide the danger,
Or wonder, till it drives you mad,
What would have followed if you had.'

Is that the choice I have to make? Death or ignorance?

But she's right. It's a choice. Everything is always a choice, isn't it?

If only I'd made better choices. If only I'd stayed home with Mom and waited for her to wake up. If only I hadn't attacked Jules.

I lie still. I don't know what to do. I shudder at the thought of going back there, back to that evening.

Maybe Crystal is right. Better not to remember. Better never to go back to that desolate rail track. My heart jumps and freezes in irregular beats. It's suddenly hard to breathe.

But if I don't know the truth, how can I ever heal?

Oh, Mom. What shall I do?

I can't bear to find out you're dead.

I'm such a coward.

Can't I face the truth?

'Yes, much better not to remember.' She puts the tin lid back over the brain bullets and puts everything in her bag. 'Better not to know why Finn doesn't come to see you.'

Finn doesn't come to see me because he's decided not to. That's the truth.

I lied to him. I kept secrets from him. He wanted naked honesty and all he got was deceit. He begged me to be real with him. Of course he doesn't come. He's probably long gone – probably a thousand miles away and still running. He's probably found a new muse by now.

Or he's in jail for having indecent photos on his phone.

I'm just not ready to accept it.

Tears well up in my eyes. *Why didn't you give me a chance to explain, Finn?*

Crystal shrugs. 'Well, don't look so sad, you did try your best.'

But I haven't tried my best. One whiff of danger and I'm giving up.

I won't give up.

Just for you Finn, I'll find out. I want to love the truth like you do. I want all that naked honesty in my life too, even if it kills me.

'No,' I whisper. 'Leave them; maybe I'll take them.'

'Are you really sure?' she says.

What is a life without you, Finn, anyway?

'I don't know what to do.' I look at her, hoping she'll help me decide.

'Don't look at me,' she says. 'I don't have any answers, Lexi. The things you want to know are all still hidden inside your head. If you want answers, the only way to find out is to eat more brain bullets.' She pauses. 'But then, that might kill you.'

'Will you stay with me, if I do?' I say. 'If I take them? If I get really ill, will you get the doctor?'

I want to remember. I can't live the rest of my life not knowing.

'Of course I'll stay with you, pal,' she says. 'I'll stay with you every step of the way. Whatever you remember, I'll hold your hand and be there with you.'

I bite my lip and nod my head. OK, I'm going to do it.

Crystal refills my tumbler of water. 'When you're ready, then,' she says. 'Better now than never, but remember it's entirely your choice.'

I remember the migraines. I remember the vomiting. The rush to intensive care. I remember the pain in my chest and the mad beat of my heart. I suddenly realise this is it, I might die. Is it really worth it? I don't want to die.

The past versus the future. Is remembering what happened to me worth losing everything yet to come?

But how can I go into the future not knowing? It's like Finn said; in the end it's only the truth that counts. The truth has a power of its own, beyond everything. I'm tired of lies, tired of deceptions and tired of not knowing and not remembering.

So this is it.

I've decided.

Crystal takes the tin back out of her bag.

The storm closes in around my hospital bed.

She opens the tin. She passes it to me. She repeats: 'This is your choice, Lexi.'

I say, 'Are you ready to call the doctor?'

'Yes.'

I take the first brain bullet. I open my mouth and place it on my tongue and then chew. And swallow. And then I take the next. And the next and the next. Until my mouth becomes too heavy and dry.

Too salty and bitter.

Crystal hands me the tumbler of water. 'Are you going to finish them?' she says.

'I think so,' I say.

'Are you sure?' asks Crystal.

'Yes,' I say, 'everything. Everything.'

I will remember or die trying.

ULTRAMARINE VIOLET

78

Massachusetts, Last Spring

The brain bullets work.

I hear the rumble of the interstate railroad. It calls to me.

Come, it urges.

Come and find comfort. Come to me. Find shelter in my dark pounding heart.

I don't know when I stop taking the shortcut to Finn's, but suddenly I am only going to the railroad.

Finn won't want me.

I am going to lie down on the track.

I'm going to wait.

That is all.

For it to be over.

That's all that's left now. My heart is pounding against my ribs.

Mom is surely dead. The air is too thin to breathe. Finn won't ever speak to me again. I've lost him. The school won't have me back. I'm choking. It's all my fault. Jules will post everything online. The kids will gossip and judge. The video will go viral. The parents will condemn and accuse. The school will show my pictures to the court. I will be charged. I will never be able to hold up my head again. I may end up in jail. I'll be on a sex offenders' list.

Charlie has murdered my mom.

And now he'll come for me.

And he won't stop until he finds me.

It's all my fault.

I sit down on the rail tracks. I don't know what else to do. I'm not even sure I can kill myself successfully. But I will try.

It is beginning to get dark.

Let the darkness come.

Am I sure?

Is dying the only solution?

The hospital room sways into view.

'They're finished,' says Crystal, but her voice is very faint. I'm hardly with her any more. The sterile whiteness is swirling in a thick fog.

She leans over me, adjusts the pillow, whispers, 'Are you OK?'

Shadows lengthen. Far out at sea, seagulls stream shorewards, squawking kitten cries. The storm brews. The air trembles. Over by Gallows Hill, the maidens are stepping down from the scaffold and joining hands in a slow dance. Round and round and round they go.

The rail track stretches before me into infinity.

There is no hope.

There is no sanctuary.

There is no safety.

However far you run, you can't hide.

You can never get it right. You will always be caught out. Your life will be cursed. You will be laid to waste upon bare ground.

Nobody will mourn me. Finn will hate me. There is no point in anything. I've ruined his life. We can't run. My mother is dead and if she survives by some miraculous chance and learns that it's all my fault, she will never talk to me again.

No, that's unfair. She will forgive me. But there will always be this between us.

She will look on me with distrust. The same distrust that she looks on every other human being.

And I can't bear that.

All I ever wanted was to be loved.

To be good enough.

And Charlie will not stop. He will not die and he will not stop, even if the police catch him, he will find a way. He will not stop until he hunts me down.

You can't hide.

I can't run any more.

So I will just sit and wait. I won't struggle to make things right or wrong. I won't. I won't decide to tell the truth or to lie. I will sit and wait; I will let fate decide whatever happens next.

I look up towards the shadows gathering over Gallows Hill. Let the gods of the hanged maidens decide. Let the God of Auntie Gillian decide. Let the gods of the wild wind out there tossing on the dark sea decide. Let the hilltops listen to their decisions. I'm done with it.

*   *   *

Crystal leans in. 'It's what you've always wanted,' she says, 'to die, isn't it?'

Yes, she is right. I want to die.

I sit and wait. The sky turns from primrose yellow to grey to indigo and pink. A hazy moon emerges over the horizon and rises slowly. It is not really dark; it's late, late afternoon, a sort of everlasting twilight.

I hear the sound of the car long before I see it.

The sound of a car and a hazy moon.

It crosses over the cutting towards me. For one minute I think it's the police. I put my hands over my ears. I do not want to hear what's happened to Mom. I want to sit here on the rails with the squawk of the seagull and wait for the train to take me away.

Carry me to another place, another time, another shore.

But there are no sirens, so perhaps it's not the police. The track that leads down to the level crossing is not used very often. Busy people prefer to take the bridge road than risk the possibility of long waits by a crossing with a closed gate.

The car stops at the top of the cutting. I hear the squeal of a handbrake, a door opening. I see a dark figure jumping out of the driver's seat.

'Lexi.' I hear the voice I know so well.

My heart leaps, then it sinks. How come he's here? He's come to shout at me, to tell me how despicable I am. He's just come here to show me that he knows all about my lies – to tell me how I've betrayed him. Lies and deception. The very things he begged me not to do. He's come to tell me I'm a witch. I flinch, but there is nowhere to run to any more and nowhere to hide, so I sit and pray the train will take me before I must face him. Why does the train not come? I've been here hours.

He races down the short slope towards me. I want to stand up and say I'm *sorry*.

'Get off the track, Lexi,' he yells. 'Get off the track. We can sort it out; just get off the track.'

I wish I could do what he wants, but I don't see the point any more, and anyway my legs were never very good at obeying me, and now they simply refuse to move.

'Lexi!' He jumps over the first rail and grabs my arm. He tries to yank me aside. 'Are you crazy?' he asks. 'This is stupid. Get up.'

Defiantly I fold my hands. 'Go away,' I say. 'It's over; you don't understand. It's all over, there's no point in anything any more.'

'Nothing is over,' he says. 'It's you who doesn't understand. Life isn't about what goes right; it's about us, our choices when things go wrong. 'I love you and I'm not gonna leave you, stupid.'

'I'm not stupid,' I say.

'You are stupid,' he says. 'You're standing in the middle of a railway track and that's pretty stupid in my book.'

I wheel about to face him, and as I do the hazy moon whizzes past me. It's not even very dark yet. I shake my head in an arc and I see his car. It's moving; I don't understand how.

It's rolling down the cutting. And as it rolls, a few metres behind it I see a figure. A shape, dark in silhouette, on the horizon.

I know that figure.

The car comes to a bit of a halt and the figure steps in behind the car and shoves it.

'The car!' I shout. 'The car!'

'Don't worry about the car,' he says. 'Get off the track, then we can talk. We can go and talk somewhere.'

But he's got his back to the car. He can't see it's moving.

'We can't,' I sob. 'The school is looking for me. You don't understand. And my mom . . . It's all finished. It's all over.'

'Lexi, we can fix anything, I promise,' says Finn. 'Just get off the track.'

I watch confused as the car bobs forward, about ten metres behind us. It picks up speed, bumps down the short, steep cutting.

'Finn,' I say, 'the car!'

He wheels round. 'Holy Jesus Christ!'

The car is on the track.

I reach my arm out for water. Crystal moves it away. 'Be careful,' she says. 'You'll spill it.'

I thrash my arm, my hand waves.

I look back up the cutting. Against the hazy moon, on the horizon, is the figure. It moves. I know the way it moves.

I wave my arm towards it.

I look towards the cutting. I know that face.

The figure turns and runs off.

Crystal stands over me. Her face looms in on mine.

I look up at her. I know that face.

Just as I knew the face on the cutting.

The two faces merge.

'Crystal?'

'Jules?'

She smiles, all teeth. I can recognise faces now.

'It's you?'

'Ah, you've remembered,' she says.

I am paralysed. I cannot move. The hazy moon whizzes by.

'It was you,' I say.

I reach for the water. I need water, I'm going to vomit.

She pulls the water away.

'It was you up there by the rail track. You released the handbrake. You pushed the car down the cutting.'

I've remembered.

'You're Jules?'

'I wondered how long it'd be before you remembered,' she says. 'How long I'd have to keep dodging your aunt. You were real slow, though. For a while I was certain you'd never remember, that I was safe.'

'Why?' I say. 'Why did you push the car down the cutting?'

Suddenly the room tilts and spins.

'You need to help me,' I say. 'I'm going to vomit.' My heart races. My mouth wells up with saliva. A bitter taste rises in my throat.

'Help yourself,' she says coldly. But the water is out of reach.

'You need to help me, Lexi!' he says. 'There's no time to waste. We've got to get the car off the track before the train comes. It will derail the train,' he says, 'it'll kill people.'

I don't want to kill anyone else. Oh, Mom. I don't want anyone else to die.

Somehow my legs understand, somehow they find the energy to stumble forward and race to the car.

Finn swings open the driver's door. 'I'll check it's in neutral,' he yells, 'and you push.'

Finn yanks at the steering wheel. I try to push. The car twists a little. It's stuck on a rail.

'Jules was up there on the cutting.' I say. 'Didn't you see her?' Then another thought strikes me. 'Did you come with her?'

'Bounce it with me,' yells Finn. 'Push at the same time. The whole community is out looking for you. She must have followed me.'

I stumble round the car. 'Let me try and steer,' I say. 'You're stronger. You get behind and push. I'll bounce it this end.'

We switch positions. I stand with a driver's side door open, my hands on the wheel.

'Why did you let Jules follow you?' I don't understand. I know I have no right to ask.

'Don't yank on the steering wheel,' warns Finn. 'It'll lock.'

I put my shoulder against the door frame and with one hand on the wheel and one other on the frame beneath my shoulder, I try and push and bounce.

'If it locks, we can't steer it.'

In the distance something rumbles.

'Hurry.'

It's too awkward. I adjust my footing. I get a grip on the edge of the car where the hinges are. The door opens to its widest.

'Push,' yells Finn.

The track beneath my feet seems to shake. I push. The car moves. It bounces up and the front wheels are free of the rails. I bounce and push again.

'Keep bouncing it,' he says.

The car lurches a little bit, but seems to be caught – maybe the back wheels are on a rail. We bounce harder.

Whether it was Jules or not, it's my fault.

'I'm so sorry,' I whisper. 'I never meant it to be like this.'

The moon hangs hazily in the late afternoon sky. Ghostly. Ominous. The car advances up and over another rail.

'BOUNCE!'

My hands are slick with sweat. My blood pounds. I start to bounce again. Face burning. Armpits drenched. All my force.

'One, two, three,' yells Finn.

Jump, bounce, push, steer. The car's a dead weight.

'One, two, three,' yells Finn.

Get it over the rail.

I yank too hard. The steering locks.

The sound of the wheels banging against the rail. The sound of the seagulls crying overhead.

'I'm so, so sorry.'

Then there's just the sound of Finn yelling and yelling and in all of that I don't hear the train.

INDIGO

79

Venice Ward, Room 4

'Help me, Jules,' I say.

I remember everything now. Everything. Including Mags's warning.

'Nobody can help you,' Jules says. 'You're dying. You chose it.'

Mags's warning of Lucrecia Borgia.

'The brain bullets?' I whisper.

'Once I knew you'd remember everything sooner or later I had to do something. I have absolutely no intention of being up on a manslaughter charge.'

'But why? Why do any of it?' I gasp out.

'Nobody crosses me. You understand. Nobody. You can try but you won't succeed, not with me.'

Lucrezia Borgia, beautiful, evil, poison.

'What did you put in them?'

'Enough potassium chloride to stop the heart of anyone on death row,' she boasts.

'Please,' I beg, 'call the doctor.'

'You'll see a doctor all right. In the morgue.'

'You won't get away with it,' I whisper.

'By the time they do the autopsy they'll hardly find anything. It's a natural compound found in salt and cereal, dumbass — the body will metabolise it.'

I can't believe it. I can't focus. I force myself to focus.

'And was it my fault if you gorged out on them?' Jules shakes her head. 'Oh, don't worry, I recorded your every word, just in case. Such a dumbass. It was so tiring, visiting you day in and out, listening to your pathetic whimpering.'

She laughs. I recognise that laugh. Even though the long fingernails are gone, even though she hides behind her new haircut with its auburn dye and frizz curls. I can recognise faces now. She can't hide from me any more.

She can't.

I know everything.

I remember everything.

These are the facts. Finn and I were pushing the car off the tracks. I was trying to bounce the front wheels over the last rail. Finn was at the back, by the trunk. He had his head down and he was pushing. At the last minute the car catapulted forward, rolled off the track and on to the stones at the edge. I stepped over the rail and steered the car so that it would not go off sideways. But I pulled too hard. The steering locked. It veered sideways. Finn was pushing from behind. I think he fell. I think the car clipped him.

Then the train hit.

The rear of the car was torn free. It was carried two hundred metres down the track. The train did not derail. I was thrown forward. Three metres sideways. Finn was not there when I looked up. I hit my head against stone. I lost consciousness. I forgot everything.

But I remember what happened.

I understand now why Finn doesn't see me.

Finn is dead.

80

Crystal taps her fingers. The thick fog swirls in and closes around me.

Mom is dead.

Finn is dead.

Let me die too.

Let me join Finn again in the greatest escape ever. I think this is good.

We will hit that long, long road and keep on running.

Finn and me. Me and Finn.

Running free at last.

Crystal chuckles.

Suddenly the noise grates. Bile rises up in my throat. *Die and let her win? No justice for Mom? No justice for Finn?*

The hand of some unseen force guides me. It has always been guiding me. All the questions and the colour-coding, the dreams, the therapy sessions, the sickness and the brain bullets. Something was always guiding me to seek the truth.

I hear the creak of rope from the gallows, straining under its precious weight. The whispers of the hanged maidens. *There must be justice against those who persecute us.*

I may have made bad choices, but Jules planned all this, planned, manipulated, exploited, twisted, lied.

Don't let her win, whisper the maidens.

Don't let Charlie win.

Give us all justice.

And the maidens are right. I must not let them win.

Dying is too easy. Living is hard. I will live and I will denounce her. And Charlie. They won't win. I won't let them get away with it. My stomach twists. Pain surges up my gullet. It's only me now who can bring them to justice.

I'm not going to die.

I refuse to.

Energy is draining out of me though. I'm too weak to even vomit any more. A cold sweat starts. It chills deep into my blood. *Just die*, it whispers.

I won't let myself. I lean over in the bed. I shove my fingers down my throat. I find my open oesophagus. Nothing happens. No surge of vomit.

I won't die.

Crystal leans forward, tries to drag my hand out of my throat. 'Stop it,' she says.

With a strength I never knew I had I bat her hand away.

I plunge my fingers harder down my throat. I feel a heave, a contraction. And suddenly I'm puking. I'm vomiting so hard and so fast I can't breathe.

Crystal screams.

I stick my fingers down my throat again. Crystal lunges at me. Choking, I push her off.

'Help,' I call, 'HELP.'

I reach for the emergency call button. One press and the medics will come running. Crystal tries to grab it off me. I grab her fingers and twist. *I am not going to die.* I will live. I twist her smooth manicured hands with my ugly scarred ones and I am stronger.

Stronger than her.

My fingers have a power beyond her hatred.

They are strong for me.

They are strong for you, Finn.

Strong for my mom.

Strong for justice.

For the truth.

For the trial.

My hands.

My ugly.

Misshapen.

Scarred.

Burnt.

Discoloured hands.

Are stronger.

And I press the call button.

THE AFTERMATH

Dear Finn,

You will want to know what happened and all about the court hearings, so here goes. There were three trials. I had to give evidence in all of them.

TRIAL ONE

<u>UNITED STATES FEDERAL</u>
<u>COURTHOUSE, SPRINGFIELD, MA</u>

Joanna Felicity Proctor v. The United States
Charges: Murder in the Second Degree
Trial Over
Verdict: Not Guilty

Joanna Felicity Proctor is my mom.

And here's the big news.

She survived!

She's ALIVE!

ALIVE!

ALIVE!

ALIVE!

ALIVE!

At first I couldn't take it in.

I was so scared.

I was so certain Charlie had killed her.

I should've trusted Auntie Gillian more. I really should.

The reason why Mom couldn't come and see me in the medical center was because she was locked up.

Yes, Finn, she was locked up.

IN PRISON.

Because . . .

And here's the even bigger news.

She's alive, Finn, and CHARLIE ISN'T!

He's DEAD.

YES, DEAD.

I can't believe it!

I still can't.

It seems at the eleventh hour, just when Charlie thought he'd got Mom cornered, she found the strength to pull out that baseball bat and defend herself.

She swung the bat and knocked him sideways.

He fell and hit his head and broke his neck.

And died.

Oh God!

I know!

There is a God!

And black magic works!

The even better, biggest news is she's been acquitted of all the charges against her, too.

I'm so grateful to all magic, to all gods, to Auntie Gillian and to all the medical staff at the center and, in a weird way, to Jules too. If not for all of them, the courts might've found Mom guilty. It looked bad, her stashing that bat in her room, like it was premeditation.

But once I'd given my evidence, told the court everything, relived every minute of every episode of abuse that Charlie ever inflicted on us, it changed the way the jury thought.

I entered all the notes I made during my recovery in

Shore Medical Center to the court as well, and you could literally see the way the judge was moved.

After that, all her lawyer had to prove was that she struck in self-defence. That she did not intend to cause him to fall and break his neck.

That's why my evidence was so crucial, that's why Auntie Gillian was so on my case!

That's why I *had* to remember everything.

How can it be, Finn, that one death breaks my heart and another makes me jump for joy?

How can I be so happy and so broken, all at the same time?

Oh, Finn, are you out there somewhere?

Do you miss me too?

The next trial speaks for itself.

TRIAL TWO

<u>UNITED STATES FEDERAL
COURTHOUSE, SPRINGFIELD, MA</u>

Alexia Clarke v. The United States
Charges: Level 1: Images depicting erotic posing
with no sexual activity
Trial Over
Verdict: Guilty

Those photos on our phones.

I'm glad at least you were spared this trial. It was really humiliating.

I've been cautioned and given a conditional discharge.

My name has been placed upon a Level 1 Sex Offenders Register for two years. The register covers convictions:

'Where the Sex Offender Registry Board determines that the risk of re-offense by an offender is low and the degree of dangerousness posed to the public by that offender is not such that a public safety interest is served by public availability.'

I've learned my lesson, Finn, but I can't be sorry for those magical hours with you in your attic. I just can't.

I will never forget being with you.

Our art was pure. It was love and beauty and passion.

It was Jules who turned it into pornography.

But the law is the law, however much I loved those pictures.

I accept that.

We were wrong to have taken photos.

Yet, I wish I still had them. You as David. Me as Venus.

You'll want to know about Jules, of course.

Well here it is, the third case.

TRIAL THREE

UNITED STATES FEDERAL COURTHOUSE, SPRINGFIELD, MA

Julia Bridges v. The United States
Charges: Murder in the First Degree and Attempted Murder
Trial: Ongoing

She's charged with murdering you, Finn.

And trying to murder me too.

I'm not sure what was going on in her head.

What worries me is if it was you and me who drove her to it? Are we guilty as well? Did we break her heart?

And would I feel the same, if you were stolen from me?

I get very confused when I think about love and pain and responsibility. And a part of me is very sorry for her.

Anyway, her defence attorney is arguing that she didn't intend to cause your death or serious injury to you.

The State is arguing she did intend to cause you grievous bodily harm and /or death through intentional and planned action.

336

I have given my evidence.

I have sworn it on the Holy Bible.

It's the least I could do for you, Finn.

You will have your truth, your whole truth and nothing but the truth.

You will.

Whatever the cost. Whatever the outcome.

Part of her defence is trying to prove that I'm unstable, that my memories are unstable and therefore I am not a competent witness.

But Auntie Gillian isn't having that. She spent the entire time I was recovering in the medical center documenting every conversation that my doctors ever had with her or me. She even kept a chart and record of every event in my stay there.

Dated. Noted. Signed.

By doctors.

Her thoroughness in all things is awesome.

Her file proves beyond doubt that apart from being poisoned, I made excellent progress and now enjoy a complete recovery.

Between us, Jules cannot hide from justice.

I suppose she thought she was in the clear, as long as I didn't remember what had happened at the railroad. And it's kind of ironic that her brain bullets, which she'd hoped would kill me off, actually seemed to help me remember. Though my doctors concur that I would have remembered everything in the end anyway.

I guess that's what she was afraid of.

The evidence against her is pretty overwhelming.

But it won't bring you back, Finn.

And I don't forgive myself for being so self-centered, so abysmally lacking in trust. I should have known you better, been surer of your love, trusted you. I should have trusted in the universe. I shouldn't have gone down to that crossing.

Today, I faced her defence lawyer. And Jules herself. During the cross-examination, I told the court everything – from her jealousy over you to the way she tried to blackmail me. I didn't spare myself either. I owned up to everything. I think you would have been proud of the way I told my truth.

Then Jules took the stand. The prosecution didn't spare her. The hardest bit was hearing how they thought she'd tracked us to the railway, planned everything, waited until she was sure we were in the direct trajectory of the car and then released the handbrake, put the car in neutral and shoved it down the incline. That's what the prosecution tried to nail her on.

She tried to squirm out of it.

But that's what happened. Those are the facts. The car's handbrake was released and she did shove it in our direction.

We may never know her real intention.

If you hadn't been so frantic to find me and to get me off the track, you might have locked the car up, seen what was happening.

You might still be here.

It was hard to stay in the courtroom and listen. Auntie Gillian reached out her hand and found mine during the worst bit. The car gathering speed, rolling towards us. The train thundering down . . .

She gently squeezed my poor fingers. I squeezed hers back and we held hands throughout the rest of the hearing.

I don't think there is any doubt that Jules will be found guilty of something. The police arrested her very quickly after the last brain bullet incident. The tin she'd brought the brain bullets in was in her hand. It was covered with her fingerprints. All the ingredients were in her mom's kitchen. Her computer showed how she'd researched ways to administer potassium and selenium.

She claims she was just trying to help me remember.

But whatever happens to Jules, it won't bring you back, Finn.

I'm not sure how there can ever be justice for you.

Good old Aunt Gillian, though, is unequivocally clear about her views on the subject. She just said: 'Let justice roll on like a river and righteousness like a never-failing stream. Amos 5:24!'

She winked at me when we were leaving the courtroom and then she said, 'Well done, child. It's been a tough time for you, but "when justice is done it brings joy to the righteous, but terror to evildoers." Proverbs 21:15.' Then she made a potato spud fist and spudded me!

It made me smile. She was trying so hard to loosen up, to be there for me.

So I bunched up my poor deformed hand into a potato spud fist too.

And I spudded her right back.

And smiled.

And I noticed that I wasn't hiding my hands any more.

Dear Finn,

It's been sixteen weeks since the accident. And every minute of it, I've felt so close to you. More than close. Almost like I've been given a chance to be with you again. Almost as if you've been here beside me, guiding my recovery.

Now I have to say goodbye. I have to let you go. How weary of this world you must be, when all that vast realm of the unknown lies before you.

Thank you for staying with me. Thank you for watching over me, my handsome, kind, awesome artist.
Finn the Beautiful.
Finn the Beloved.

Farewell.

And one day, if the fates will it, I shall see you again, and stay beside you for ever.

Always and always.
Your Lexi

Acknowledgements

Huge thanks to:

Margaret Bateson-Hill
Ruth Eastham
Emma Greenwood
Naomi Greenwood
Sophie Hicks
Caroline Johnson
Kitty Kettle
Lena McCauley
Anne McNeil
Karen Owen
Chitra Soundar
Jessica White

Sarah Mussi is the multi-award winning author of over a dozen teen and YA novels. Her first title, *The Door of No Return*, won the Glen Dimplex & Irish Writers' Children's Book Award and was shortlisted for the Branford Boase, amongst others. Her second novel, *The Last of the Warrior Kings*, was shortlisted for the Lewisham Book Award and inspired a London themed walk. Her brilliant thriller *Siege* was nominated for the CILIP Carnegie Medal (2014) and won the BBUKYA award for contemporary YA fiction and received many short-listings. Her title *Riot* won the Lancashire Book of the Year Award 2015. *Bomb* was listed in *The Guardian New Best Kids Books* list and shortlisted for two other awards including the Lancashire Book Award 30th Anniversary.

Sarah grew up in the Cotswolds, went to school in Cheltenham and graduated with a BA in Fine Art from Winchester and an MA from the Royal College of Art. She won a scholarship from industry to study textile art in indigenous use in Cameroon. Sarah trained as a teacher in English and art, and lived and taught for fifteen years in West Africa. She now teaches literature part time in Lewisham and offers author talks and visits. Her latest trilogy, *The Chronicles of Snowdonia*, is a series of dark romantic thrillers set on Snowdon, featuring the timeless myths of Wales, King Arthur and the *Mabinogion*. The first book, *Here be Dragons*, has already been showcased in the People's Book Prize.

Sarah delivers workshops at writers' conferences and festivals. She tutors aspiring authors for Golden Egg, Bloomsbury, Creative Words Matter and SCBWI and talks to school students about her teen and YA novels, and the important topical issues they raise.